VERIDIAN STERLING FAKES IT

a novel

JENNIFER GOOCH HUMMER

LAKE UNION
PUBLISHING

Text copyright © 2024 by Jennifer Gooch Hummer
All rights reserved.

Published by Lake Union Publishing, Seattle

www.apub.com

Amazon, the Amazon logo, and Lake Union Publishing are trademarks of Amazon.com, Inc., or its affiliates.

ISBN-13: 9781662518997 (paperback)
ISBN-13: 9781662518980 (digital)

Cover design and illustration by Kimberly Glyder

Printed in the United States of America

VERIDIAN
STERLING
FAKES
a novel # IT

ALSO BY
JENNIFER GOOCH HUMMER

Girl Unmoored

Operation Tenley

For Madison, Daisy, Tatum,
and Craig:
True works of art

Exaggerate the essential; leave the obvious vague.
—Vincent van Gogh

ONE

Veridian Sterling hit the ground wrist first, hip second. One or two people looked down at her like they could, if absolutely necessary, stop to help her. She avoided eye contact, grabbed the van Gogh, and stood. The light was turning. Hobbling her way across the street, she made it to safety before the first taxi could run her over. New York was a beast.

On the sidewalk, Veri inspected the painting. She hadn't even known it was in there, but it looked fine—luckily it had landed face up. She balanced her portfolio on her knee and slid the painting back in, this time remembering to zip the case closed. When she picked her head up again, she was standing in front of the 528 Gallery: the next one on her list.

The assistant at the desk smiled at her. "Hello, welcome to 528." She could've been a runway model, like every other gallery assistant in New York City. "If you have any questions, please let me know."

"Hi thanks yeah, I do." Veri nodded down to her portfolio. "I'm an artist?" She said it like maybe she wasn't. "And I was hoping to show you my work."

The gallery assistant pinched her lips, attempting to look sorry. "Aww. I'm afraid my boss only sees new artists a few times a year. Maybe if you come back next month, we can get you on her list."

"Great." Today was not going well. Some might say it was going *very* not well. This was the third gallery this morning to blow her off. She lowered her voice. "It's just, I might not be in the city next month. These rents . . . am I right?" It had worked yesterday: one assistant had dipped her head in sympathy and agreed to take a look at her portfolio—not that it had helped. "Is there any way I could just quickly show it to her today?"

"Well, I mean . . . she's not here." The assistant pushed some paperwork aside. "But I guess I can take a look."

"Amazing, thank you." Veri placed her portfolio down on the desk and spun it around to face the assistant, who flashed a smile and started flipping through the pages. "Most of these are *photos* of my work, obviously," Veri said, trying not to hover but doing it anyway. "I usually work on a forty-by-thirty canvas. So, you know, pretty big."

The assistant stopped flipping. "Is this—?"

"Oh, sorry," she said, embarrassed. "That's not supposed to be in there." She reached for the painting, which she could see now had a smudge of dirt on the back, but the assistant took a closer look at it.

"Van Gogh's *Landscape with Couple Walking and Crescent Moon.* You really nailed it."

"Thanks." Veri was taken aback. "It was an assignment, at Rhode Island School of Design?" She waited for the assistant to be impressed by her college, but she only studied the van Gogh copy more intensely.

"I'm a huge van Gogh fan. The trees look like they should be in *The Lorax.*"

"Totally." Now Veri was the one who was impressed. "Not a lot of people know this one."

"Anyway." The assistant dropped the painting back onto the plastic page and slid the portfolio away. "528 is mostly contemporary. Your genre isn't right for us."

"But your website had some realism—"

"It's not right for us. Sorry." The assistant glanced over Veri's shoulder to greet someone new. "Hello. Welcome. Let me know if I can help." She shifted the paperwork back to the center of her desk while Veri zipped her case closed, mumbled a "thanks," and stepped outside.

On the sidewalk, she grabbed the tobacco pipe from her pocket and noticed an entrance to the park at the end of the block. Her ankle was still throbbing, and she knew she should probably sit down and take a look at it.

The first empty bench had been tagged with tiny red mushrooms. She could practically smell Professor Wells's disdain whenever someone mentioned graffiti. Street artists should not be considered artists. *Vandals, all of them!* Secretly, she agreed. Anyone could spray-paint a bunch of mushrooms on a park bench in the dark of night.

After sitting, she rotated her ankle to assess the damage. She couldn't get a visual of it under her Doc Martens, but it was moving around okay. Actually, her wrist hurt more. She rotated that, too, then crossed her legs and sat back.

This morning had started out cool but was getting uncomfortably hot. October in the city was finicky. Chilly mornings became humid lunchtimes, which became chilly afternoons again. The 1940s wool army coat she'd found on eBay felt heavier, and her eyes stung from the sun. She should go home. Her portfolio would need its own seat on the subway, and rush hour this morning had been a body slam of commuters. Still, though, she might as well try the last gallery on her list. It was only a few blocks away.

She fished her baseball hat out of her backpack and slipped it on. Across the way, a mime was delighting a group of tourists and students. Seeing the college hoodies made her heart wobble. Upperclassmen at the Rhode Island School of Design had warned her that she would miss college more than she could imagine after she graduated. She hadn't believed them at the time, but now, a year and five months out of school, she did. Adulting wasn't exactly fantastic. Plus it was expensive. Living with her mom was free, and even still, her minimum wage job barely covered her costs.

"Mind if we sit here?" Two girls in NYU gear looked down at her. They wrinkled their noses when they spotted the tobacco pipe. "Is that real?"

"Yeah, but I don't smoke it."

"So, it's like a nervous tic thing?" Her friend jabbed her in the ribs. "Sorry."

"No worries." Veri stood with her portfolio. "Have a good one, ladies."

"You too." The girls huddled over their phones as soon as they sat.

Back on the sidewalk, Veri kicked her leg up to press the crosswalk button. Even with her portfolio tucked under her arm, she was the first one across the street.

"Veri!" Someone was yelling her name. "Veri, hey!"

A familiar figure hurried across Seventy-Eighth Street toward her. "Phoebe?"

"So good to see you." The two hugged. "I haven't seen anyone from school since we got out. It's not like you're hard to spot, though." She meant the pipe.

Veri plucked it out. "I haven't seen anyone, either, actually. You look amazing as usual."

Phoebe was tall and thin, with dark-brown skin and soft brown eyes. Why she wasn't a model, Veri had never understood.

"Thanks. So do you. There's no one else in the world who could look as snatch as you while chewing on an old-man pipe."

"Thanks." Except it didn't seem like a compliment, the way Phoebe's top lip lifted ever so slightly. "Hey, so what are you doing up here? Don't you live downtown?"

Phoebe pointed her thumb over her shoulder at the building across Seventy-Eighth. It was another gallery. Pieces of abstract art, squiggles upon squiggles upon squiggles in bright fluorescent colors, hung in the windows.

"Do you work there?"

Phoebe scoffed. *"Please."*

"Phew." Phoebe didn't seem like the type to work *in* a gallery. It screamed of desperation to be an artist working as a gallery assistant—like working as a casting director when you wanted to be an actor. "Wait, so those are *yours*?" Veri nodded toward the abstracts.

"They have one of mine in the back, the way back. It's like a tiny pink Jackson Pollock. I only agreed to do it for my uncle's new kid." She shook her head the way all fine arts majors did whenever they talked about abstract art. Phoebe did watercolors, mostly landscapes. "It took me, like, three seconds to make."

"At least you're getting shown." A trickle of jealousy caused Veri's voice to contract. Phoebe shrugged like it was no big deal, even though they both knew that it was. A year out of school and her work was already in a gallery, even if it was just pink drips.

"What about you?" Phoebe smiled, overly so, down at her portfolio.

"Nada." Veri shrugged.

"That sucks." Phoebe had been one of the more down-to-earth students in their dorm. Most of the other students were phony and competitive. They'd tell you that your work was amazing and then trash it behind your back, only to copy it on their next assignment. "Hey, I didn't know you and Derek broke up. I saw him a few weeks ago. My uncle wanted to pay me in Bitcoin, and he's the only one I could think of who knows about that stuff."

Derek's name made the back of her throat clench. "It was mutual. No big deal," she said with a shrug.

"So, it's not a bad thing."

Veri brushed the idea away. "To be honest, I broke up with him." It was a partial lie. Derek had pretended to be surprised, even though in the last two months of their almost two years of dating, he'd gone for days without even texting her back. It started out hot and heavy while they were still at school, but then Derek got a job working for a crypto company in Connecticut, which meant they could only see each other when the other one offered to visit. Plus, Veri guessed he was cheating on her. He texted her an eggplant emoji out of the blue one day in August, and when she question marked it, he didn't respond. He didn't respond to the next ten question marks either. Finally, she ended it in a text: exactly what he deserved. When he came to Hoboken a few weeks later to collect his favorite hoodies, she told him it was better that they broke up now, before she went to live in Chicago. This was a lie. Allison, her roommate and best friend, had already taken over the internship that Veri had accepted at the museum (they didn't seem to care who the intern was as long as they were a RISD graduate), so she wasn't going anywhere anyway—but he didn't need to know that. Veri and Derek didn't speak after that, and she stopped following him on social media. It had taken her until the end of September to stop wishing he'd be hit with a bus full of crypto coins.

"Okay, good, because he asked me out, which was kind of weird."

"Cool. You should go for it, Phebes." She tried not to look surprised. Derek had never liked Phoebe. *Why do you even hang out with that girl? She's got no talent and just ass-kisses her way through school because her dad's some rich prick.*

"Naw, I'm good," Phoebe said. "He's nice, but ah, not my type." She pressed the crosswalk button with her elbow. "Text me. We should get together soon." She waved and hurried back across the street in her knee-high boots.

Veri took another look at the squiggle implosions in the window before starting down the sidewalk again, thinking about Derek and wondering how many girls he'd hooked up with since they'd broken up.

By the time she reached the final gallery on her list, she'd convinced herself that Derek wasn't worth the brain space he was taking and noticed a white canvas in the front window. NEW SHOW COMING SOON was hand painted across it in black. She checked her phone to see if the Hattfield Gallery had closed, but it didn't mention anything on their website, so she started toward the front door and spotted a penny on the ground. When she leaned over to pick it up, a pair of shiny brown dress shoes stopped on the opposite side of it. "Right, that's mine."

Veri looked up. A guy, hot, around her age, in a dark suit and skinny blue tie, was looking down at her.

She ripped the pipe out of her mouth and backed away. "Oh, sorry, I just saw it there—"

The guy flashed a perfect smile before scooping up the penny and spinning it around in his fingers. "Hold on, I bodged it. This isn't mine." His British accent made him even hotter. "Must be yours."

"Oh, um, not really."

"Yeah, go on, then."

"Okay." She took the coin.

"Riz-D," he said. "Rhode Island School of Design."

How did he know that? Was she in school with him? She'd definitely have noticed him; there weren't exactly a ton of crisis-level-hot Black British guys hanging around. "Your cap," he said, reading her mind and nodding up to her baseball hat. She touched the brim of it, like she didn't remember she was wearing it. "So that would make you an artist?" *Ah-tist*. He looked down at her portfolio and glanced into the gallery. "Your work's in there?"

"I wish," she chuckled.

"Right." He nodded, taking a step back. "Well, consider that your lucky penny, then. Might be a good omen." He capsized her heart with that smile again, and she waited until his tall frame disappeared around the corner before dropping the penny and the pipe into her coat pocket and opening the gallery door.

Another blonde runway model assistant was standing over a desk talking on a landline. She cringed when she saw Veri. "We don't have a bathroom," she said, covering the receiver.

"I'm hoping to talk to the owner?"

"Sign in next to your name."

Veri's eyes went wide. Her *name*? Had one of her professors contacted the gallery about her? Or maybe the owner had already heard of her. It wasn't that impossible, considering she'd won the Schumaaker Award for Best Artist in her graduating class. Not to brag, but it *was* the most prestigious award at RISD.

The assistant's forehead folded together. She tapped the clipboard on the counter and said "Yes, Myra; I'll make sure" into the phone.

A dozen names were written on the clipboard, all of them crossed out. "I don't see my name here. I think this gallery would be perfect for me, though. My genre is social realism, and I have a totally original series of paintings to show. It's called the *Walk Out* series. Each of my figures are walking out of the scene, literally off the canvas. It's a focus on the transient energy left behind after a subject leaves—"

"Sorry, hold on a moment." The assistant covered the receiver and sneered at her. "Do I look like I want to hear your word vomit?"

"No . . . ?"

"Write your name down and come back tomorrow."

The assistant sat in her chair and wheeled over to her computer screen, while Veri wrote her full name, Veridian Sterling, under the others and noticed a stack of business cards. She took the top one and saluted with it. "I shall do just that."

The assistant rolled her eyes and covered the receiver again. "Look. A little advice. Don't try to impress her; it's just an assistant job. The pay sucks. But there's plenty of old rich dudes walking through the door."

Assistant? "Oh . . . sorry, I thought—" She looked around the space. Single words, all in black, were hand painted across otherwise plain white canvases, just like in the front window. FINICKY. FABULOUS. FEROCIOUS. *Duh,* Veri realized. NEW SHOW COMING SOON *was* the exhibit. "I'm not— Thanks anyway." She turned around and hurried out the door.

On the sidewalk, a thin white man wearing a New York City baseball hat, white jeans, and a white jean jacket was struggling with a large canvas. Underneath the protective bubble roll, Veri could make out the same hand-painted writing across it. This one read FAKES. "Hey, do you mind?"

Veri held the door for him.

"Thanks much," he said, stepping inside.

"You got it." Veri let the door close and watched through the window as the assistant stood and greeted him. She pointed to her left, and the man disappeared around the corner with his bubble-rolled canvas.

On her way back to the train, Veri felt her stomach bottom out. That was it: the last gallery she could pitch in the city. She'd promised her mother she'd have an apartment by now. In a few weeks, she'd have nowhere to live—and worse, no art studio to paint in. She'd have to resort to plan B, but first she was going to have to come up with one.

When she reached Seventy-Eighth Street, she spotted Phoebe again, this time walking away from the abstract gallery with a guy. It was Derek; she could tell by the navy blue coat he was wearing, the same one they'd bought together at a flea market. She was about to shout out their names, until they grabbed hands. Veri did a double take. Hadn't Phoebe just told her that Derek wasn't her type? She waited until they were halfway down the block, then crossed the street and noticed a photo of Phoebe and her squiggles in the gallery window. *Phoebe Jones, "The* Derek *Series"* was the title of her show.

"Oh *come on*," Veri groaned. They were all Phoebe's paintings. Every single squiggle upon squiggle, on every wall that she could see, was Phoebe's. It didn't look like there was a pink Jackson Pollock knock-off in the back either. The assistant at the desk spotted Veri and waved, signaling *We're open.* Veri backed away, wishing she had never even come into the city this morning.

Today was definitely going *very* not well.

TWO

On the subway, Veri sat next to an older man with a cane. She turned her music up and watched another man leap onto the train just before the doors closed. Instead of sitting, he stood by the door, unzipped his pants, and started fondling himself. "Jesus H. Christ," the man with the cane bemoaned. When he stood, Veri followed him to the other end of the car. She'd missed many things about New York when she was in Rhode Island, but disgusting men wasn't one of them.

By now, her hot anger over Derek and Phoebe had cooled into a steady simmer of confusion. How was it that they were the least likely couple she could imagine, and yet Phoebe had named an entire series after him? Even if they all looked like a migraine inside an explosion of neon, you didn't name your paintings after someone unless that someone was important to you.

It was suddenly sweltering in the train, and Veri shimmied off her coat. The man with the cane leaned over and picked something up. "I think you dropped this, young lady."

It was the Hattfield Gallery card.

"Thank you." She shoved it back into her coat pocket before accidentally glancing over at the sex criminal again.

When the subway screeched to its next stop, Veri jumped out, hurried down past two more cars, and stepped back inside the train again. She scrolled through her Instagram account, VerisArt. Her *Walk Out* series had a total of ten paintings. Her favorite was of a businessman with a briefcase leaving a train station late at night. His right leg was already out of frame, while behind him on the ground was an abandoned red stiletto. *Night Appointment* had the most likes (562), plus eighty comments. Each one of the ten paintings had a link for purchase in the profile. As yet, none had been purchased.

A few stops later in New Jersey, Veri got off the PATH for good and hurried down the stairs to the parking lot. A protest was going on. A few dozen people, mostly in plaid jackets and beanies, were holding up signs and chanting about climate change.

"Veri!" someone yelled. It took her a moment to figure out who it was: Jamie Spring from Hoboken High School. Jamie hurried over with her sign, which read *Carbon Kills*. "Hey, girl boss." They hugged each other with their free arms.

"Did you plan all this?" Jamie was one of the first kids she knew to get a nose ring. She always had offbeat hair colors too. Today it was fuchsia.

"Yeah, me and the rest of us at Climate Crew. The nonprofit we started. Hey, do you have time to hang with us?"

"Not really, I've got to go meet my mom. But I mean, go climate!"

"Hell yeah." Jamie fist bumped her. "How about a selfie." She pulled out her phone and tipped her head into Veri's. "Play dead." Veri hung her tongue out the corner of her mouth and closed her eyes while Jamie snapped their photo.

"Awesome to see you, Jamie."

"You too." She lowered her sign. "Are you still working at Weekly Dry Cleaners? My dad said he hasn't seen you there in a while."

"Yeah, but only two days a week. I'm trying to get a gallery gig in the city, so I've been taking some days off."

"So dope. Well, if you ever want to join us at Climate Crew, you know where to find us. You could make some freaking amazing signs."

"That sounds cool." Veri hiked up her portfolio and hurried off.

She'd lied about wanting to get involved in the nonprofit but told the truth about seeing her mother. Butterfly + Beds was around the corner from the Hoboken train stop, and her mother would be expecting her to stop in and say hello.

Veri spotted her standing in the front window, hanging teacups in midair. "How are you doing that?" she asked from the other side of the glass.

Her mother read her lips and tugged on a clear fishing line, which Veri could now see was hanging from the ceiling. "Can you notice it from out there?"

Veri shook her head.

"Good." She waved her inside. Belinda Sterling was forty-three, going on undetermined. Some days she could pass for thirty-three easily, with her dark hair and clear skin. Other days, usually just when she woke up and right before bed, Veri noticed her eyes looking puffier and a few new wrinkles around her mouth. Watching her mother age kind of terrified her. She was Veri's only parent.

Inside, the air smelled like perfume. The store was a more expensive version of Anthropologie but had somehow managed to survive in Hoboken for over ten years. Apparently, Hoboken, New Jersey, was no longer the working-class kid sister to New York City that it had been when Veri was first born. Most of their neighbors were upset about the millennials knocking down the iconic old brownstones, but her mother didn't mind. She argued that it would make their brownstones all the more valuable for whenever she decided to sell, which Veri had thought would be never, but two weeks ago she learned that it meant *now*.

Her mother brushed something off the puffy white blouse she was wearing, one of the same kind displayed on a row of hangers nearby, and stepped down from the windowsill in her black ankle boots. "I'm sure I'll get an earful from that one if they don't hold." She nodded toward Janet, the store manager, standing behind the register and checking out a bearded white guy wearing a North Face vest. "So tell me, honey. How did it go?"

"Swimmingly," Veri said. "The only thing anyone was even slightly interested in was one of my van Goghs that I didn't even know was in there. Like, what, they're going to show it in the gallery so I can get arrested for plag*art*ism?"

Her mother smiled. "Plagartism" was a word they'd come up with for whenever anyone wanted to buy Veri's renditions of the great masters. Just because Veri could copy the most recognizable paintings in the world didn't mean she would sell them. "What if they got into the wrong hands?" her mother would argue. Veri eventually figured out that her mother also wanted to keep the paintings for herself, evidenced by the fact that her best copies were hanging in their house.

"I think I've gone to every gallery in Manhattan at this point."

"I'm sorry." Her mother pulled her into a quick hug. She smelled like the Butterfly + Beds room sprays, the rose scent. They had bottles of them all over their brownstone. Lavender + Currant was the most popular, but she and her mother preferred the Rose. "Even your great master artist idols were rejected hundreds of times before they sold their first painting."

"Not all of them."

Her mother tipped her head, doubtful. "I think I remember Gustave Courbet was rejected one hundred and ten times before he ever sold a painting." She'd been a fine arts major at RISD, too, which meant her chances of being correct were pretty good.

"Okay, maybe. But at least he wasn't getting beaten out by squiggles and blobs. *None* of the galleries I went to had paintings of actual things."

"Sometimes squiggles and blobs can be beautiful," her mother argued, while starting to gather up fishing line. "Are you hungry?"

"Hell, ya. I'm a starving—and about to be *evicted*—artist." It sounded bratty, so she added, "Unless I come to Cape May with you, I mean."

"*Veri.*" Her mother shushed her and started toward the back of the shop. Her mom hadn't given her two weeks' notice yet, and she wasn't going to until the paperwork on the new store was signed. Two of the three women she was partnering with had also worked at Butterfly +

Beds, and all of them understood that her mother was risking the most by quitting. She was the only one not divorced from a hedge fund guy. She was also the only one not divorced, but only because she'd never been married.

"Oh, Belinda, dear." Janet waved from the register. "You're going to have to stop your little window project now and unpack all the boxes in the back room. We're having our managers' meeting, and we won't want to be interrupted."

Veri's blood ignited. Her mother was way too elegant to be spoken to in such a condescending manner, especially from an old "Karen" like Janet, who could have waited thirty more seconds for the bearded guy to leave before barking out the order. That was the point, of course. Her mother had been bossed around by jealous Janets for years (two of her previous managers were also named Janet), and buying into Divine Homes was her ticket out.

"Sure thing." Her mother smiled anyway.

In the back room, she finally groaned at the boxes stacked up against the wall. "Looks like I'll be here for a while. I have to tag all these items before I leave. But listen, honey. I was thinking tacos tonight. Would you pick up a few things on the way home?"

Veri nodded and shifted her portfolio around. Her mother handed her her bank card.

"No, I got it, Mom." Veri's stomach pinched. She'd promised her mother she would pay for half the groceries now that she was out of school, but her tiny savings account was taking a big hit. Weekly Dry Cleaners paid minimum wage. It was a lame job, just running the register, but she'd worked there since high school after her friend Amy Weekly had gotten her hired.

Her mother forced the card on her anyway. "How about you cook a few nights this week instead?" She didn't wait for an answer. She disappeared into the break room, and Veri headed out, glaring at Janet and her overly aggressive stack of turquoise bracelets on the way.

Back at the brownstone, Veri dropped her portfolio by the stairs and headed into the kitchen, which somehow still smelled like the onion bagel she'd toasted that morning. She grabbed a sparkling water from the refrigerator and sat down to check her phone. There were three new comments on her website—all spam. VerisArt was over two years old, and she hadn't received a single inquiry from an actual person. "*Yet,*" she told herself as she cracked open the plastic bottle and glanced up at the self-portrait of her great-grandaunt placed above their kitchen table.

Gray haired and stoic looking, Bunny Bonheur wore an army-style jacket, black slacks, and black lace-up army boots. Her hair was in a messy bun—or whatever they called it in the early 1900s—and a tobacco pipe hung from her mouth. She used to dislike this painting of her mother's distant relative, until she'd learned about suppressed female artists of the eighteenth and nineteenth centuries—many of them not even allowed to own paint supplies—and realized she was related to one. In solidarity, Veri had bought her own pipe and ramped up her resolve to become a successful artist herself.

"Life update, Bunny." She nodded to the portrait. "Another day of rejections. End of update."

She sat back in her chair, and the two chewed on their pipes together, wondering the same thing: how in the world Veri was going to find an apartment in New York City and start paying her own bills.

THREE

A buzz woke her up. It was a number she didn't recognize, but the area code was New Jersey. She let it go to voicemail, flipped over her phone, and dropped her head back onto her pillow. It was 8:00 a.m. Even now, many months later, her instinct was to roll out of bed and rush to class. Up until the final semester of her senior year, she'd had two early-morning studio sessions.

When her voicemail chimed, Veri rolled over and listened to it.

"Yes, hi. Is this Veri from VerisArt.com? This is Mildred from Middle Street Gallery." Veri's heart jumped. "I took a look at your art site, and we'd like to see the one . . . ah, let's see here . . ." A keyboard started clicking. "Yes, the one with the subway stop. So if that's good for you, doll, come in any time. We're here every day. Rain or shine, as they say."

"Yes!" Veri high-fived the empty air. "Mother fracking yes!"

She threw off her covers and hurried into the hallway. The smell of coffee wafted up the stairs, which meant that her mother was already awake and, most likely, had already gone to work. She'd been leaving the house by seven fifteen for the majority of Veri's life. In her earlier years, Veri remembered her mother making her breakfast and walking her to school. But somewhere around sixth grade, she would wake up to an empty house, with her mother already commuting into the city for her job at Bloomingdale's. It was only when Veri was a senior in high school that her mother found her job at Butterfly + Beds, much closer to home.

As suspected, her mother's room was empty. There was a small copy of a Raoul Dufy sailboat painting on the wall. This was one of the last paintings her mother had reproduced in college and the only piece of art she'd liked enough to frame. It made Veri proud every time she saw it—a tiny window into her mother's past life as an artist.

In the bathroom, Veri brushed her teeth and rolled on a double layer of deodorant. She wasn't as pretty as her mother, but she wasn't the worst-looking human either. Her father, she'd been told, was fairly hot, though. Of all the things her mother remembered about him, it was his large Italian nose that she recalled the most. Thankfully, Veri hadn't inherited it. The only photo she had of him was from her mother's freshman winter program in Florence, which she kept hidden in her drawer. Roberto Rossi died in a motorcycle accident a few years after his one- (or maybe two- or three-) night stand with the young American student, Belinda. He'd never admitted to being Veri's father and had squirmed out of any DNA tests by living overseas, where they were neither prevalent nor mandatory. Nineteen-year-old Belinda dropped out of college and went home to Ohio to have the baby alone.

Veri would never know her father, and now, she had no time for a shower either. Back in her room, she looked up the Middle Street Gallery address. It was one bus stop away, just on the other end of Hoboken. There was no website for the gallery, but maybe it was new. Who cares. They wanted to see her art.

She threw on cargo pants and a clean white button-down and stepped into her Docs. In the kitchen, she made a quick cup of coffee and nodded up to Bunny. "Life update: could be a good day." She leaned against the counter and read a text from her mom. **Left the grocery list on the table.** Veri glanced out the window. The two maple trees were almost completely orange and red by now, and a pink Barbie bike had been leaning up against one of them for months. Their courtyard was shared with another brownstone. The family with the little kid had moved in after she went to college, and they never seemed to be home.

The door into the garage studio was slightly ajar, and Veri headed in with her coffee. Her mom's VW lived on the street and was rarely driven except to move it to the other side of the street to avoid street sweeping. Copies of Veri's favorite paintings by Vermeer, van Gogh, Monet, Cézanne, and Courbet were taped onto the cement walls. As a kid, she'd spent hours studying how each of these artists created their masterpieces. *How to Paint Like the Great Masters*—the entire series, seven books in all—was lined up on the top of a wooden dresser filled with art supplies. Mildred had asked for *Night Appointment*, so Veri wrapped it in bubble roll, grabbed her wool army coat, and headed out the front door.

The Middle Street Gallery sat in between a hardware store and a Jersey Mike's Subs. The sign above it was peeling. Through the open door, Veri could see tables and chairs, a lot of them, everywhere. The place was filled with secondhand furniture. Long mirrors were leaning up against walls, and piles of random objects sat on every available space: sconces, dish racks, and lamps. Wrong address. Had to be. Veri turned around to head back to the bus.

"Veri Sterling?"

A woman appeared in the doorway. She looked to be in her sixties, with a wide girth and a welcoming grin. Mildred. "Come on in, doll," she said with a wave.

"Thank you."

They were the only two people in the musty-smelling store. Veri felt her nose sting and tried to suppress the trigger, but three sneezes came out in quick sharp succession.

"Gesundheit, doll. My goodness."

"Excuse me. I always sneeze in threes."

It sounded like a children's book title, but Mildred didn't acknowledge the rhyming. Instead she fiddled with a lampshade on a table. "I'm sure your mother told you: we usually take seventy-five percent, but for you, we'll do fifty."

"My moth— She did, yeah." Veri covered her surprise with a tight nod. "Thank you."

"Of course, when she asked, we were tickled to see her daughter's crafting. Let me show you where we can put it."

Crafting? Veri followed Mildred past a million more random items—a mismatched set of ceramic planters, a piece of wooden fence, a nightstand with a glass bowl on top of it—to the back of the store, where she shut a door to expose the wall behind it. The sign on the door read *Office of the Boss.* "How about here, doll?"

"Um, okay."

Mildred seemed to ignore the man wearing a cowboy hat who walked in and stood behind the register. Husband, Veri thought. When she pulled off the protective bubble roll, Mildred frowned at the painting. "It's bigger than it looked on your www page."

She meant her website, Veri guessed. "It's thirty-six by thirty-six?"

Mildred looked at the wall space again. "I think it's going to be too tight."

"Shoot." Veri feigned disappointment.

"I'm sorry, doll. We wanted something more like twenty-four by twenty-four. Could still be, what, in the twenty-, thirty-dollar range, you think? We're getting a mirror in today that needs to fit back here too." She lowered her voice. "Gorgeous gold plated. You'd love it."

"Sounds nice." Veri smiled through her sticker shock. *Twenty dollars?* Her website had *price upon request* for each painting, but obviously Mildred had come up with a price on her own.

"So I'll tell you what—you think you could paint us something that's twenty-four by twenty-four? We love cats. Ever paint cats?"

"I don't have any at the moment, but I could come up with something."

"Ever hear of an artist named Harry Craine? I think I got that right. There was a movie made about him. He only painted cats. You think you could paint us something like that?"

"Sure, I mean, I can check him out."

"I'll save this spot for you." She tapped the wall and looked past Veri. "Frank! Put a sticky note here. Write 'Spot taken for cat' on it."

The man behind the register opened a small tin box, pulled out a pen and sticky notepad, and scribbled on it without saying a word. Veri slipped her painting back into the bubble roll.

"Me and him love cats. We got a Persian and a feral. The odd couple. I don't know what all the hype is about dogs and you young people. No one wants cats now, but we love 'em." She led Veri to the front of the store, picking up a pair of pink candlesticks on the way. "Give these to your mom for me, would ya? I saw her eyeballing them when she came in."

The candlesticks were heavier than they looked. Veri slipped them into her backpack before shifting her painting under her arm again. "Thank you. I'll call you when the painting is ready."

"No need. We're always here. Bye, doll."

Outside, Veri heard Mildred shout, "Frank! The sticky note!"

She started down the sidewalk, telling herself not to be too disappointed. At least she hadn't had to sell her best painting for twenty dollars. And at the very least, the new cat project gave her an excuse to buy more supplies.

As she stood outside Hoboken Art Supply, she googled Harry Craine. There was no such name, but a *Herman* Craine came up as an artist. Mildred was right: Herman Craine was obsessed with cats. He did hundreds of paintings of cats before he was admitted to a mental institute for schizophrenia. Veri scrolled through images of playful kittens on beds, cats jumping over furniture, and cats hanging out with lots of other cats on top of a piano. She guessed Mildred would like a painting similar to any one of them.

The store looked empty but for the teenage clerk. After grabbing a cart, she started down the aisle. Art supplies had been her birthday and Christmas presents for as long as she could remember. At RISD, she'd known kids with unlimited funds, but she'd had to be disciplined. Her full scholarship did not include supplies, and her mother maxed out her cards more than once getting them for her—she'd found the statements in the trash. And the Weekly Dry Cleaners salary only went so far. Still, as usual, by the time she reached the checkout counter, her cart was overflowing.

The clerk mumbled a hello and stared at her cleavage. Veri frowned. There was nothing he could possibly see through the white button-down and wool army coat, but he couldn't stop looking at her chest. She grabbed the tobacco pipe out of her pocket and slipped it into her mouth. It was an instant creeper-detractor. The clerk looked away and kept his eyes glued to the register for the remainder of her purchase.

"Is that it?"

"Yup." The total flashed on the card reader, and she felt her face flush: $653. She didn't even have half that much in her account. "This is so embarrassing." She slapped her forehead. "But I forgot my wallet."

"You got like Apple Pay or something?" The clerk finally looked at her at eye level.

"I don't. Listen, sorry about this. Do you want me to put it all back?"

"I can hold it for you."

"Um . . . you know . . . probably not." She slid the subway painting out from the bottom rack of her cart. "This is mine. I brought it in with me."

The clerk shrugged. Veri started for the door. "Thanks sorry bye."

Around the corner, she exhaled. $653? She dropped her pipe back in her pocket and felt the business card in there again. "Myra Hattfield. The Hattfield Gallery," she read out loud. She started to rip the card in half, but stopped herself. *Myra Hattfield.* Now that she thought about it, she could swear she'd heard the name before. Maybe she was a teacher—or went to Weekly Dry Cleaners.

She searched for more information on her phone. The Hattfield Gallery was voted in the top one hundred galleries in 2015. Plus . . . *Myra was a Rhode Island School of Design graduate.* It didn't say what year. When her mom got home, she'd have to ask her if she'd ever heard of Myra.

FOUR

When the doorbell rang, Veri hid around the corner until she heard the delivery guy walk back down their front steps and drive off in his car. Then she grabbed the Thai food she'd ordered for dinner and brought it into the kitchen. Her mouth started watering from the spicy scent, but she'd watch more *Interesting Builds* and wait for her mother as promised.

Their TV screen was over the fireplace, and the baby blue linen couch, plus two matching chairs and a recovered wood coffee table, were all from Butterfly + Beds. It was an average room, except for the ceiling. Veri flicked the architecture show back on again, flopped onto the couch, and dropped her head back. She never got tired of looking up at it. According to the *Hoboken Reporter*:

> *The Creation of an Artist* is stunning: an absolute gem of a ceiling design inspired by Michelangelo's Sistine Chapel panel, *The Creation of Adam*. In this mother-daughter interpretation, "God" is a baroque-style goddess wearing flowing purple robes; she reaches down from the heavens to hand a paintbrush to an eager young female artist (also in baroque clothing), who holds a palette in one hand and extends the other up to the paintbrush, without quite touching it. With the expert detail around the panel, including gold leaf columns and chunky flying cherubs, this is perhaps the most exquisite ceiling in Hoboken.

Veri had memorized the review. Also, a copy of it was framed on the wall.

It had taken them one year to complete and three and a half neighbors to help build a mini scaffolding. Mr. Stevens died halfway through the project, but the scaffolding survived. The entire 800 block of Bloomfield Street was invited to the unveiling party; one neighbor even offered to buy the brownstone so they could own the ceiling. Besides the newspaper article, *The Creation of an Artist* got them an appearance on News 12, plus their ceiling's own Instagram page. It had probably also helped Veri get the scholarship at RISD, too, considering she wrote her college essay about the making of it.

A text from Allison pinged on her phone. Hey girl, started at The Pie Place. It sucks. Whatever. Come in tomorrow

Veri: Totally will!

Allison: Did you look on StreetEasy app yet?

Veri: I will soon

Allison: KK. Roomies forever.

The best surprise about freshman year had been Allison. They'd decided the school had placed them together after they'd each written "Hard to live with, love frozen food" on their housing applications. Allison and Veri had remained roommates for four years.

Roommates.

She sat up.

That was *it*. One of her mother's freshman roommates was named *Myra*. She slid off the couch and grabbed her mother's freshman—and only—college yearbook.

"Myra Hattfield . . . Myra Hattfield . . . you have to be in here somewhere. Aha!" She found the photo of an eighteen-year-old Belinda standing with two other freshman girls in front of a sign that read *Welcome to Rhode Island School of Design*. One of the girls was someone named Daphne Rennit, and the other, shorter one was Myra Hattfield.

The Ring app chimed on her phone, and a second later the front door opened. "I'm home."

"Mom!" Veri hurried into the kitchen and found her mother opening the refrigerator door. "Myra Hattfield," she said, holding the yearbook open. "Owner of the Hattfield Gallery."

Her mother squinted at the photo, closed the refrigerator, and twisted open her bottle of sparkling water. "She's difficult, Veri. We haven't spoken in years. I thought we were cooking tonight," she said, spotting the bag of food on the counter.

"I kind of forgot to get groceries, and *are you kidding me*, Mom. She was your roommate! And now she owns a gallery."

She agreed with a nod and went to sit at the table, looking a little pale. Veri knew she should let her mother decompress for a bit, like she usually did after work. Except tonight, she couldn't.

"Mom. I haven't been able to get past a single assistant-slash-supermodel in a *single* gallery yet. All I'm asking is for her to take a look at my portfolio."

Her mother kicked off one of her ankle boots. "I promise you, Veri, you'd be better off getting a meeting with her on your own."

"I don't think you really grasp how many RISD kids get shows because of connections." She sat opposite her mother and turned the yearbook around to face her. "I ran into my ex-friend Phoebe, who already has her own show, but I looked it up, and it's her *uncle's gallery*." It was true. Another small fact that Phoebe had neglected to tell her. "Also, I just found out that Derek was cheating on me with Phoebe the *whole time* we were going out. Which is pretty *heartbreaking*. I've been pretty sad about it, actually . . ."

Her mother yawned: not exactly the reaction Veri was hoping for. "That's terrible, honey." She kicked off her other boot, and Veri waited to see if she might think it was terrible enough to call Myra. Instead, she took a sip of her sparkling water and rubbed the back of her neck.

"It just confirms how smart it was of you to break up with him, though. Men like that are never worth crying over."

"Oh, come *on*, Mom!" Veri banged the table harder than she meant to. Maybe it was the result of all the galleries brushing her off or the frustration of knowing she needed to get another job pretty soon, but suddenly Veri felt bitterness bite her in the throat. "How could you not tell me about Myra?"

"*Veridian*," her mother said sharply. She looked exceptionally tired tonight. "For one thing, I haven't stayed in touch with anyone from school since I left. And for another thing, I'm sorry I don't have connections in the gallery world for you, but Myra Hattfield won't make up for it."

Veri looked away. Her mother always seemed to have connections when it involved local places like Weekly Dry Cleaning or the *Hoboken Reporter*, but ever since she'd been pitching galleries, there had been none. Belinda Sterling was a great artist—she was probably even better than Veri was—but she'd thrown it all away. When Veri was two years old, Grandma Kay had offered to pay for a nanny so Veri's mother could go to Ohio State and finish her degree. The shame young Belinda had brought on her mother had been forgiven, but Belinda refused the offer. And the subsequent offers. After Kay died, her mother used what little money she'd inherited to buy the brownstone and, up until now, had worked herself to the bone getting bossed around by Janets. Divine Homes was the first ambitious career move she'd ever attempted, and while Veri was proud of her, she wasn't about to follow in her mother's footsteps and give up on her art career.

"Mom, please. I've been to almost every gallery in the city, plus the Middle Street 'Gallery.'" She put "gallery" in air quotes. "And I mean, thank you for that, but even *they* don't want my stuff unless I paint a *cat*."

Her mother's eyebrows popped up while Veri continued on with her rant.

"I won the *Schumaaker* Award. They don't give that to people who draw squiggles with Popsicle sticks. They give it to the best artist in the school. *I* was the best artist in the school, and I can't get a show because I paint actual *things*?" Veri sat back and crossed her arms.

After a beat, her mother shook her head. "The self-pity, Veri, is so unbecoming."

They stared at each other for another uncomfortable moment. "Why didn't you just go back to school?"

"Come on, Veri. You know why. And *you* had four *years* to make connections. In fact, you could be making connections right now in Chicago."

"It was an internship at the *gift store*." Veri rolled her eyes.

"At one of the best museums in the world."

"Allison hated it, Mom. Best decision I ever made was not taking it and giving it to Allison instead."

A commercial blared out from the TV room.

"You're talented, honey. But a lot of people are talented."

That hurt. Veri stared down at her Doc Martens, and her mother went to the sink with her sparkling water and took out a wineglass instead. "Look, honey, if what happened to me happened to you, I'd encourage you to think twice about doing what I did and dropping out. But at the time, I had things to prove that meant more to me than getting a degree or having people tell me my paintings were good. I wanted to prove I could be . . . *not* a terrible person. *Not* a terrible mother."

Grandma Kay was verbally abusive, her mother had admitted a few years ago. "But you're nothing like her, Mom. And you're such a good artist. You could have done both."

"Not back then." Her mother looked at an old photo of herself with a toddler Veri on the refrigerator door. "Now can we eat? Janet had me reprice all the sales racks today, and I didn't have time for lunch." She started spooning Thai food into ceramic bowls with yellow bees on them, more Butterfly + Beds products. After a moment she said, "I'll call her, Veri. But don't say I didn't warn you."

"Wait, for real?" Veri clapped.

Her mother nodded into the bee bowls. "Now what's this about a cat painting? I used to love painting cats. I was a little obsessed with it, actually."

Veri told her all about the Middle Street Gallery while they ate their Thai food together.

FIVE

The same assistant-slash-supermodel was sitting at the desk the next morning, this time doing her nails. Veri backed away from the window and tried to calm her nerves. She didn't expect to be this anxious. Her phone buzzed in her backpack, and when she saw who it was, she forced herself to answer.

"Hi, Mr. Weekly." She cringed. "Sorry I haven't asked to be put back on the schedule yet; I was about to call you later."

"You're fired," he said. He was a gruff man, but she'd never heard him like this.

"What?"

"I can't have employees like you, Veridian. Your mother is still welcome as a client."

"I-I'm sorry, Mr. Weekly, but I'm not sure what you're talking about."

"Climate Crew? I can't be targeted by my own employees."

"Targeted? I didn't . . . *what?*"

"It's on the social media."

She scrolled through her phone. There it was—the selfie Jamie Spring took with her and the *Carbon Kills* sign. Both of them were playing dead, with their heads tipped together and their tongues out. *Boycott @WeeklyCleaners* was written across the top of it.

"Mr. Weekly, I had no idea . . . it was just a selfie."

"This business is hard enough without all you wake-up people. Your mother, though, we value her business." He hung up.

She considered DMing Jamie but slipped her phone back into her backpack instead, then gathered herself together and walked up to the door. The scent of nail polish assaulted her as soon as she stepped inside. "Hi, excuse me. I have a meeting with Myra Hattfield."

"She's on a call," the assistant said without looking at her. She was wearing just the right amount of makeup, with sparkling chandelier earrings.

"No problem."

The assistant continued gluing decals onto her nails, little ghosts, while Veri shuffled her portfolio case to her other arm. There was nowhere to sit.

"Emma!"

The assistant froze mid-decal and hurried over to the office door in her stiletto ankle boots and black catsuit. "Yes?" She pressed her ear to the door.

"I'm calling out your name *so you will come in.*"

Emma opened the door and disappeared, leaving Veri to look around the gallery. The FAKES painting she saw getting delivered was on the wall now, and the rest of the artwork looked the same but with different words. Three paintings, FINICKY, FABULOUS, and FEROCIOUS, were on the right side of the gallery, and FANCIFUL and FULGID were on the left. "Fulgid"? She googled it quickly. It meant something having to do with rapid flashes of light.

The office door opened again. "You can go in," Emma said. Her face was slightly pinker, and her sky-high cheekbones looked a little deflated.

"Thanks."

Myra Hattfield sat behind a pristine glass desk with a phone pressed to her ear. She was impeccably dressed in a navy blue Chanel pant-suit, her dark, professionally blown-out hair stopped just above her shoulders, and she looked short—five foot two at best. This was definitely the same person she'd seen in her mother's yearbook.

"Darling, say no more." Myra's hand flicked in the air while she spoke. "You need not do a thing. Leave all to me, my wonderful . . . yes . . . of course. *Je t'embrasse . . .*" She hung up the phone, along with her fake smile, and eyeballed Veri from head to toe, starting with her messy ponytail, down to her wool army coat and black jeans, and finally to her new black Converse sneakers that she'd been saving for a special occasion. "You must be Belinda's daughter. Sit."

There were two clear acrylic chairs in front of her desk. Veri sat in the closest one and lay her portfolio across her lap. "I really appreciate your time, Ms. Hattfield."

"I'm sure you do." Myra leaned forward and tapped the glass. "Let's have a look."

Feeling her heart beating in her throat, Veri stood, unzipped the case, and placed her portfolio down on the desk. Myra slipped on reading glasses and opened to the first page: the artist's mission statement, along with her education, awards, and the internship Veri had won for the museum in Chicago. Myra flipped past all of it without reading a word and leafed through the rest of the pages at breakneck speed, not lingering on a single photo of her work. "I'm not interested in realism. Your mother should have told you that." Myra did not look up.

"Yes, but . . . my *Walk Out* series focuses on the energetic disruptions left behind after a subject leaves the scene. As you could see a few pages back, um, there, sometimes it's a dog running out of frame." She couldn't possibly have seen the English bulldog leading its owner out of the park in the millisecond she'd flipped past it. "It's not traditional realism. My genre is more like *energetic* realism. How a seemingly static space can change when different energies arrive." She wasn't sure if she should keep talking, and she couldn't even tell if she was still breathing.

Finally, Myra took off her glasses and sat back. "Indeed." She paused, sounding like she might be reconsidering. Finally, a gallery owner who understood her artistic vision! "But." Myra sat forward again and slapped the portfolio closed. "It won't sell."

"The thing is—" Veri felt her throat sour. Myra Hattfield was her one and only connection. "It's like part of a greater theme of reality. We humans think that a place is alive when we're in it, but what if that same place only comes to life after we *leave*?"

Myra sighed dramatically. "Amusing, intriguing, blah blah, but it won't make a cent."

"But—"

"I can't sell the genre, Veridian." She opened the portfolio again and pulled out the van Gogh assignment. "However, *this*"—she held it up—"is good."

"Oh, no . . . um, that's not supposed to be in there." Veri groaned to herself. She'd forgotten to take it out again.

"Well, it's your best piece." Myra dropped the painting back onto the plastic page and slid the portfolio across her desk. "You've wasted a trip into the city, I'm afraid. Assuming your mother still lives out in Hoboken."

"She does, yeah." Veri zipped up the portfolio, along with her last bit of hope.

Myra clasped her hands together. Her long nails were painted in bright red. No wedding ring. "Your mother mentioned you won the Schumaaker Award. Impressive."

"Thank you." She felt like she was going to cry.

"Well . . ." Myra's voice trailed off in a *We're done here* kind of way.

"Ms. Hattfield," Veri said, pushing on. "I have some plein air that I didn't include here. No people or animals in them. I could come back later and show you?" Truthfully, she only had one painting of a poppy field, but she could paint another landscape by the end of the day.

Myra stood. "I have five years' worth of artists lined up to show in my gallery. If you were my daughter, I would have suggested you get into graphic design. Everyone wants a website these days." She stepped out of her office, and Veri followed.

Sitting at the desk, Emma didn't even notice. She was watching something on her iPad with AirPods tucked into her ears. "It's a crime that I pay her at all," Myra groaned. "You know, Veridian, I *am* looking for a new assistant, though. I'm about to fire this one." She nodded to Emma, still oblivious to them. "I'm sure your mother could use the extra income. She never did go back to school, did she?"

"Actually," Veri answered, pretending not to be insulted, "she's about to buy her own home design store, so she's killin' it." She thanked Myra again and started for the front door.

"Emma!" Myra snapped behind her. The assistant must not have heard her this time, either, because the next thing Veri heard was Myra's office door slamming shut.

By the time Veri got down into the subway, she was fuming. She should never have asked her mother to make that call. Her mother was right. Myra was no help—worse than no help, actually.

A lone trumpet player was belting out jazz notes deeper down in the tunnel. He was good. Exceptionally good, in fact. As good as any professional trumpet player she'd ever heard. When she reached him, she pulled out a few dollars and dropped them into his upside-down hat. His gray hair was clipped short, and his eyes were closed, lost in his own sound, but when Veri backed away, he opened his eyes and winked at her. She acknowledged his thank-you and continued down the tunnel to her train track, heavyhearted for this talented man who was too old now to ever make it big.

~

The train down to Thirty-Fourth Street was being rerouted. Along with the rest of the people waiting on the tracks, Veri let out an audible groan after the announcement.

"Screw you, New York!" someone yelled.

There was a collective push up the stairs. Instead of getting on another train, Veri decided to walk downtown. It had turned into a breezy, beautiful October day. Plus, she hadn't worked out since . . . truthfully, she couldn't remember the last time she'd gone for a run.

On the sidewalk, a group of people were standing in a semicircle and staring down at the ground. A graffiti art tour, she realized. A middle-aged skateboarder type was talking. "Each street artist has his own tag. These mushrooms stenciled on the sidewalk, those are Mushroom Man's tag."

"Banksy's a woman!" Veri shouted before running across the street.

A few blocks later, Allison waved at her from the patio of the Pie Place. Veri hurried over, plucked out her pipe, and hugged Allison's tiny frame. People were always assuming she was a ballerina. With her sandy-blonde hair up in a high bun and her long slender arms, no one would ever guess she was a sculptor.

"Dang, girl. Can't we please stop rockin' that pipe? You look like Sherlock Holmes's pasty-white little sister." Allison stepped back and scanned Veri's wardrobe. "And puh-*lease*. You can't even see your boobs under that coat. If I had those, I'd be flaunting them."

"I look smashing." Veri tugged on her army coat and looked down at Allison's T-shirt: THE PIE PLACE: SO GOOD IT'S A CRIME. "So how is it here?"

"Barely better than cleaning up the kiddie art room at that museum all day without even getting paid. Thanks for letting me take your internship, but I'm so glad I quit." A man—likely Eastern European— sitting at a two-top behind her was holding his check in the air, looking mad. "At least I can afford some supplies now."

"Why did they make it seem like we'd graduate one day and be Jeff Koons the next?"

"I don't know, girl."

Veri lowered her voice. "Guess what I just found out. Derek's been sleeping with Phoebe!"

"Wait. Phoebe Jones, the actual *goddess* who paints landscapes?"

"Yup. Except now she does abstracts and calls them *The* Derek *Series.*"

"Shut up."

"I swear." Veri held up her palm. By now, the man with the check was waving it. "Hey, there's a guy behind you looking pretty mad."

"He's an ass. Ignore him," Allison said. Veri tried to, but the guy was glaring at her now too. Allison gestured down to her portfolio. "Derek's a dick. I've always said that. Any luck with the galleries?"

Veri shook her head. "I got an offer to be a gallery assistant, though. *Pff.* As if."

Allison grabbed her arm. "Wait. For real? How much does it pay?"

"Um, I didn't ask?"

"Hey, waitress!" the man shouted. He was standing up now, waving the check.

Finally, Allison turned to him. "I'll be right there, *sir.*" She spun back around to Veri. "You should take that job, V. This one sucks. Text me if you don't want it, cuz I'll take it in a second." She walked backward for a few steps before turning to take the man's check and struggling through the doorway with his empty plates.

Back at the brownstone, Veri lay on her bed and pulled the Hattfield Gallery card out of her coat pocket. Something dropped onto her chest. It was the penny she'd found on the street: the one the flirty hot guy had said was his. Remembering his British accent made her smile. *Well, consider that your lucky penny, then. Might be a good omen.* She turned the penny over in her hand. A lucky penny. A good omen. He was wrong, obviously, but also . . . maybe . . . he was kind of right. At this point, she didn't have her dry cleaning money to count on anymore, and even though her mother hadn't started pushing her to get a job yet, she knew it was coming. Watching Allison get harassed was sobering and sad, but if she didn't get some other kind of income soon, she'd be applying as a waitress herself.

She put the penny on her bedside table and picked up her phone.

SIX

All the way into the city, Veri's stomach felt like someone was trying to jump-start it. Her mother hadn't made her feel any better either. "Working for Myra won't be easy, if it's the same Myra I remember," she'd said last night while draining the pasta.

Now, Veri stepped out of the train and headed toward Eightieth Street. The wind was off the charts, and her cheeks wobbled against it while she fought her way up the street.

"Ew." Emma sneered at her when she walked through the front door. "What is that?"

Veri looked down at her jeans without holes, her wool army coat, and a graphic T-shirt. "You mean this?" She pointed to the T-shirt. It had different types of doughnuts for each day of the week.

"You're going to get me rehired." Today, Emma's cheekbones were shimmering with some sort of opalescent makeup, and her eyelashes looked like they were two thousand miles long. Veri wished she had at least put lipstick on. Her minimalist makeup strategy might need to be reconsidered for this job. "Hold on." Emma disappeared around one of the gallery walls and came back with an elegant yellow poncho in her arms. "Here. Put this on."

It was soft as butter. Veri looked up at her. "You sure? This is pretty nice."

Instead of answering, Emma slid the portfolio case out of Veri's other arm and hid it under her desk. "When you work at a bakery, you don't bring in your own muffins. Shoe size?"

"Seven?"

Emma slipped off her high heels. "Today you're a nine."

Veri stepped back. "I'm fine with my Converse."

Emma thrust the shoes into her chest. "I've been trying to get fired for three months. You're the only one she's agreed to hire. I'd give you my kidney if I had to." Emma swiped everything off her desk—phone, iPad, AirPods, nail polish and nail files, an unopened diet soda—and into a reusable Whole Foods grocery bag.

"Couldn't you have just quit?"

"God, no. Not if I ever wanted to pay my rent again. Getting fired by Myra makes you *legit*. What are you waiting for? Put it on."

Veri took off her army coat and dropped the cashmere poncho over her doughnut T-shirt. "So soft," she said, stroking it.

"Shoes," Emma ordered.

Veri slipped out of her Converse and into the ridiculous heels—and stood like a dog forced into a Halloween costume. Emma stepped behind her, gathered up her hair, and secured a messy bun with one of the elastic bands around her wrist. "There. This will have to do. Oh, wait, how about lipstick?" She plucked a stick out of the Tory Burch backpack on her chair.

Veri shook her head. "No."

Emma didn't argue. "You should at least wear some gloss."

"What's my job exactly?" Veri still hadn't moved in the stilettos.

"Get her whatever she wants before she knows she wants it." Emma picked her pink trench coat up off the back of her desk chair. "And try not to die of boredom."

"You're not leaving right now?"

Emma was already out the door. "Hey!" Veri started to follow. Her ankle gave out on the first step. She threw the shoe off and hobbled out the door wearing one high heel. "Seriously?" she yelled in the middle of the sidewalk.

Emma, in bare feet, raised her arm in a wave without looking back. "Sorry, not sorry!" she shouted before disappearing into an Uber waiting by the corner.

"Really mature," Veri mumbled, then limped her way back into the gallery.

Inside, she found the other high heel and wobbled around to Emma's desk. The only item left on it was a daily calendar. Myra's office door was closed, so there was no way to tell if she was in there or not. She looked closer at the calendar. *Auction*, on Thursday, November 7, was the only appointment, and that was weeks away.

Veri sat down at the desk and clicked on the computer screen. It had a password log-in. "Of course," she mumbled. She opened the desk drawer to search for a sticky note or a scrap of paper, anything with a password written on it. Nothing. She tried *Hattfield Gallery*, but the computer laughed at her. She tried *Myra Hattfield*, in upper case, lower case, and as a single word, but none of those worked either. She tried *what have I done to myself?* but again, nothing happened.

"Who are you?" Myra walked in the front door wearing a brown mink coat and oversize dark sunglasses.

Veri stood quickly, wobbling in the heels. "Veridian Sterling?"

"You look different. Good. Come."

Myra disappeared into her office, and Veri wobbled in after her, wondering if the mink was fake, but Myra didn't seem the type.

After chucking her coat onto one of the acrylic chairs, Myra sat at her desk. "Now, Veridian. Get me up to date."

"Um, okay." How could Emma have left her to be eaten alive by Myra Hattfield like this? "Not much . . . has happened . . . I think the mail came?"

Myra rolled her chair closer to the desk and clasped her hands on top of it. She kept the dark glasses on. "If you ever tell me that again, I will have you arrested for theft."

Veri swallowed. Her forehead prickled with the beginning stages of regret. *Run away,* she thought. *Turn around and hobble right out the front door.* "Got it," she said.

Myra lowered her glasses. "There were hundreds of girls who wanted this job, Veridian."

"Yes, Ms. Hattfield." Veri waited for Myra to tell her to call her "Myra," but she didn't. "The only thing is, um, Emma forgot to leave me a list of my duties."

"Hello?" a male voice called out in the gallery.

Quickly, Myra pushed her sunglasses up again and waved Veri out of the office. "Greet that person. I'm not here."

"Okay." Veri wobbled out and shut the door behind her.

A pale-faced man with a pink buzz cut, wearing a white hoodie and skinny white jeans, was in the middle of the gallery. He looked oddly familiar, standing with his hands on his hips and staring at the wall, or more specifically the FAKES painting. Veri considered taking off the high heels but decided it would be worse to go barefoot. "Hello. Welcome to Hattfield Gallery. Can I help you?" Should she even say that? Was she supposed to say anything?

The man turned to her. He was in his fifties. Maybe even his sixties. "Delivery."

He wasn't carrying any food. "Oh, sorry, I think you have the wrong address. We didn't order anything."

The man frowned at her. The lines in his face were miles deep. You could go cross-country skiing across his forehead. "Where's Emma?"

"She no longer works here."

"Who are you, then?"

"Veridian." She started back over to the desk. This guy had a bad vibe about him. She needed to look like she was too busy to talk.

The man dropped one hand from his hip and pointed at her. "*Veridian.* Between green and teal on the color wheel."

"Yes." Veri flashed a smile, then started flipping through the calendar pages for no reason. "If I can be of any assistance, let me know."

"That's it?"

"Excuse me?" She looked up.

"That's all you're going to say. You're not going to try to sell me anything?"

"I just . . . don't want to hover. Is there something in particular you would like me to say?"

The man looked back at FAKES. "What do you think of this?"

"What do I—you mean like personally?"

He nodded. He seemed as bothered by the painting as she was. "You think it's shit, right?"

Checking to make sure Myra's door was still closed, Veri lowered her voice. "Well, I mean, how long can it take to do that? You could make like twenty of these in one day."

Suddenly, the office door swung open. "Beck!" Myra cheered, throwing her arms out and air-kissing him. "I thought I heard your voice."

Beck. This was the same guy who'd brought FAKES into the gallery the other day. She hadn't noticed his pink hair then, or maybe he hadn't dyed it yet, but it was definitely him: Beck Becker. His signature was on the bottom corner of every canvas. She had just insulted the artist.

"You've met the new girl?" Myra gestured to Veri.

"We were just catching up," Beck Becker said. Veri waited for him to tell Myra that she'd already dissed his art, but he didn't.

"And you have a new piece for me, darling?" Myra clasped her hands into a beg and batted her eyelashes at him.

Beck Becker nodded. "It's in the van. I'll get it."

"This one can get it." Myra flicked her eyes at Veri, who snapped to attention.

"Sure, I can get it." And while she was at it, she could jump into an Uber like Emma did and never come back.

"Van's to the left. Oh, and there's only one in there; I left the other nineteen at the studio." He winked at her.

Myra perked up, delighted. "You have more for me?"

"Inside joke," Beck said.

Myra took Beck's arm and led him over to another one of his hand-painted **F** words, where they huddled together, whispering, and Veri wobbled out to the sidewalk.

The street was noisy. The sound of honks punched the air. Her skin was prickling from dry sweat, and the cashmere poncho wasn't helping. When she spotted the van parked a few cars away, it dawned on her that Beck Becker had not given her his keys. The back door opened anyway, and she attempted to slide the large canvas out, but it was heavier than it looked. She yanked on it a few times, hardly moving it at all.

"Can I help you with that?"

It was the hot guy. He was wearing a dark suit and blue tie like the last time she'd seen him.

"Y-yeah, um, thanks," Veri stuttered. "I thought it would be, ah, not so heavy."

He killed her again with his smile, lifted the canvas with both arms, and pulled it out of the van; **FERMENT** was written across it. "So you *did* get your art in there, after all," he said, nodding to the painting.

"Oh, this isn't mine. I just work there. Or, well, I did, for like three minutes, before I scraped this thing up."

There was a black line along the side of the canvas where Veri had tugged it across the van floor. The hot guy used his suit sleeve to wipe it off. "Not at all. It's tip-top." A truck driver honked loudly enough for both of them to look over and see that a town car was blocking him.

"Take it easy. Go around." The hot guy waved at him. The truck driver gave him the finger and gunned it around the car.

"Wait, is that your town car?" Veri asked, realizing it just now.

"It'll be fine there for a second." He started for the gallery with the canvas, and Veri hurried after him in her best wobble and opened the door for him. She wanted to say that she could take it from there so Myra wouldn't see him, but as soon as he stepped inside, she heard Myra say, "Tate?"

"Hello, Ms. Hattfield. I was just helping your new assistant."

"Her name's Veridian. Greenish teal. That's her name," Beck Becker said, standing next to Myra in front of FULGID.

"Where would you like me to put this?" Tate asked Veri.

"There is fine." Myra answered, pointing to a spot on the wall.

Tate placed FERMENT down, and Myra sauntered over to it. "Oh, Beck! It's wonderful. Isn't it, Tate?"

"It certainly is." Tate turned away to hide his smirk, while Myra and Beck Becker started discussing the merits of the word "ferment." "It can mean to stir something up, as in a great excitement," Beck said. "But, at the same time, it can also mean to sour on something, to make it grotesque."

"Sheer brilliance," Myra said.

"See," Tate whispered. "Nobody's getting fired."

"The day is young," Veri whispered back. "But thank you again for helping me out."

"There you are, Tate." A well-tanned man in a long camel-colored coat appeared in the doorway. He was in his forties or fifties—who could tell—but whatever his age, he was handsome. Like *seriously* handsome. Like the kind of handsome that plays James Bond. He was tall, with dark-brown hair worn loosely in a side part, and his square jaw had probably killed the ladies more than a few times. His piercing blue eyes had definitely seen the inside of a soul or two.

Myra spun around. "Charles?"

Now it was Tate who looked nervous. He straightened up, growing an inch taller. "Sorry, Mr. Winthrop. I was helping Myra's new assistant."

"It's all right, Tate." Charles stepped over to Myra and kissed the back of her hand. She blushed enough for everyone to see.

"You still have the penny?" Tate whispered to Veri.

"Um. Maybe. I'll check when I get home," Veri lied. It was currently where she'd left it on her bedside table, balanced on top of a chunky piece of pink quartz—the love stone of crystals, apparently. Her mother had brought a few home from work one day.

"This," Myra said, clearing her throat, "is Beck Becker. One of my artists."

"Charles Winthrop." He stuck out his hand. "Pleasure to meet you."

"Yeah, you too, bro."

After they shook hands, Myra said, "Charles was living in London for years, but he's finally back in New York. He is one of our finest art dealers." She looked like she wanted to say more, but instead she said, "And this is all Beck's work." She motioned around the gallery.

"Wonderful," Charles said politely. "I'd love to stay and hear more about it, but"—he turned back to Tate—"I need to head over now."

"Of course, sir," Tate said, giving Veri a quick smile and opening the front door for him.

"Found something at 528 Gallery, have you?" Myra asked with a bit of snark to it.

Instead of answering, Charles smiled at both Beck Becker and Veri. "Nice to meet you, Beck, Myra's new assistant." He dipped his head at Myra. *"Myra."*

Myra blushed again, and as soon as he was gone, her mood visibly plummeted. "Veridian, I need you to go to the bank for me." She pulled a thick envelope out of her Chanel bag. "This is to be deposited. It's *imperative* that it's in before four o'clock. Also, my usual at Blue Unicorn. Plus one for Beck."

Beck, looking relieved now that Charles was gone, pointed at Veri. "Make sure it's *organic* oat milk." He followed Myra into her office and shut the door behind him.

When everyone was gone, Veri threw off the high heels and slid back into her Converse. She kept the poncho on, though. She grabbed her backpack and walked over to the window to make sure the town car had left. When she walked by the van, she saw that the back door was still open. She slammed it shut with her foot and walked on, wishing she'd never asked her mom to call Myra.

SEVEN

The Blue Unicorn was all the way across town: she'd tracked it on her phone while she passed at least ten Starbucks and a dozen other coffee bars on the way. She'd forgotten her AirPods in her army coat, so she had to entertain herself by thinking about Tate. He wasn't a lawyer or a boring Wall Street suit; he was a driver, which made him even hotter.

On the next block, Veri came upon a poster-size advertisement for an upcoming Cézanne exhibition at the Met. An image of Cézanne's *Tall Trees at the Jas de Bouffan* was on the poster. She'd copied it a few times in high school, but it was her mother who'd pointed out how Cézanne saw nature not as a moment in time but as a reproduction of shapes. *"See how he paints the trees like pieces in a jigsaw puzzle? The lines are at a forty-five degree angle. Nothing in nature is at a forty-five degree angle."* It was the beginning of cubism, although Cézanne probably didn't know it at the time. *"Also, the Prussian blue was Cézanne's favorite blue."*

Her phone buzzed in her backpack, and she panicked. She'd been gone for thirty-five minutes, and it was probably Myra asking where she was. She'd have to remember to make a unique ringtone for her.

It was from Allison, though. Send me that gallery asst info?

Without responding, Veri slipped the phone back into her backpack. She felt guilty, but she didn't have the heart to tell Allison she'd taken the job just yet.

The Blue Unicorn didn't have a sign, only a tiny blue unicorn in the upper-right corner of the window. Inside, it smelled like coffee and sawdust. Other than that, it was like any other overpriced coffee shop, with menu boards written out in white chalk pens.

A thirtysomething guy with bleached hair and a tattoo sleeve greeted her at the register. "What can I get you?"

She opened her mouth to speak but then closed it. Myra hadn't given her her order. "Ahh . . ." She moved her eyes across the fake chalkboard.

"What sounds good?" the guy asked, not impatiently, which was refreshing for New York.

"The thing is, it's not for me. My boss forgot to tell me her order."

"Wanna ask her? Take your time." He started wiping down a steam nozzle.

"She's not the texting/calling kind of boss. She's more of a Miranda Priestly kind of boss."

She didn't expect him to know who she was talking about, but he rubbed his tattoo sleeve and called down to the other barista working the end of the line. "Hey, Bridge, what's the Miranda Priestly again?"

"One no-foam skim latte with an extra shot, searing hot. And I mean *searing hot*," the barista rattled off.

"That's amazing."

"So you want that?"

"Yeah, sounds good. Make it two, though, one with oat milk . . . oh shoot, I mean *organic* oat milk."

The guy rang her up. "So you work in fashion?"

"Art gallery." She slipped off her backpack and pulled out her wallet. The coffee was eighteen dollars. Veri plucked out the emergency twenty that she kept folded behind her license. "You still take cash, right?"

"Bitcoin, cash, Venmo. Hell, maybe we'll start taking *art*. Fractional shares of the *Mona Lisa*, am I right?"

"It's okay," Veri said as she handed over her twenty. "I don't need change. Thank you for sleuthing with me."

"Yeah, no problem. I'm an artist, too, by the way. Which gallery?" He looked at her with a mixture of desperation and possibility. She wanted to tell him the truth, that there was zero chance she could get him a show at the gallery. She felt bad about it, but why give him any hope? She looked down at his hands and clucked her tongue.

"Sculptures only," she said. "Ugly stuff," she added quietly, "but a job's a job." His nails looked too clean to be a sculptor. It was an educated guess. Allison's nails had been constantly cracked and stained at school.

"Preach," the barista said with a nod.

The next stop was the bank, which she almost forgot about after leaving the Blue Unicorn holding the two *searing-hot* coffees. It was obvious to her now that she should have gone to the bank first. Only a few people were inside, and all of them were tellers, looking bored.

"Can I help you?" a man with slicked-back hair looking like he had just graduated high school asked before his fellow teller could.

Veri placed the *searing-hot* coffee on the ledge. "I need to deposit this." She pulled out the thick envelope and slid it under the glass partition, noticing a drip of coffee on the poncho.

"ID, please," the teller said without picking up the envelope.

"It's not for me. I'm depositing it for my boss."

"We won't be able to accommodate you."

"Wait, what?"

He shook his high school head. "We won't be able to deposit it unless your boss is here."

"Oh yeah. She's standing right back there. She has an invisibility cloak on, though."

The teller did not look amused.

"Look, I'm sorry," Veri said sincerely. "It's my first day, and she told me to deposit this huge wad of cash and that it was *imperative* it gets in today. She didn't tell me anything else. So could you just let me deposit it, and next time I promise I'll bring a note or whatever."

"I'm sorry. We can't accept cash from a third party."

"Fine. You know what?" She wiped her damp forehead. "That's fine. My boss is mean anyway. I don't even know if I'm going to make it through the day. I'm probably getting fired the minute I get back because her coffee, which I bought with my emergency twenty, is gonna definitely be cold. And even though it's like supposedly *cool* to get fired by Myra Hattfield, I think that only applies to models." She swiped up the envelope and started to gather the hot coffees. "Oh, and I ruined a cashmere poncho too."

"Where's Emma?" A man in a blue suit with a *Manager* pin on his lapel appeared behind the teller.

"She quit," Veri said. "I'm Myra's new assistant."

"She *quit*? But her modeling career?"

"I mean, she was *fired*."

The manager looked relieved and elbowed the teller. "Go ahead, take the cash, Michael."

"Thanks." Veri put the coffees down again and slid the envelope under the partition.

"Myra's a good client," the manager added before disappearing in the back.

It was $25,000 in cash. She nodded along with the teller when he double-checked the math with her, then took the receipt and the coffees and walked all the way back to the gallery, wondering if Myra was a drug dealer.

Another envelope was taped to the front door, this one with her name on it. *Veridian.* Veri balanced the tepid coffees in one hand and tried the door. Locked. She pulled off the envelope and plucked out the single key.

Once inside, she found a note from Myra on her desk. *Next time take a key. If anything gets stolen while you're gone you're responsible. Also you'll have to pay me back for the coffees that never came. Close tonight at*

6pm and arrive by nine thirty am every morning on the dot. I don't tolerate
tardiness and I can check on the cameras.

"Cameras?" She spotted a small camera in the ceiling on the back
wall, aimed at the front door. She was being *watched*. She dumped the
cold coffees—that Myra definitely hadn't paid for—in the trash and
sat at her desk. What had she done? She never should have taken this
job. Allison would be better at it anyway. She pulled out her phone and
started to text her, when her mother's text pinged in. Mr. Weekly called
me. You mixed up someone's laundry the last time you worked. You owe
him $800 now. Says he'll sue you if you don't pay. She added the emoji
with the head blowing up, twelve times.

Great. That was *eight hundred* dollars that she didn't have. She
threw her phone on the desk. At least she hadn't texted Allison yet.

～

Myra called at 5:55 p.m. "Veridian, update me. Who came in? Any
serious offers? I'm in the car, so speak up."

In the five hours since Myra had left her with nothing to do, Veri
had stared at the computer screen, either playing video games or doing
some online window-shopping. Only two people had come into the
gallery—a Japanese couple who spoke no English and left after five
minutes. "Two people and no," Veri told her.

"Two people. Are you sure?"

"Yes. I didn't leave the desk except once, just to, you know, the
bathroom." The only bathroom was through Myra's office. Not knowing
the camera situation, Veri had talked herself out of needing to go until
around four o'clock, when her bladder was at stage critical.

"Anyway, Veridian, tomorrow I want you in at nine."

"Okay."

Myra hung up.

She called right back.

"Did Emma give you her key?"

"She must have forgotten," Veri said, *as she was sprinting down the sidewalk.*

"That girl. Fine. Use the one I left for you. And make a copy of it by the time you get in in the morning."

She hung up again. Veri clicked off her phone. How was she supposed to get a new key by nine in the morning when she had to leave for the PATH at eight? She looked up locksmiths in Hoboken. One a few blocks from her stop was open until 7:00 p.m.

It was dark by the time Veri got back to the brownstone—and cold again. "Tell me all about it," her mother called out from the kitchen when she walked in the front door.

"How were you ever roommates with her?" Veri dropped her backpack by the stairs.

Her mother chuckled. "You're welcome." She was sitting at the table paying bills.

"She has not even a *shred* of niceness in her." Veri gave her mother a quick hug and got the orange juice from the refrigerator. She hadn't had any food all day, except for the bag of potato chips she'd bought at the train station. She took a pinch of the buttered pasta warming on the stove. "I'm so hungry," she mumbled.

Her mother took off her reading glasses and sat back. "How does she look these days?"

"Short." Veri noticed a moving box in the corner of the kitchen, and she fished some crackers out of the cabinet. "And mean."

Her mother grinned. "Short and mean."

"Wait, so you're already packing?" she asked through a full mouth of crackers. She took a closer look into the box. Cookbooks and old sketchbooks were piled up to the top.

"I'm still waiting for this Realtor to get back to me, but I thought I might as well start cleaning things out. You should too, Veri. It always takes longer than you think." Her mother sat up again and opened more bills. "We've lived here for a long time."

A ripple of sadness moved through Veri's chest. "My whole life."

Her mother turned to face her. "I know, honey. I'm sad about selling too; you know I am. But you would've gone to live in the city sooner or later, and I won't get another chance like this . . . probably ever. The ladies could easily buy it without me."

Veri brightened up for the sake of her mother. "They need your design skills for Divine Homes just as much as they need the money for it." Veri picked a warped sketchbook out of the box. The pages were filled with a younger Belinda's watercolors: apples, bananas, and oranges. "Hey, is it normal that the artist pays the gallery owner to show their work?" Veri dropped the sketchbook back into the box and plucked out another. This one had sketches of animals, including cats. She remembered she still needed to do the cat painting for Mildred.

"I told you, honey. She's slippery."

"Rude *and* slippery," Veri said. "I'm going to take a shower."

"Okay, and one more thing." Her mother stopped her before Veri started up the stairs. "The ladies want me in Cape May tomorrow, so I'm driving down for a few days. I'll let you know once I'm there when I'll be back."

As soon as Veri got into her room, her phone pinged. It was a text from Allison. Meet @ The Pie Place for breakfast tomorrow? I found an apt for you, gurl!

Veri: Really? Where?

Allison: Tell you tmmrw See u @ 8

Veri gave the text a thumbs-up and collapsed on her bed. Today had been exhausting. How was she supposed to make it through the rest of the week?

EIGHT

The Climate Crew was extreme, but no one could deny that they were fighting a just cause. It was too hot for October. Veri unbuttoned her army coat and hurried down the sidewalk to the Pie Place. Allison, in a long skirt and loose sweater, looking gorgeous, waved from a table on the patio.

"I've been dying to try this place as a civilian," she said after they hugged. "They wouldn't even give us free frickin' pie."

"Why are you talking past tense-y?"

Allison placed her hand flat down on the table.

"What the Krispy Kreme is that?" There was a rock on her finger. A very large, very shiny diamond. "Is that *real*?"

"Hell yeah. But it's like the kind they grow in labs or something, so no squirrels were killed."

"You mean it's not a blood diamond."

"Ew. And yeah, this girl's off the market."

Veri grabbed Allison's hand for closer inspection. "I feel I am missing some key details here, Allison. Two days ago, you couldn't pay rent."

"Improv class, V. I went in Chicago and met someone."

"Wait, what?" She dropped Allison's hand. "Why didn't you tell me this before?"

"I couldn't. I mean I was dying to, but he needed to tell his kids about me before I could say anything. It was killing me, but he made me swear. He's a doctor." She admired her own ring. It sent off a million rainbow flashes.

"A doctor at improv class? Does he play a doctor on TV?"

"Doctors can have passions too, Veri. He's pretty funny, like, *very*, Veri."

"'Funny' is not exactly a doctor's most important trait, you know."

Allison shrugged off the comment. "So obviously I quit this place. I won't need that gallery job either."

"Good. Okay, good. That's good."

"What's up with you? Why are you saying 'good' so many times?"

"I took it, actually. The job."

"Oh. Is it gross?"

"Very." Veri nodded.

A tall, skinny waiter came up to their table. "So did you tell them yet?"

Allison clasped her hands under her chin and grinned up at him. "Yeah. And they're glad to see me go, Jeremy. I told them you'd take all my shifts. This is my friend Veri."

"Hey," Jeremy said without making eye contact. He looked nervous to be talking to girls.

"She'll have the mocha peppermint coconut pie. Trust me." Allison winked at her.

"Whipped cream?" Jeremy asked.

"Like a mountain of it for her," Allison said, sitting up and smoothing her sweater down over her hips. "And just coffee for me. I gotta keep this banana boat in check, you know, for the dress." Jeremy walked away, nodding down to his notepad. "So this is what I want to tell you, V. I'm moving to Montauk. Monday through Thursday. On weekends we'll go to Palm Beach."

"Huh? Is this guy a thousand years old?"

Allison gazed down at her ring. "He is indeed older. But nothing too shrively. And at least he doesn't sit around smoking weed all day and playing video games like every single guy our age does."

It was true: that *was* what most of the guys in college had done. Not Derek, though. He was usually nerding out and coding on his computer. "But wait, what about your sculpting career?"

She rolled her eyes. "As if sculpting were an *actual* career. I know we dreamed of being famous artists with studios in our country houses, but like, come on. I'll just settle for *having* a country house."

"I wish I didn't care as much as you don't."

Allison sat forward. "Here's the deal. I need to sublease my place now that . . ." She flashed her ring again. "It's in Harlem, fully furnished. And as you know—and *still* have not come to see it for some lame reason—I've only lived there not even two weeks actually."

"If I can afford it, yeah, totally. But like, for real? You're moving?"

"I'll miss you too." Allison grabbed Veri's hand. "But Montauk isn't that far. Plus, maybe I can set you up with one of his bougie friends." She paused. "So listen, I'll send you the details on the apartment. You can think about it for like a week; then I have to put it on StreetEasy."

Jeremy came back with the pie and coffee. "I picked up three of your shifts," he told Allison.

"Thanks," Veri and Allison said at the same time.

He shrugged, then pulled out his notepad and walked over to a table at the end of the patio. A father and daughter had sat down a few minutes earlier. Veri watched the father giggle with his daughter, who kicked her legs under her seat. Sometimes when she saw dads and daughters, she watched them like they were from another planet.

"Hello, calling Veri," Allison snapped at her.

"When's the wedding?"

"No date yet."

Veri moved the piece of pie into the middle of their table.

"Have some of this, then."

"You're a bad influence." Allison frowned.

"You're welcome."

They both dug in.

NINE

Myra held up her black Amex. "Tell him to stay here, Veridian. We'll be ten minutes."

She waited until Myra had slid all the way out of the cab before handing the driver the card. "I'm sorry, sir. Do you mind waiting for us?"

"I keep meter running," he agreed.

They had driven all of five blocks. Myra wasn't much of a walker.

"Hello?" Myra knocked. "Estrella?"

The door opened a few inches before getting stuck. A woman with tight blonde curls rolled her eyes at them. "*Attendez*," she said in a thick French accent. "The door keeps . . . *merde*! Mortimer!" she yelled, then whispered, "He's death so I yell for nothing." She closed the door again.

"He's dead?" Veri asked.

"She means 'deaf.'" Myra was getting impatient.

This time the door opened all the way, and the Frenchwoman, who looked to be around thirty, waved them inside. "Come, come, *viens, viens*."

It was an art studio, packed with easels and paint and canvases. The floor was covered with thick tarps, one of which had jammed up the door, and the air was thick with paint fumes—Veri's favorite scent.

"You're looking lovely, Estrella," Myra said.

"*Merci.*" Estrella had stacks of silver rings on every finger and wore a pink miniskirt with white sparkling tights and a T-shirt with a photo of

Blondie on it. Veri smiled to herself when she noticed they were wearing the same Doc Martens. Myra had scoffed at Veri's just this morning when she arrived at the gallery. "This isn't a music festival, Veridian," she'd said. "I'll expect you to dress more professionally from now on."

"I love your shoes," Veri told Estrella.

"You are the new girl?" she asked.

Veri nodded.

"You look so cool," she said.

"Thank you. So do you—"

"We have a cab waiting, so just a quick glimpse, Estrella," Myra interrupted. "Dying to see it."

Estrella led them to a large canvas with soda cans and dental floss glued onto it. The background was painted a grape purple, with bits of silver leaf placed arbitrarily around the soda cans. It looked like a group project from a kindergarten class, but Myra's hand flew up to her cheek. "Estrella! Absolutely stunning," she cried.

"Mortimer thinks it is perfect for the Broad." Estrella nodded at her work.

"Great idea." Myra clapped. "Veridian, remind me to set up a meeting with Eli's people."

"Yes, of course." She pulled out her phone and texted it to herself.

Estrella stared at Veri. "You are so young."

Not sure if that was a question or not, Veri said, "Yes, I'm a recent college graduate, so not that young."

"Estrella went to RISD," Myra said, stepping up to the canvas of chaos to study it more closely.

"Really?" Veri perked up. "Me too."

"Didn't we all," Myra murmured. "Now, Estrella dear, where can I find Mortimer? Is he here somewhere?"

"Mor-ti-mer!" Estrella yelled in no discernible direction.

An old man stepped into the room. He looked to be about seventy, with a slim comb-over. His tan linen pants matched his linen shirt, which was unbuttoned down to his navel to show off his gray chest hair.

Two thick gold chains with crosses hung in between his small mounds of man-boobs.

"Mortimer, darling, it's divine. Uncanny!" Myra chirped like a chipmunk.

Mortimer pointed an arthritic finger at Myra. "Un*canny*. That is a good one." He had bad teeth. He walked over to Estrella and pinched her butt. "She's a talent. She has many talents, in fact."

The man could be Estrella's grandfather.

"And this young one is who?" He looked at Veri with his beady eyes.

"The new girl, Mortimer," Estrella said.

"Well, we do have some other stops to make," Myra said pointedly. "Mortimer, do you have something for me?"

He pulled a folded check out of his floppy linen pants—Veri tried not to think about what else was under there—and handed it to Myra, who slipped it into her Chanel purse without looking at it. "You'll have it delivered by next week?"

"That we will." Mortimer air-kissed Estrella, and she brushed down his sagging cheek with all her silver rings.

Myra headed for the door.

"Nice to meet you, um, both," Veri said. If they said anything, she didn't hear it. The cab was still idling outside, and Myra waited for Veri to open the door for her.

As soon as they'd driven away, Myra said, "Set up the call with Eli Broad's people." She slid on her dark glasses. "Then cancel it. They're never going to consider that trash."

"Okay." Veri couldn't stop herself from cracking a smile.

"Don't be too smug, Veridian. At least Estrella gets to show her glue collage, or whatever the hell that was, at the gallery. Someone will probably pay a premium price for it now."

"It's just . . . who's going to take her seriously after that? Doesn't seem worth it, that's all."

Myra looked at her over the top of her glasses. "You know, your mother might have said the same thing once, and now she does windows." Veri was stunned. Myra turned away. "Oh, and I was sorry to hear she's selling the brownstone. I know how much she loves it."

"She told you?"

"She mentioned she was moving, yes." Myra clucked her tongue. "Being a single mother sounds . . . well, happily I'll never have to know, single or otherwise."

"It's because she's opening the store in Cape May," Veri said defensively. "And she *designs* windows."

The cabdriver started swearing at a person jaywalking in front of them, and Myra's cell phone rang. "Oh, and before I forget, Veridian, set up a call with David Geffen. I'd like him to consider a Beck piece." She looked at her phone and answered it quickly. "Beck, darling, I was just thinking about you."

Veri texted the Geffen note to herself and clicked off her phone, fuming. Myra's snarky window comment was too stupid to take seriously, but still, it struck a nerve. Her mother was already sounding stressed down in Cape May. She'd left a voicemail this morning.

After returning from Estrella's studio, Myra sent Veri back to the bank to deposit Mortimer's check: $75,000. The bank tellers were all too happy to take the money this time. Myra was gone by the time she got back to the gallery, and the rest of her workday was totally uneventful, except for a few people who left almost as quickly as they'd entered, one man even saying, "I told you, Jean, junk." At home, Veri put her Chipotle order in the refrigerator and grabbed something to drink. The box full of her mother's old sketch pads was still in the corner. She picked out the one filled with animals and brought it into the garage with her, deciding she might as well start on the cat painting for Mildred now.

After flipping through the pages, she found a perfect sketch to use as a model for Mildred's painting. There were three cats, two curled up on the floor and one stretched out inside a windowsill, all looking like they were smiling. It seemed like something Mildred would love. A newspaper article fell out from between the pages, and Veri recognized the man in the photo right away.

New to the Scene was the headline, with a black-and-white photo of a younger Charles Winthrop looking less refined but just as handsome. *Rhode Island School of Design senior, Charlie Winthrop, stands ready to take the London art scene by storm.* The article went on to congratulate "Charlie" for his acceptance into the London School of Economics.

"Oh my God." She snapped a photo of the article and texted it to her mother. This is the art dealer I was telling you about! Do you know him?

She waited for her mother to respond, but when none came, she slid the article back in between the pages and started sketching out the cats.

TEN

When Veri arrived at the gallery the next morning, the door was unlocked. "Hello?"

Her skin prickled when no one answered. But then again, if someone wanted to rob a gallery, they might want one with better artwork in it. "Anyone here?" she asked a little louder.

She heard a voice. Myra's office door was open a crack, and it sounded like she was on the phone. "Do you want to tell me now why I'm here at this godforsaken hour?" Veri grinned at Myra's comment (it was nine thirty) and went to her desk as quietly as she could. Suddenly overnight, it now felt like winter outside, and her cheeks burned from the cold walk.

"But are we sure it's authentic?" Myra continued. "Yes of course the provenance would prove it's real . . . Well, in that case, we'd better find the painting before anyone in Hong Kong does. That entire country is obsessed with finding his ear, for Chrissake . . . *You're sure* it's not just a rumor, because realistically it will fetch tens of *millions* . . . Now, why would you even ask me that . . . of course I won't tell a soul. I'll start making inquiries . . . subtle ones . . ."

Veri kicked her boot against the desk leg by mistake, and Myra's tone changed right away. "I have to click off now . . . ciao ciao. Veridian?" she called out. "Is that you?"

"Hi." Veri poked her head into the office. Myra's face was pale and totally devoid of makeup. Her eyes looked flat, and dark circles sat under them like empty hammocks. Even though her hair was still blown out, it lay in disarray around her shoulders. She was in matching "leisure clothes," from what Veri could see.

"How long have you been out there? Were you listening to my phone call?" Myra's tone was aggressive.

"I just walked in," Veri lied. "I didn't hear anything." *Ear. Painting. Millions.*

Myra narrowed her eyes at her for a moment, then looked back at her computer screen. "I'd kill a small child for coffee."

"Sure," Veri said. It was Myra's way of ordering. "I'll be quick."

"No." Myra looked over at her again. "Don't be quick. I don't need coffee, actually; I need privacy." The black Amex appeared in her hand, and Veri took it from her. "The At Home store downtown, on Broadway. Go get me a candle. Bamboo—their signature brand. Just one. Nothing else."

"The At Home store, downtown, got it. Do you—should I lock the front door?"

Myra started dialing on the landline. "What time do we open?" she asked sincerely.

"Nine thirty . . . I mean, it says that on the window, but ah, you can open whenever."

"Lock it. Now go. I need to make some calls."

After she shut the door, Veri grabbed her backpack and army coat, then stepped outside and locked the gallery door with her new key.

According to Google, the At Home store looked like Butterfly + Beds on steroids. Everything in it was beautiful and overpriced. According to NYCityMap, it was a thirty-minute train ride. Just as she started walking toward the station, a car honked behind her, and the passenger-side window of a black town car lowered. "Hello." It was Tate.

"Should I be worried that you're always double-parked outside the gallery, much like, let's say, a stalker?"

"Mr. Winthrop's office is around the corner." He slid down his Ray-Bans. "Plus, we share a penny, Veri. It's the only way I get to see it, unless you'll grant me visiting rights?" He added a smile, and Veri's ability to form words momentarily died. This man was *gorgeous.*

Behind the town car, delivery trucks were forced to merge into the next lane. "You're causing a lot of traffic, you know."

Tate threw his hand up. "Just another day in the life of a driver. So where are you headed?"

"To a store downtown." She looked in the back seat. "Are you waiting for Mr. Winthrop?"

This morning, her mom had finally texted her back about Charles: Yes, he was Myra's boyfriend, she'd said. I didn't know him that well but he was the big man on campus. Cape May is gorgeous today. Wish you were here.

"He's in a meeting. Let me drive you. It's freezing out."

Veri shivered the very moment he said it. Her nose was dripping, and she'd left her gloves on her desk. "What if he comes out and you're not here?"

"I'll tell him I was assisting a young woman in need." He opened the passenger door from the inside, and Veri slipped off her backpack and slid into the front seat. "It's like winter just started overnight, d'you know what I mean?" He was in his usual outfit of blue tie and dark suit. He started up the car again. "So where are we headed?"

"Union Square. Myra needs a candle," Veri chuckled. When he didn't laugh back, she got nervous that she'd sounded too glib. "Hey, so I found an article about Mr. Winthrop yesterday. He went to Rhode Island School of Design too."

"Yes, he's told me he went there before he went to London."

"Is that where you met him? In London? I mean, you're British, right?"

"Bermudan, actually. But to be fair, I moved to London when I was little, or just outside of London, rather."

"Wow, Bermuda. That must have been nice."

He tipped his head. "Honestly, I hardly remember it. But Mr. Winthrop promised my father he'd hire me if he ever moved back to New York, and he did."

"Cool. How long have you lived here?"

"I went to NYU, and now I'm at Stern. My final year." A yellow taxi blared its horn, and Tate scowled into the rearview mirror. The taxi honked again and then swerved hard around the town car, only to get stuck behind another town car in the lane next to them. Tate remained as calm as a cucumber.

"You're like Yoda-level calm," Veri said, amazed by his reaction.

"Only when there's a guest in the car." He gave her a side-smile, tapped his thumb on the steering wheel, and changed lanes again. The traffic was moving faster than normal, or maybe Tate just knew how to get around better.

They reached the store after a few more near misses with yellow taxis and Ubers. "You sure you don't mind waiting? I can take the subway back," Veri asked after he'd double-parked.

"I'm sure." He rested his left wrist on the steering wheel and looked at her. "I'd be waiting uptown if I wasn't waiting here. That's what I do. Take your time."

"Okay, but if you have to go, just text me."

"Sounds like a plan." He handed Veri his phone, and she put her number in before handing it back. It was more awkward than either of them let on. She could tell by how he cleared his throat when he sent her a text. Tate, her phone pinged. And then it pinged again: Donovan.

Veri stepped out of the car and went inside.

By the time she'd bought the world's most expensive candle, Tate was standing outside, leaning up against the passenger door waiting for her.

"All set, then?"

"Yeah, thanks."

He opened the door, and when he got back into the driver's seat, he frowned. "So you were right: Mr. Winthrop does want me back."

"Oh no, you should have texted me."

"No worries at all. I told him I was with you, running errands for Myra."

Veri narrowed her eyes. "He's really not mad?"

Tate started the car. "No, but I am. I was going to suggest taking a drive around Central Park."

That was a flirt. You don't want to drive around the park with someone unless you want to at least figure out if they're single or not. "That would've been great." She tried to sound slightly disappointed, even though her mind was racing. Tate was the single hottest guy she'd ever driven in a town car with, and also this was the only time she'd ever driven in a town car. She wanted to sneak a photo of him and send it to Allison, but she didn't want to risk it. She needed to play cool.

Tate shifted in his seat. "By the way, how is our penny?"

She pretended not to know what he was talking about for a moment, then dug around in her coat pocket and pulled it out. "I can't believe I still have it," she lied. She'd tucked it back into her coat pocket after her first day of work, hoping he'd come back to the gallery and ask about it. "I mean, I *think* this is it."

Tate inspected it while trying to keep his eyes on the road. "That's our boy," he said. "Would it be all right if I visited with him for a bit? I'll return it at dinner."

"Dinner?" she asked, confused.

He grinned at her. "I'd love to."

"Ah," Veri said. "I see how you did that." She forced herself to look out her window so he wouldn't see the shock holding her face hostage. This perfect specimen of a man was asking her on a date. It was possibly the best day of her life.

"So . . . would you like to sometime?" Tate asked, sounding nervous now.

"Sure . . . yeah . . . definitely," she answered. "I'm pretty much free every night." She groaned at herself. *Pretty much free every night?*

"Great. Is it okay if I text you? I won't know my schedule for next week until the weekend."

"Totally get it. Myra's schedule's busy too," she lied again.

"She's probably going to the Met show as well." There was an awkward pause between them until Tate said, "All the way downtown for a candle, then?"

"She needed 'privacy.'" Veri air quoted "privacy" and immediately remembered: *Ear. Painting. Millions.* "Hey." She shifted in her seat to face him. "Can I tell you something? But you can't tell anyone."

"Absolutely." He seemed excited by the idea.

"I think I overheard Myra talking about a painting that someone found."

"Isn't that part of her job?"

"No, but I mean like an important one. I think it might be a van Gogh."

Tate slammed on the brakes, inches from rear-ending a taxi. The taxi driver blared his horn, and Tate stuck his middle finger out the window. Tate looked mortified. "Sorry about that," he said. "I'm not always such a rubbish driver, I promise."

"No worries." Veri let go of the dashboard and resituated herself. "I would never even dare to drive in this city."

Tate, still looking flustered, apologized again. "Not quite Yoda-level calm now, though, am I?"

She grinned. "I've never seen Star Wars, to be honest."

"What? That's a crime against humanity."

They spent the rest of the car ride talking about their favorite movies.

ELEVEN

Veri sent off the email blast, pushed back her chair, and leaned down for her backpack. When she sat up again, a figure was standing over her. She jumped.

Charles Winthrop held up his palm and stepped away from her desk. "I am truly sorry. I didn't mean to startle you. Veridian?"

Veri nodded and collected herself. "It's okay. Myra isn't here right now, though. Would you like me to call her?" He couldn't possibly be interested in Beck Becker's work.

"I'll call from the car."

Looking past him, she didn't see the town car through the window, but Tate had to be close. It had only been a few hours since he'd asked her out for dinner, and she'd already texted Allison: Have news!

Charles pointed to the open sketchbook on her desk. "Cats?"

She felt her cheeks flush. In between the emails Myra had instructed her to send, she'd been sketching out more cats for her painting—all with those same little smiles that her mother's cats had. "It's for a commission." As soon as she said that, she wished she hadn't. "I mean yes, these are cats."

He looked impressed. "Myra mentioned that you're very talented."

This floored Veri. "It didn't seem like that when I showed her my portfolio."

He nodded sympathetically. "She's a hard sell, but I know she admires young artists who try to impress her, so don't give up." Charles Winthrop gestured to the wall where **FAKES** was hanging. "Do you suppose he went to art school, this Beck Becker fellow?"

Veri scoffed. "Well, he definitely went to first grade."

Charles didn't laugh. He just kept staring at the painting. Veri felt a pinch in her stomach. There were *cameras* in the gallery, and Charles probably told Myra everything she said. "Sorry, I shouldn't have said that."

"If you hadn't, I would have. It's refreshing to find someone your age with such an appreciation for, let's say, the old talents." He paused. "Perhaps you might be willing to share your discerning eye with me at gallery openings, auctions, things like that. I'm interested in what your age group finds appealing."

"I mean, sure. I'd love to. Anytime." She nodded too enthusiastically.

"Good." He put his hand on the counter. Veri spotted a gold signet ring on his pinkie. No wedding band. "Now the truth is, I didn't come here to see Myra. I wanted to ask you something, if I may."

"Yeah. Of course. Hit me." Ugh. *Hit me?*

"Oh, but before I forget." He dipped his hand into his camel coat pocket. "From Tate." It was the penny. She took it from him, and he lowered his voice. "Do you know who Myra was talking to, about the missing van Gogh painting?"

Veri was too surprised to answer. Tate promised he wouldn't say anything. She looked past Charles and out the window again. So *that's* why he was here. To ask about the missing painting. "Tate's not out there," Charles said, reading her mind.

"Mr. Winthrop, if Myra finds out I was eavesdropping, she'll probably—"

"I won't say a word, and if she fires you, *I'll* give you a job. Not that you'll need it, Veri." He nodded to her sketchbook. "I can see you have real talent."

He sounded genuine, but a warning sign flashed in her head, and it must have been obvious. He placed his hand over his heart. "I shouldn't have asked you, Veri. I'm sorry. Mea culpa."

"No, it's okay. I mean, you're an art dealer, so it makes sense. It's just that, honestly, I have no idea who she was talking to."

His eyes dropped to the floor for a second before he nodded. "Of course. Thank you anyway. And I hope you won't be mad at Tate. He's a terrific young man. Hard worker." He started for the exit.

"Wait—" She stood. "Do you think it's true, though? A real van Gogh painting being discovered, like, out of the blue? It seems like they would've all been found by now."

He stepped back up to her desk. "It's not the first time I've heard this. That's why I'm so curious. As you probably know, van Gogh only sold one painting during his lifetime, so it's certainly plausible that there are more that we don't know about yet, maybe packed away in basements and such. Plus"—he smiled a smile that could melt DILF hunters everywhere—"I really hope so. He's a personal favorite of mine."

"Mine too."

Charles looked pleased about that. "I always feel my heart flitter a little when I'm standing in front of his work."

It was such a strange thing to say, but not to Veri. "One of my professors used to call van Gogh's technique 'virtual brushstrokes' because you're practically swept *into* his movements. Sounds kind of crazy, but it made sense to me."

"I'd say that's a perfect observation," Charles said. Their matching enthusiasm seemed to spark a joy in both of them. Veri felt a genuine lift in her mood.

"Do you know what the painting looks like?" she asked.

"I know that it's called *Girl in Yellow on Beach*. And that van Gogh modeled his subject after a woman in Gauguin's painting *The Siesta*, which I'm assuming means the woman in the painting with her back turned to the viewer. You know the history between the two artists?"

She nodded. "Best friends until Gauguin ghosted him, and van Gogh did a painting of two chairs to reflect their personalities: a sad one for himself and an eloquent one for Gauguin. Van Gogh was crushed, and Gauguin was, or at least seems like he was, kind of a jerk." Veri had never liked Gauguin's work, but she didn't want to offend Charles in case he did.

"Sad, indeed," he said. "*Girl in Yellow on Beach* was to be sent to Gauguin as a gift, but after van Gogh's suicide, it never made it to him. That's all we know." He paused. "Did Myra mention if she'd looked the painting up on ArtsData?"

Veri shook her head. "I didn't hear her say anything about that. I'm not sure what that is."

"Ah, I see," he said. "That says a lot, then."

"What do you mean?"

He lowered his voice. "ArtsData is a secret directory of all stolen and missing art and artifacts. It's intended for government agencies that work on global art crimes, but a few lucky others have managed to get access to it as well."

"Wait . . . so Myra has an account?" Veri whispered.

"I wouldn't know." He winked. "But I do know that Myra's grandfather worked on a few of these cases as an informant before he died." He checked his watch. "Well, it's been a pleasure talking with you, Veri."

"Thank you . . . it was also lovely talking to you . . . a-also," she stuttered.

He started for the door.

"Actually," she blurted out. "I wanted to tell you, Mr. Winthrop, I think you went to school with my mom."

He raised his thick eyebrows, intrigued. "Oh?"

"At RISD. She was one of Myra's roommates."

He tipped his head in thought. "She had two, I believe."

"Belinda Sterling. I forget the other one's name."

He looked like he didn't remember either of them. "I remember that she had two, but I'm afraid I wasn't on campus very much my senior year."

"Right. Forget it, sorry." This was embarrassing. She should never have expected him to remember her pretty but shy mother. "No worries." She brushed the idea off with a wave and started going through the mail that had already been gone through.

He pushed open the door. "Take care of that penny. I promised Tate I would say that. Not sure what all this penny talk is about."

And with that he was gone.

She waited for a few moments before clicking open the computer and googling *ArtsData for missing artwork.* Every link sent her to chat sites complaining about not being able to access it. Charles was right: ArtsData wasn't available to the public. She sat back in her chair. There was no doubt about it, though: Charles's wink was meant to tell her that Myra had access to it. She shook her head at the thought of finding a missing van Gogh. It would absolutely rock the art world. Forget the cameras, she decided. If Myra caught her searching around on her computer, she'd make something up.

Myra's office smelled like expensive perfume today. Veri sat at her desk and clicked on her keyboard. It was password protected. She groaned and went back to her own desk. She knew she should be mad at Tate for telling Charles about the missing van Gogh, but actually, now she was glad that he had. At least she knew the name of it.

She clicked open her phone and searched *where to find lost paintings.*

The Art of the Pawn came up first. *Lost something of value? Art. Jewelry. Coins. Find it here.* She clicked on the link. The Art of the Pawn was only a few blocks away.

TWELVE

Leaves were starting to fall and Veri's teeth were chattering when she finally spotted the Art of the Pawn's sign. A bell clanked on the other side of the door when she pulled it open, and the air inside smelled thick with old smoke and heated arguments, but it was warm.

"How you doin'?" the very Italian man behind the glass counter said in greeting. He looked sixtyish, wearing a black button-down shirt under a black leather coat. His full head of hair had to be bottle dyed, and his bushy black eyebrows were the same unnatural color.

"Good, thank you." She was the only customer in the small cluttered shop. Glass displays were lined up in the corners and against the walls, all of them packed with random items like trophies and deer heads and gold necklaces. It reminded her of Middle Street Gallery but with weapons. Three swords hung on the wall behind the glass counter, and a sign read **WE BUY GUNS**. "I was wondering if I could ask you something."

"Shoot," the guy said, gesturing for her to continue.

Veri held out the penny. "Let's say this was a super-rare coin that I found like in between an old attic wall or something, and I knew that a lot of people would want it but I had no idea where to sell it. What would happen next?"

The man took the penny and inspected it. "I'd tell you that it's just a penny." He handed it back.

"Yeah, but what if it *wasn't*. What if it was something valuable? Like, super valuable."

"That you found in between a wall?"

She shrugged. "Or in someone's basement." She checked for cameras in the ceiling.

"Are we talking about stolen goods?"

"Undetermined."

The guy paused. "Look, young lady." He leaned on the counter and lowered his voice. "Are you telling me you're in trouble or anything? Cuz I don't do trouble here."

"No," she said. "Nothing like that. I swear. I'm talking *hypothetically* about"—she paused—"a painting that looks like this." She googled Gauguin's *The Siesta* on her phone and held it out for him. "Except this lady here with her back turned to us is wearing something yellow and sitting on the beach, instead of in the jungle."

He crossed his arms over his chest. "You buying or selling?"

"Finding."

The man exhaled. "Usually, I got a guy. I got a lotta guys. I got a guy for just about everything *in fact*. You need papers? I can get 'em for you. You need jewels? I got you covered. But"—he placed his palm on his heart to accentuate his sincerity—"in the case of art and the like, while I'm always up for a finder's fee, I think you gotta ask on the black."

"Black?"

"Black art market." He looked surprised that she didn't know the term. "Fancy name is 'underground auctions.'" The bells clanked against the door again, and an elderly woman wearing a plaid cape stepped in, carrying a trophy with a gold bowling ball on it.

"How do I find one of those black markets?" Veri asked quietly.

"They're hidden in plain sight all around the city." He slid down the counter and held out his arms. "I'll take that from you, Mrs. Swisher." He took the trophy and placed it on the glass countertop.

Veri started for the door. "Thanks for your help."

"Anytime." He nodded to her. "You got something else you need help with, you just come back and ask for Pawlie. With a *w*, not a *u*." He pointed at himself with his thumb.

On the way out the door, Veri heard Pawlie say, "So your husband was a bowling champ too, Mrs. Swisher."

~

On the train on the way back to Hoboken, Veri studied Gauguin's painting on her phone and sketched out a few ideas of what van Gogh's *Girl in Yellow on Beach* might look like. It was thrilling to think she was sketching a van Gogh that hardly anyone even knew about yet. The woman seated next to her on the train watched her draw. "You got talent, sugar."

When Veri reached her brownstone, a **For Sale** sign was hanging on their front stairs. Her mother must have found that Realtor—which meant they really were going to move.

Voices filtered out of the kitchen. She shut the door and put her keys on the table.

"Veri, is that you?" Her mother's voice sounded too upbeat, the way she spoke to customers at work.

"Yup."

"Can you come in here for a quick sec? I want you to meet Carol."

Carol. Carol Pellowith. Her name was on the bottom of the **For Sale** sign.

Carol Pellowith was sitting at the kitchen table across from her mother. She wore white high heels to match her white pantsuit. Her platinum blonde hair, which made her look older than her (probably) sixties, was in an updo, and she wore dark-rimmed glasses.

"This is Carol, our Realtor."

"Hello, young lady." Carol Pellowith's cheeks looked overfilled. She held out her hand without standing. "Pleased to meet you."

"You too." Veri shook her limp, cold hand.

70

"Carol comes highly recommended. The Altairs sold their brown-stone in under a month," her mother said.

"That's great." The Altairs were their neighbors who'd shared their courtyard before the millennial parents and kid with the bike moved in.

"And in this climate, I think we can do even better with your brownstone." Carol raised her drawn-in eyebrows and smiled.

Veri grabbed a bottle of water from the refrigerator and gave them both a quick nod. "Nice to meet you, Carol."

"And you," Carol said.

She shifted her backpack and headed out of the kitchen. As she was about to start up the stairs, her phone pinged. It was Tate.

CW says you're not mad. Do I believe him?

She never kept her read receipts on, so she could easily ignore him, but she'd been waiting all afternoon to see if he would apologize for ratting her out. She sat down on the first stair and texted: Maybe.

Tate's three dots repeated for a few seconds. Finally he texted: Drats. I knew he was wrong. How can I make it up to you?

Drats? Veri grinned at her phone. Adorable, but she wasn't going to let him off the hook that easily. She was starting up the stairs again when she heard Carol Pellowith say, "Now, remind me again, how much was the loan for your daughter's college?"

Carol Pellowith must not have been *that* good; she'd mixed up her clients. Veri had gotten a full scholarship.

"A hundred and thirty thousand," her mom answered quietly.

Veri stopped in place.

"I'm trying to get there, Belinda, but I think it's going to be tough to end up with six hundred and fifty-thousand to buy into the store in Cape May with your partners, especially now that you need a little more than a hundred thousand to pay back those school loans. And then there's my fees, of course, so now we're up to three-quarters of a million dollars that you're hoping to profit from the sale. But after your second mortgage and the tax revaluations, plus the capital gains tax, I think the best we can do is for you to come out even."

Her mother was silent for a moment. "So even if we get what you think we will, I'm going to end up with nothing in the bank? That doesn't seem possible, Carol." Her voice was breaking. "I'm going to need somewhere to live in Cape May, and we don't expect to see a profit at Divine Homes for at least a year."

"Aw, sweetheart, I see this happening more and more these days. Usually, it's with widows who can't sell their homes because they can't afford to relocate. So listen, Belinda, let's put it on the market and see what kind of offers we get. Who knows, maybe we'll get enough over asking for you to still relocate and buy into that dream store, which sounds lovely by the way."

The kitchen chairs screeched, and Veri hurried up the stairs. *What college loans?* She hid around the corner, waiting for Carol to leave. A text pinged on her phone. Tate again. **How about dinner? Anywhere in the greater Manhattan area.**

"Thank you so much, Carol," she heard her mother say. "I so appreciate all your help."

"Thank *you*, Belinda. Trust me, we'll get some good offers. And that *ceiling*. Gracious God alive, it's *gorgeous*," she exclaimed. "No one's going to paint over it under my watch."

As soon as Carol was gone, Veri hurried down the stairs. "Mom. What's going on? What loans are you talking about?"

Her mother turned white. "You heard that?"

"I got a scholarship, and you, in the nicest way"—she paused— "didn't go to college. So what school loans is she talking about?"

"Come into the kitchen, honey."

"What loans?"

"Okay. Look, I didn't want to tell you, ever, because I knew that you might not go if I told you the truth," her mother said. "And I really wanted you to go, for me as much as for you. So one of us did." She smiled weakly.

"I got a scholarship." But even as she said the words—which she'd said so many times before, to so many people—she suddenly knew it wasn't true. The anguish on her mother's face confirmed it.

Veri threw off her backpack. "You lied about my scholarship? That's . . . I don't even *know* what that is."

Her mother took a step forward, and Veri backed away. "Listen, Veri. You did get a scholarship for the first semester."

She could feel her eyes shifting left and right while she tried to remember. She and her mother had opened the letter together. Veri didn't even read it all the way through before cheering and hugging her mother. It was like winning the lottery. She wouldn't have been able to attend RISD without a scholarship. Now, Veri looked back at her mother.

"So basically, you just told me that my entire life is a sham. I'm not even a good enough artist to get a scholarship."

"Honey. If you'd let me explain. It's what colleges do to get you to go. They give kids a first-semester scholarship so they'll come to their school. You're not the only one."

Veri shook her head. "And now I have to live with the fact that you can't buy into your *store* because of me and my loans?"

"You heard—?" Her mom looked devastated for a second before putting on a brave face. "You know what? Maybe it's just not meant to be. It was always an ambitious idea. And this way neither of us will have to move. The school loans are very manageable; I've been paying them off slowly. The only reason I would've needed to pay them all off now is because my partners won't allow me to have any debt going into the purchase."

There was a pause while they both considered what this all meant: Her mother's dream of owning her own store was about to be crushed. Veri felt sick.

"Dinner's in half an hour," her mother said finally.

"I don't want dinner, Mom. I need to get started on my cat painting." Veri ran upstairs and shut her door. When she heard her mother's bedroom door close, she sat on her bed and fumed. In a million years, she would never think her mother would ever betray her like that. She could have gone to community college or skipped college altogether. Or found her own way to pay for tuition.

Her own way to pay for tuition.

She ran back down the stairs and grabbed her backpack. Then, back in her room again, she pulled out her sketchbook and flipped it open to the drawings she'd done on the PATH: *Girl in Yellow on Beach.*

Her phone pinged again.

Nightclub? A show on Broadway? You pick. It was Tate, still trying to apologize.

Veri thought for a moment, then wrote: Actually, I think I might have an idea.

Tate texted a question mark.

It could be fun, Veri added, then panicked. What if it sounded like she meant sex? She added, it's driving somewhere fyi.

Tate: I'll drive you anywhere you want to go. Is tomorrow night okay though? Gotta work tonight.

Veri: Sure thanks!

Tate sent her a thumbs-up emoji plus a soon-arrow emoji, which made her cringe a little at his dad vibes while also finding him endearing. It didn't matter, though. What mattered was that she was going to get him to take her to an underground auction.

As soon as she clicked her phone off, she shook her head. What was she thinking? It was a dumb idea. Famous paintings didn't just show up at underground art auctions. Did they?

THIRTEEN

Veri had just finished putting on her first layer of mascara when she heard a car honk outside. She cupped her hands against the bathroom window and spotted a black town car double-parked. Tate was early. Ugh. She threw on the outfit she'd picked out, ran a brush through her hair, and hurried downstairs. Before he could knock, she pulled the front door open. "Hi."

"Hello. Sorry I'm early. I thought there might be more traffic." Tonight he was wearing jeans with a plain blue T-shirt under a silver Lululemon puffer coat. Veri groaned under her breath. He was even sexier in his casual clothes, and she needed to stay focused on her plan.

"It's totally fine." It was awkward, the way they didn't kiss and also didn't shake hands. "I just have to grab a few things upstairs." She also had to finish doing her makeup.

He wiped his feet on the doormat and stepped inside. "These old brownstones are wonderful. Are you moving?"

It was the **FOR SALE** sign outside. "Maybe. It's a long story."

"You live here with your parents?"

"Just my mom." Tate looked embarrassed. Veri was used to it. "Nothing bad, just no dad. Can I get you anything? Something to drink?"

"You're quite sure you don't prefer I wait in the car?"

"Of course not. My mom's not even here."

He looked over at the ceiling in the TV room. "That's insanely cool." He started walking closer and stopped. "Is it okay to look?"

"Of course."

Tate walked into the middle of the room and dropped his head back. "Unreal." This was the same reaction everyone had when they first saw it. "This is bloody awesome."

"Thanks. My mom and I did it when I was in high school."

"It looks like—" He paused.

"*The Creation of Adam*," she clarified. "From the Sistine Chapel."

Tate circled underneath it. "Have people *seen* this?"

"It's on my Instagram. You sure I can't get you a beer or something?"

"No thanks, I'm driving *somewhere*. I hope I'm dressed for the occasion. You'd have told me if I needed to wear a tuxedo, yeah?"

"No tuxedos. Come on, Tate, I'll grab you a sparkling water."

He smiled. "I think that's the first time you've ever said my name." His soft brown eyes could melt glaciers.

"What. Really?" It definitely was.

In the kitchen, he begged off the sparkling water she held out for him and spotted the studio through the open garage door. "Mind if I have a look?"

"Sure. It's a mess in there, though."

"Never trust a pristine studio, according to Mr. Winthrop."

"I agree," she said, grinning. "Be right back." She hurried out of the kitchen and up the stairs.

In the bathroom, she fluffed up her hair and paused to look at herself in the mirror. Undereye concealer was necessary. Myra hadn't come into the gallery today, and she'd spent the time alternating between being angry at her mother for lying about her scholarship and searching for information on the lost van Gogh. Nothing came up. She'd tried to log in to ArtsData, but again, nothing.

She put on lip balm and smelled her underarms. Not bad. She looked at herself in the floor-length mirror. Black turtleneck and black jeans.

Downstairs, she found Tate standing in her studio with his hands in his pockets. "You were right. You're very good."

"When did I say that?" She was mortified.

He side-grinned her. "I'm only playing . . . but you *should* have a show." Tate pointed to her cat painting. She'd finished it last night, long after her mother had gone to sleep. "I like these little kittens too."

"Thanks. I did that one on commission, actually. We should get going." His compliments were making her overheat in the turtleneck.

"Just know that I am duty bound to tell Mr. Winthrop if I find a brilliant new artist."

She ushered him out of the studio and closed the door behind them.

When they were both settled into the front seats of the town car, Tate said, "Okay. Time's up. Where are we off to?"

"An auction."

"An *auction*?" Tate scowled, clearly disappointed.

"Underground, though."

"I was hoping for something a little more food related. Can I ask *why* at least?"

Veri hesitated. "I've just always wanted to go to one?"

Tate narrowed his eyes. "I think you must know about the finder's fee."

"The what?"

He paused, looking sorry he mentioned it. "Mr. Winthrop is offering a hundred thousand dollars to anyone with information on the van Gogh painting you overheard Myra talking about."

"*For real?* But Myra made it sound like a secret." Her mind was spinning. A *hundred thousand dollars?*

"I guess you can't keep a secret like that in the art world," he said. "So if I take you to an underground auction, you'll forgive me?"

"Yes." That $100,000 would pay back most of her school loans. Her mother could still buy into Divine Homes. She could move into the city and rent Allison's apartment. All she had to do was get some information on the lost painting.

Tate buckled his seat belt. "Even though I doubt you'll find anyone with any information on it, an underground auction it is."

"Wait. So you *do* know one?"

"I'm not sure if it's quite *underground*, but it's definitely not Sotheby's." Tate started the engine, and loud music blasted. "Sorry." He turned it down. "When the boss isn't here . . . you like Drake?"

"Love him." After she'd buckled her seat belt, Tate started driving.

These are the things they discussed while Tate drove them out of the city and Veri kept thinking about giving her mother $100,000:

1. Food. Tate loved Italian food. Veri told him she preferred Mediterranean, even though she should probably like Italian because her father was that—Italian. Off Tate's worried look, Veri told him once again that growing up without a father was fine. And also, he was dead and she'd never met him. But still, it was fine.

2. Tunnels. Tate actively avoided them if at all possible: the result of early-childhood trauma wherein he was stuck inside the Blackwall Tunnel for six hours because of a flat tire.

3. Boyfriends—of their mothers. Tate's mother had had two before getting married to his stepfather. Now he had a stepbrother who was younger and planned to move to America for university as well. Veri explained that her mom had had a few boyfriends, too, but she always managed to keep them relatively secret, and she never remembered any of them ever spending the night.

"No boyfriend currently?" Tate asked, then quickly added, "Your *mum*. I meant your *mum*."

"Nope," she said. "Neither of us," she said casually, without daring to look at him.

Moments later, they spewed out of the Queens–Midtown Tunnel (where Tate had definitely looked stressed) and into the chaos of Queens. Tate knew of one, well *maybe* one, underground auction in the area. He'd taken Charles to the address a few times and overheard him discussing bids afterward.

A few turns later, the town car stopped in front of what Veri could only describe as a decrepit doorway in Danger-Ville. Garbage was piled up on the sidewalk, and graffiti—not the artistic kind—was sprayed across every door. CHECKS CASHED HERE signs blinked in a few windows along the block.

"There." Tate pointed to a door with bars across the entrance. "Not quite sure how underground it is, but like I said, it's definitely not Sotheby's."

"Thanks." Veri started to unbuckle her seat belt, but Tate zoomed the car forward.

"Are you crazy? You said you'd forgive me if I bloody *drove* you to one, not let you go *in*."

"But—"

"How about I take you out for dinner now instead?"

Veri's phone pinged. She looked down at it and was immediately sorry that she did. "It's Myra. She never calls me. I'm not answering." Veri looked at him. "You always answer, I bet."

"Not always." He paused. "Actually, always," he admitted.

Myra called back. This time, Veri answered. "Myra?"

"Veridian. Thank God. We have a flight out Sunday morning. I'll send a car to Hoboken at six a.m."

"*What?*" She looked at Tate, who frowned back. She asked, "What flight?"

"Do not tell me you are out of town." Myra was breathing heavily. It sounded like she was somewhere crowded. "Christ, I hate Saks. Pack light. Three nights, tops. Maybe a week."

"Where are we going?"

"Florence . . . ," she huffed.

"*Florence?* As in *Italy?*" Veri looked wide eyed at Tate.

Myra huffed louder. "Are you stupid? What other Florence is there?"

"Oh sorry. . . I'm just surprised." She was shocked. Veri had never been to Europe. And Florence—that was where her father was from.

"If you aren't prepared for travel, I'll hire another assistant." Something chimed in Myra's background. An elevator. "Veridian?"

"No, yeah, of course I'm prepared."

"I'm going into an elevator . . . the car will . . . there at six . . . don't forget . . . passport . . ." Myra hung up.

Veri stared at her phone.

"You're going to Florence?" Tate asked.

"Sunday morning. That's insane." She looked at him. "I'm sorry, Tate. Would you mind dropping me off at the gallery?"

He looked upset. "You sure? A quick dinner?"

"Yeah, I'm really sorry. I'm kind of having a panic attack that my passport is expired. I put it in my desk drawer to remember to get it renewed, but then I forgot about it."

"I should take a look at mine, too, now that you mention it." He shook his head and started driving again.

Veri swallowed, feeling nauseous. Passport. *Passport.*

Her passport wasn't expired. She just didn't have one.

FOURTEEN

Tate pulled the car over in front of the gallery.

"I am so sorry again, Tate."

"Like I've said a few times already—exactly fourteen, but who's counting—it's no problem at all. And you promised dinner when you get back from Florence."

Tate said he was surprised she had never been, considering what a fan she was of the old masters. Veri pretended to listen while he talked about Florence's cathedral during the drive back into the city. Secretly, though, her underarms were dripping. She kept them pinned in tight to trap any potential odor. Myra had sounded serious when she'd said she was going to fire her if she didn't go on the trip. Emma should have warned her that travel was part of the job.

After Tate opened the door for her, she said "Thanks again" and reached into her pocket. "Hey, so, how about you take care of our penny while I'm gone." She'd planned on giving it to him after he took her to an auction.

Tate beamed, and they hugged quickly. Already, drivers were honking at them. "Let me know when you're back," he said, shutting her door.

She pretended to shuffle through her backpack until Tate drove away. Instead of unlocking the gallery door, she called her mother and got her voicemail. She hung up. Veri already knew what her mother would say: *I kept telling you to get a passport, Veri, for exactly this very reason.* She had. A few times. Veri started down the street, toward the only possible solution she could think of.

The Art of the Pawn stayed open until eight on Fridays. Pawlie was leaning on the glass counter staring down at his phone. It took him a moment to look up after she walked in, which seemed a little lax, security wise. He scanned her body—boobs to shoes, to be exact—before he straightened up and said, "Help you?"

"I was in here the other day asking about artwork that's maybe lost?"

Two deep lines appeared in between his bushy eyebrows. "Didn't recognize you. In a *good* way. Where's the pipe?"

"I'm on a date," Veri said sheepishly. "Was." She bobbed her head. "Maybe."

"So hey, you find that painting?"

"No. I—" She lowered her voice, even though she was the only one in the store. "I have a bit of a passport malfunction. By which I mean, I need one and I don't have one."

He flipped his phone over on the glass and crossed his arms "You lose it?"

"Never had one. But now I need one."

"There's a US Passport Hub downtown. But make an appointment. I see suckers wait in that line for hours."

"Normally a great suggestion," she said. "The thing is, though, I need it in like thirty-six hours. By Sunday. Morning. Six o'clock to be exact."

Pawlie looked sympathetic. "That *is* a predicament."

She lowered her voice. "I was wondering if, because you said you got *guys* for everything, you might have one for passports."

Pawlie leaned his large belly over the glass and whispered, "You sure you're not running from somethin'?"

Veri held up her hands. "I swear. It's for work. My boss told me an hour ago that we're going to Italy on Sunday, and . . ." She stopped herself. This was stupid, and illegal. "You know what, I'm sorry for even asking you. I'm just gonna let her fire me. Thanks anyway." Veri started for the door.

"Hey, yo, hold on there." Pawlie looked worried. "Ain't nobody gettin' fired on Pawlie's watch. All right, listen . . ." He looked right and left and lowered his voice, making Veri question exactly how alone they were. "I do, in point of fact, got a guy for that."

"You do?"

He threw his arms out. "Whaddya think I ain't got a guy for that? Come on now." He grabbed a pen and paper from the counter behind him. "This guy's nothin' pretty to look at," he said as he scribbled, "but he'll help you get what you need. Now you're in luck, cuz the DMV, she's open till noon tomorrow in Yonkers, and he'll be there."

"Yonkers?"

"Beggars can't be choosers. You got a car?"

"Not really."

"That's a strange answer. Most people know if they got a car."

"Okay, no. I don't." There was no chance she was going to ask Tate for a ride to Yonkers. After she got fired by Myra, which was becoming more realistic by the minute, she'd probably never see Tate again. Or their penny. Or that finder's fee.

"Don't matter. It's only an hour away by train." He scribbled something else on the paper. "You can walk to the DMV from the station. But right now, you gotta go down to Viktor's, with a *k*. He's a Russian guy. Go to Viktor's on the corner of Eighth and Fourteenth for the flowers. He'll know which ones when you tell him I sent you." He folded the paper and handed it to her.

"You want me to buy flowers right now?"

The bell on the door clanked behind her.

"It's all written down there for you." In a louder voice he said, "Evening, ma'am, what can I do you for?"

A woman in a long white coat came up to the counter. A handbag hung from her wrist, and she wore white leather gloves. "Yes, I'm looking for some silver candlesticks."

Jennifer Gooch Hummer

"Oh sure. Just one sec while I finish up with this young lady." Pawlie nodded to the note in Veri's hand. "Just do what it says. You'll be fine."

On her way out the door, she heard Pawlie say, "What kind of candlesticks are you interested in, ma'am?"

The woman responded, "I said I was *looking* for some. *Mine.* They were stolen last week. I'm trying to locate them."

As soon as she was outside, Veri looked at the note. *"Five thousand dollars?"* she muttered.

She was supposed to give $1,000 to Viktor at the flower store on Eighth and Fourteenth, and $4,000 more to someone named Mark Trailson at the Yonkers DMV. She groaned. She was supposed to give *$5,000* to total strangers? Even after getting paid today, Friday, her first direct deposit, she didn't have anything close to that in her account. Oh, and Mr. Weekly had texted her again asking for the $800 she owed him for someone's missing clothes. She could tell Myra the truth, that she didn't have a passport, but then she'd get fired. And actually, she *couldn't* get fired now, since she needed Myra's contacts to keep searching for the van Gogh. Someone in her inner circle had to know something about the painting. Staying employed by Myra was worth the $5,000.

She slipped Pawlie's note into her pocket and started for the bank. She still had her mother's bank card in her bag. She could take the money out of her savings and pay her back before she ever found out. It was risky, but it was the only option she could think of at the moment.

It took an hour on the train to get downtown, but Pawlie's directions were perfect. Viktor's flower stand was on the corner just outside a tobacco shop. Veri was shaking when she approached it, both from stress and cold. No one was manning the stand. "Hello?"

"Help you?" A gray-haired man popped his head around the corner.

"I'm looking for Viktor?"

"It is me." He spoke with a Russian accent.

"Pawlie from the Art of the Pawn told me to come see you."

Viktor grunted. When he exhaled, Veri could see his breath. He looked like he could use a year's worth of hot meals. "Pawlie," he repeated.

Veri nodded eagerly. "Art of the Pawn Pawlie, with a *w*, yes."

"Okay." He stepped out from around the flowers. He looked even thinner in his baggy gray clothes. Veri took a step back and watched him pluck around at his wall of bouquets, until finally he pulled out blue carnations with a few sprigs of baby's breath. If someone had asked Veri to pick out the cheapest-looking bouquet, it would be this one. "You have the money?"

Veri nodded. She'd been clutching the wad of cash in her coat pocket. "Then you give it to me now."

A thousand dollars for dyed blue carnations.

She placed the money in his palm. He, in turn, handed her the ugliest flowers on earth.

"Goodbye." He disappeared around his flower wall again.

"Wait . . . um, excuse me?"

He popped his head out. "Help you?"

"Yeah, so that's it?"

"You want buy more flowers, woman?"

"No." She clutched the carnations. "Definitely not," she added quietly.

He disappeared again, and Veri reversed course back to the subway stop.

By the time she got back to the brownstone, it was late and she was only slightly less frazzled.

"Hey, honey," her mother called down from upstairs. "You're home late."

"Yeah, I texted you, Mom. I had to do some more random errands for Myra." Her stomach sank as she remembered how she'd taken the $5,000 from her mother's savings account.

Her mother appeared at the top of the stairs in her faux-silk bathrobe. She looked like she'd been lying in bed for a while, her hair messy around her face. "It's almost nine o'clock on a Friday night." She started down the stairs in her bare feet. "What on God's earth is she making you do?"

"I don't know, Mom. Just her usual overly demanding stuff that she should hire a TaskRabbit for but doesn't because I chose to work for her." Right away, Veri was sorry she'd said it. Working for Myra was terrible, but it was nothing like working for the Janets. Her mother nodded toward the bouquet in Veri's hand and smiled. "Aw, honey. Is this because of our fight?"

Veri looked down at the flowers. "Totally, yeah. I felt bad about it." And now that she'd thought about it for a day, she did. She couldn't ever remember a time when her mother had made her feel even slightly guilty about living the college life that she never could. In fact, whenever she came back from school, her mother wanted to know everything—who her friends were, what she was studying, and if she could see her latest projects. It was annoying, and sometimes Veri even told her so. Remembering this now, and all those snotty little eye rolls she'd given her, made her feel like the human equivalent of a Shrinky Dink. "Mom. I really am so sorry." Her eyes burned. "I wish we'd talked about it, though, before you made all these sacrifices, and maybe we would have decided it wasn't that important for me to go."

"But it *was* important, Veri." Her mother pulled her into a hug, and Veri could smell the rose-scented salt bath she must have just taken. "I loved every minute of living vicariously through you. It was almost selfish of me." Her mother squeezed her harder. "But it was wrong of me not to tell you about the loans, and I hope this means you'll forgive me." She took the bouquet and grinned at it. "Interesting choice."

"All that was left." Veri smiled, suddenly remembering the gift card envelope sticking out of it. "Oh, sorry, I didn't have time to write anything." She plucked the envelope from the plastic fork and shoved it into her pocket.

Her mother gave her a peck on the cheek and started for the kitchen. "There's a greek salad in here for you." She nodded to the refrigerator and grabbed a vase for the flowers. "Oh, and honey, I know this is a nuisance, but Carol Pellowith is having an open house here on Sunday. I'll be in Cape May. I'm staying for the week this time, leaving on an early train in the morning. I told the Janets I was having laser eye surgery and needed the week off. They were not happy."

"It's fine. I'll be gone on Sunday, anyway."

Her mother brightened. "Fun plans with friends?"

"Yep . . . with Allison." She felt gross from all the lying. Her mother put the vase on the kitchen table, and Bunny Bonheur looked down at the bouquet like the garbage flowers that they were. "Hey, Mom, is it okay if I just go collapse on my bed? I'm not really hungry."

"Of course." Her mother followed her out of the kitchen. "Thanks again for the flowers."

"You're welcome."

"They're lovely."

Veri nodded and started up the stairs. Now her mother was the one lying.

FIFTEEN

It was eleven o'clock, the train had taken almost two hours, and she could already see that the DMV was packed with people sitting in plastic chairs or standing in lines. Veri clutched the blue carnations in one hand and used the other to pull open the door. There was no chance she would get through the line by the time it closed at noon. A sign on the wall read *No Guarantee You Will Be Helped if You Arrive Thirty Minutes Prior to Close.* But Pawlie had already thought of that.

Ignoring the killer looks from people standing in line, she held up the bouquet and hurried over to window A. "Excuse me. Flower delivery for Mark Trailson?"

The DMV woman glanced at the flowers, then spun around in her office chair and yelled, "Trails, someone thinks you're pretty."

A chair rolled out backward from behind a cubicle, with a skinny middle-aged man sitting in it. It must be Mark Trailson. He looked like he'd seen some things in his day, and none of them good. "Those for me?" he called over.

"Yes, sir." Veri nodded.

"Come round this way." He disappeared again, and as soon as Veri stepped into his cubicle, Mark Trailson motioned to a chair on the opposite side of his desk. "Take a seat."

Wishing she'd remembered antibacterial wipes, she pulled the chair out and handed him the bouquet. "These are from Pawlie."

"Yeah, I got that." Mark Trailson took the bouquet from her and plucked off the envelope attached to the plastic fork, which she'd put back on again after her mother had left this morning. Forty $100 bills were folded up inside. The envelope was suspiciously bulky, but no one was looking anyway. "Beautiful note. Nice of him," he said deadpan. "You got a contact for me to text a thank-you for the flowers?"

"Yes, sir." She gave him her phone number.

Before she'd left for the train this morning, she'd used an empty canvas as a backdrop and took a timed selfie. It looked pretty close to a legitimate DMV photo. Her phone pinged. Mark Trailson's text read: thanks for flower.

She texted him back with her selfie and Thank you agin for helping to locate my nanna inside the park yesterday. She is home safe now, exactly as Pawlie had written it out. She didn't know if "agin" might be code, so she left it as is.

She felt her pulse thumping in strange parts of her body and scanned the corners of the ceiling. Cameras, everywhere. Mark Trailson scribbled something on a blue sticky note, hidden under his palm, then ripped the note from the pad and folded it once. "Changed my mind." He handed it to her. "Texts are so impersonal. Hand deliver this thank-you note for me instead. Four p.m. today. Make sure it's *after* four p.m. He's got jiujitsu till three. Have a great day."

Mark Trailson did a 180-degree turn in his chair, stood up, and disappeared through a door that read *Employees Only*. Veri opened the sticky note. It had a name and address in Queens. Another trip to Queens? She slid the note into her pocket and headed out of the DMV.

On the oppressively hot train ride back into the city, Veri looked up the address again. It was the same address where Tate had driven her to the underground auction. She wanted to text him, but she didn't want to tell him about the fake passport.

She killed some time at a Starbucks in Queens and arrived at the address a few minutes after four o'clock. She knocked on the door and stepped back. A man on an electric bike zoomed past her on the sidewalk, and the smell of weed trailed behind him. Other than Mark Trailson and Pawlie, not a single other person in the world knew where she was. The first instructions on Pawlie's notes were to turn off her tracking.

No one came to the door. She knocked harder. She'd be fired by this time tomorrow if she didn't get the passport today.

Finally the door opened, revealing a man with a face like a skeleton, wearing a dark suit that looked a few sizes too large for him. "Can I help you?"

"I'm here to see Mr. BC?" It sounded stupid, but that's what Mark Trailson's note said: *Name is Bob Cole but call him Mr. BC.*

"Is Mr. Cole expecting you?" The man had a slight New York accent and gray slicked-back hair.

"I don't know," Veri answered. "I was told by the guy at the DMV—"

"Who?"

"Mark Trailson? He's a guy at the DMV? He told me to be here at four?" She half expected Pencil-Thin Man to shut the door in her face. Instead, he pulled it open and ushered her in.

The foyer looked like an entrance to a grand hotel, with black-and-white tiles and an elaborate flower arrangement on a gold console table directly in the middle. Along the walls, white marble statues of nude men flexing their muscles alternated with giant gold mirrors. A gold handrail curved up a set of marble stairs, emphasizing a colossal crystal chandelier hanging from the second-floor ceiling.

Pencil-Thin Man wasted no time. "This way," he said, leading her to a mirrored door in between two of the nudes. She followed him down the stairs to another large room where the walls were painted a deep coral and a stone fireplace painted in canary yellow was tucked into the back wall.

"Mr. Cole will be waiting for you in there." Pencil-Thin Man extended his pencil-thin arm toward an open doorway to the left. "Please."

Veri hesitated.

"Please, young lady," the man repeated.

"Thank you." Veri headed for the doorway. Murder seemed probable.

Inside, a man in jiujitsu attire sat in a black velvet club chair with an iPad on his lap. Not as frail looking as Pencil-Thin Man, he appeared to be as old: at least in his seventies. Instead of gray hair, his was jet black and thick. Probably a wig. His legs were crossed, and he wore brown slippers with gold *H*s: Hermès.

"Come in." He waved to Veri. "You'll forgive me if I don't stand." He tapped his knees. "The cold weather makes them worse."

"No, of course not. I mean, yes, the forgiving part." *C'mon, Veri.*

"Please, come sit," he said. She slid by him and sat in the matching club chair. A small glass side table separated them.

"Excuse the attire. Jiujitsu." He motioned down to his white bathrobe ensemble with a navy blue belt.

"Mark Trailson sent me?" Her voice came out thin and shaky.

He nodded as if this was old news. "Had to see for myself what a Veridian looks like. My little granddaughter, she's named after that ice witch, Ellie?"

"Elsa?"

"Yes." He nodded. "Why not Elsa for you?"

"My mom's favorite color is veridian. It's blue green, like the ocean in winter." Her voice *was* shaking.

Bob Cole threw his hands up in delight. "See, now I'm glad I asked. The ocean in winter!" He looked back over at the doorway, and Pencil-Thin Man reappeared. Without any further directive, the man walked in and held his scrawny arm out to Veri.

He was holding an American passport. "Th-thank you," she said.

Pencil-Thin Man backed up and stood by the door. Bob Cole uncrossed his legs and placed the iPad on the table. "Are you traveling for business or pleasure?"

"Business, sir."

He flicked his eyebrows, seemingly impressed. "And what kind of business would that be, Miss Veridian like the ocean in winter?"

"I work in a gallery in Manhattan."

"Which one?"

She hesitated. "The Hattfield Gallery?"

"Myra, of course. I owe her a phone call, in fact."

"You know Myra?"

"It's my job to know everyone in the art world, Miss Veridian. And at least until authenticators are replaced by those . . ." He looked over at Pencil-Thin Man. "What are they called again, Ronald?"

"NFTs, sir. Nonfungible tokens."

"Crypto things. At least until I'm replaced by them, it's everyone in the art world's job to know *me*." His big belly jiggled under his jiujitsu outfit when he chuckled, but Veri must have looked worried, because Bob Cole's expression turned serious. "I'm guessing that you're questioning how I can be a legitimate authenticator while also facilitating emergency passports?"

She was more worried he'd tell Myra that she'd been here, but she nodded anyway. It was a good question, now that she thought about it.

"Your passport is real. I just got it to you quickly." She hoped he couldn't tell how relieved she was to hear it. "Is there anything else I can help you with, Miss Veridian?"

"Actually," she said, "can I ask you something, Mr. Cole?"

"Please." He nodded.

"As an authenticator, does anyone ever come to you with long-lost paintings, or like previously unknown ones?" She suddenly panicked that Myra might have already contacted him about the van Gogh. "I mean like a Monet or something, that they found in, let's say, their basement?"

"All the time." He laughed. "Of course, they're never real, well almost never, but that doesn't stop some people from lying about them. It's a shame, but there's always someone somewhere trying to pass off copies as authentic."

"Plagartism." Veri nodded.

He lifted an eyebrow.

"Sorry, that's just something that my mom and I say. It's dumb . . ." She felt the blood rush to her cheeks.

"Clever. Now, would you mind if I ask *you* something, Miss Veridian?"

Veri nodded. "Please."

"Would it be all right if I suggested your name to my daughter for her next little girl?"

"Totally," Veri said. "That would be a compliment."

"Excellent. It was lovely to meet you, Miss Veridian. Ronald will see you out." Instead of shaking her hand, he kissed the back of it.

"Thank you, Mr. Cole. I think you just saved my job."

"I'm glad to hear it."

Outside, Veri waited until she was around the corner to open the passport. There it was: the selfie she'd taken this morning, plus her real birth date and social security number. She tucked her passport into her backpack and headed home to get ready.

SIXTEEN

After twenty minutes of standing in line, Veri finally made it to the front.

"Checking in?"

"Hi, yes. I wasn't able to check in online for some reason." It had been so annoying. She'd tried to check in right when she got back from Bob Cole's house, but the system wouldn't let her. She tried again before her car arrived at six this morning, and still, it wouldn't allow it.

"Where are you headed this morning?" the ticketing agent asked, with her bright-pink nails hovering over her computer keyboard. The airport was packed with people and children and giant carts of luggage.

"Florence. The nine o'clock flight."

The agent started clicking the keyboard. "Name?"

"Veridian Sterling."

Click. Click. Click. After a pause, the agent said, "Your ticket has been canceled."

"What?" Myra was going to lose her mind. It couldn't be canceled. "It can't be canceled. My boss is probably already on the plane."

"It is."

"Maybe it's my passport number?" She hadn't given the number to Myra yet, so that would make sense. She pulled her roller bag closer, rested her backpack on it, and took out her passport. The agent didn't take it. She read off the screen. "Purchaser called to cancel the ticket at 6:02 this morning."

"But she sent the car?"

"I'm not sure about that. Sorry. Your ticket has been canceled. Anything else I can help you with?" She spoke loudly enough for the young couple waiting in line behind her to hear. Their cart, piled high with five bags, was already rolling toward her.

~

It was 10:02 by the time her cabdriver got her through the morning traffic and Veri pulled her roller bag into the gallery. Myra had responded to her text (You canceled my ticket?) with Yes. Still need you at the gallery today. Gave you the day off yesterday.

She'd paid $5,000 for that day off. For a fleeting second, Veri considered asking Bob Cole if he would take the passport back. She'd seen enough crime shows to know what might happen if she did, though.

"Hello?" Veri called out now. "Myra?"

Myra's door was open a crack. She heard fragments of Beck Becker's voice.

She left her roller bag by the door and walked quietly to her desk.

"Beck, darling, I need to get to work now." Myra sounded annoyed, and a moment later, Beck appeared in the doorway. When he saw Veri at her desk, he shoved both hands in his pockets and sneered. "How long have you been here?"

"Maybe three seconds?"

He was wearing all white again, but it did nothing to hide his dark vibes.

"Beck, who are you talking to?" Myra called out.

"Your assistant."

"She's late. Send her in."

"Better get in there," he barked, looking happy to give her an order.

"You're a half hour late," Myra said when Veri stood in her doorway.

"Sorry, the traffic . . . what happened? Why did you cancel the trip?"

"Don't cry over spilled milk, Veridian. You'll get there someday." She paused. "Maybe."

"But you sent the car?"

Myra glared at her. "And then the trip was no longer needed. So *now*, as you can *see*, we are here."

"Got it." Veri backed out and shut the door. "Oh, Veridian, I'm sorry you spent five thousand dollars to get *an emergency passport that you didn't need*," she mumbled to herself while shoving her roller bag under the desk.

As soon as she sat down, Veri spotted a woman attempting to open the front door while balancing a large portfolio under her arm. She jumped up and opened it for her. "Can I help you?"

"I'm looking for the owner. I was hoping to show her my portfolio."

Veri recognized the nervousness in her voice. She felt bad for this middle-aged artist, who wore cutoff jean shorts down to her knees and black socks with her Birkenstocks. Myra would laugh in her face. "I'm sorry, but we're not considering right now. We have a five-year waiting list, to be honest."

The woman nodded, dejected, and Veri was about to apologize again when Myra's voice caught them both by surprise.

"Don't be silly. Come on in. We're always looking for new talent." Myra, standing in the doorway, was *smiling*. It was the first time Veri had seen her teeth: small but straight. Veri looked back and forth between the two. What was happening? Myra was never nice to anyone who walked into the studio unless they were potential buyers or Charles Winthrop. "Now tell me. What genre, dear?"

"Mostly realism. A bit of plein air."

Myra clapped. "We adore realism! Let's have a look. Come with me." Ignoring Veri, she led the artist into her office and closed the door.

Veri's head was swirling. *Mostly realism. A bit of plein air?* Wasn't that *exactly* what Veri had said when she asked Myra to look at her own work? And now Myra was saying nonsense like *We adore realism*. Myra wasn't just mean; she was cruel. "I'm getting that finder's fee if I have to kill someone," she mumbled under her breath, imagining Myra's shocked face when she did.

Back at her desk, Veri searched through more emails sent to the gallery before her time, looking for any clue about a lost van Gogh. Nothing. She considered contacting Emma to ask her if she remembered hearing about it, but she didn't want to risk her finding out about the finder's fee. Unless she'd become a top runway model in the two weeks since she'd been fired, chances were good that she could use $100,000 too. Frustrated, Veri sat back and scrolled through her phone, soon noticing a text from her senior adviser sent months ago, checking in to see how she was doing.

Hey Ms. Hill, Sorry I just saw your text. I'm great, working in New York. How are you? Any promising new students? She kept the text purposely vague. Working in New York could mean painting too.

A few minutes later, Myra's door opened, and the artist, looking cheery, shuffled out in her Birkenstocks. "Have a good day!" Veri waved.

After she was gone, Myra called her into her office. "Veridian, I'll be giving her a show. Don't look at me like that. It's my gallery; I can show whomever I please."

"Of course." She wasn't about to give Myra the satisfaction of saying more. She noticed some slight bruising around Myra's eyes, especially around her crow's-feet. Botox injections, Veri realized. All the Botox in the world couldn't wipe away the mean on Myra's face.

Myra's cell phone rang, and when she saw who it was, she answered right away. "Charles, darling. Hold a moment." She shooed Veri out of her office. "Well yes, someone thought they found the provenance, and I was all set to go . . . Florence, that's right. Yes, Veridian's here now too." Veri closed the door slowly and put her ear up to it. "But the authenticator at the Uffizi said it was a fake, so the man was obviously only after the finder's fee you're offering."

Girl in Yellow on Beach. That's why they were going to Florence so suddenly—and why the trip was canceled just as suddenly! Veri listened to Myra start clicking on her keyboard. "I've looked on ArtsData already once today, but I'll look again right now . . . yes, darling, right now . . . I'm logging in this very minute." Veri heard more clicking on the keyboard. "Okay now. Let me see . . . Oh, hold on a moment, darling, someone's calling me on my other line . . . Okay, I'll call you back if I find something. Ciao ciao . . . Hello, this is Myra Hattfield?"

Veri backed away, but before she'd made it to her desk, Myra's door blew open. "My apartment's on fire!"

"What?"

Myra held the phone away from her ear. "It's the fire department on the phone."

"Oh no, is there anything I can do?"

Myra tucked back inside her office and rushed out again with her Chanel puffer coat on her arm. "Thank you so very much, Captain Reinhardt. I'm on my way." She flew out the front door, and a second later, Veri's phone rang. "I forgot my gloves. See if they're on my desk."

"Sure. Hold on." Veri hurried into Myra's office. "They're here."

Myra groaned. "I need you to put them in my desk drawer, top right. They're Brunello Cucinelli. They cost more than your wardrobe . . . taxi!"

"No problem." Veri picked up the gloves—definitely the nicest gloves she'd ever felt—and slipped them into the drawer.

"Oh, and make *sure* my computer is closed." Myra raised her voice—"Taxi!"—and hung up.

After a pause, Veri said "Bye," just in case. It seemed impossible that someone as snarky as Myra could have survived out in the wilds of humanity for this long.

Veri was starting to leave her office when she noticed Myra's computer screen. ArtsData was still open on the page, and *Van Gogh lost painting* had been typed into the search bar at the top.

"Oh my God." Myra had left her ArtsData page open. She leaned onto the desk and kept reading:

These five van Goghs disappeared during the Nazi period. All remain lost.

The five paintings include The Painter on the Road to Tarascon, which had been hidden inside a salt

mine in Stassfurt, Germany, to keep safe from Allied bombings. After Stassfurt was liberated on 12 April 1945, fire broke out in the mine where the painting was kept. It is suspected that the fire was set to disguise the looting.

"What about *Girl in Yellow on Beach*?" she mumbled. She scrolled through the photos of the five missing pieces, but none of them were of a girl in yellow on a beach. She dropped into Myra's chair, deleted the search line Myra had typed in, and wrote *Girl in Yellow on Beach* instead. Right away, information popped up.

Veri jumped out of the seat. "Oh my God!" It was a photo of a tattered-looking piece of paper that listed dates and information about the painting.

1888: *Girl in Yellow on Beach* painted in 1888 by Vincent van Gogh, artist, born March 30, 1853, Zundert, Netherlands.

June 1893: *Girl in Yellow on Beach* donated to artist Paul Gauguin, born June 7, 1848. Delivered to his residence in France.

1903: *Girl in Yellow on Beach* sent to Wilhelmina Jacoba van Gogh in her residence at a psychiatric residence in Ermelo, Netherlands, where it remained for four decades.

1941: After Wilhelmina van Gogh's death in 1941, *Girl in Yellow on Beach* went missing.

"Omigod. Omigod. Omigod." Veri shook out her palms and sat again. Her heart was beating in her throat. She scrolled lower, but there was no photo of the painting, nor were there receipts or signatures of ownership—all things one would normally expect to see in a provenance, but it was at least *something*. And it proved that the painting was real. Plus, she looked closer at the screen: in 1893, the painting *had* made it to Gauguin after all. She googled Paul Gauguin on her phone. He died suddenly on the morning of May 8, 1903, the same year that the painting was sent to van Gogh's sister at her psychiatric residence, where it stayed for four decades. It certainly seemed possible that it could have gone missing after Wilhelmina's death.

Veri sat back in Myra's chair. Charles hadn't said anything about the painting making it to Gauguin in France or finding its way back to his sister in the Netherlands. *But this seemed like information he would definitely pay $100,000 for!*

Veri couldn't believe her luck. If Myra had seen this already, wouldn't she have told Charles? Veri needed to think. Charles had told her ArtsData was a secret government account. What would happen if she was caught stealing information from it? She considered taking a screenshot of the page and sending it to herself, but that could leave evidence in Myra's history. Instead, she snapped a photo of it on her phone. Next, she rewrote *Van Gogh lost painting* in the search line, exactly the way Myra had typed it in, and watched the page return to the same screen that she'd left it on. When Myra clicked open her computer again, she wouldn't suspect a thing.

Back at her desk, Veri's mind was racing. She needed to get this photo to Charles right away, before Myra or anyone else found the same information. But how? If she delivered it to him personally, he might figure out that she'd found it on Myra's ArtsData account and then not pay her the finder's fee. It seemed too risky. She could ask Tate to deliver it, but he'd already proven he wasn't good at keeping secrets, at least not when it came to Charles Winthrop. Her mother—no way would Veri ever get her involved.

She'd have to deliver it anonymously. She needed to find out where Charles lived. All of Myra's desk drawers were locked, so no luck finding an address in there. Tate was her only option.

Hey I need to ask you something. Text me when you can.

She sat back and stared at the evidence on her phone. *Girl in Yellow on Beach* was real!

A moment later her phone rang. "False alarm, Veridian. Someone's dryer blew up in the apartment below, apparently." Myra told her she wasn't coming back in for the rest of the day, though, "due to the fire stress."

"No problem, feel better," Veri said, hurrying out to lock the gallery door. Maybe she could find more information on Myra's computer now that she was gone for the day. As soon as she sat at Myra's desk again, though, she groaned. She was locked out of her computer for good. It was a momentary stroke of luck that Myra had left it open when she'd run out.

Later, when Veri got back to Hoboken, the open house was just ending. She'd forgotten all about it, and her mother was in Cape May.

Carol Pellowith, in a dark-blue pantsuit, was talking on her doorstep to a young couple with a baby. Veri waited in front of the neighbor's house until the couple waved goodbye and pushed their mini-bathtub-size stroller down the sidewalk. When Veri started up her stairs, Carol said, "Hello! Welcome! The open house is closed, but I don't think the owners would mind if we did a quick tour."

"It's my house?" Veri pulled off her wool beanie.

Carol's smile fell off. "Oh, honey, I didn't recognize you."

Carol followed her in, leaving the door open and letting the heat escape.

"I'll just get my things." Carol zoomed past her into the kitchen. "I'd say it was a fairly successful showing; I'll call your mother and give her the details." She grabbed her bag off the kitchen table. "By the way, the clients raved about the ceiling. I think it's going to sell the place. It's always a plus to show off the sellers' talents. Makes the client think they'll buy the house and suddenly inherit their genius too. Subconsciously, of course."

After she was gone, Veri ordered pizza and stepped into the garage studio. Tate hadn't texted her back yet, and she needed to add a finish to the cat painting. Mildred had left another voicemail this morning asking about it, and Veri was determined to deliver it to her tomorrow: her first real day off in what felt like forever.

As soon as she got out the glaze, her phone pinged.

Tate: What's up buttercup? No Italy?

Veri: Changed her mind I guess.

Tate: What are you doing rn?

Veri: The cat painting ;)

Tate texted a cat emoji plus a queen emoji back. Veri chuckled. Allison would think Tate was hilarious.

Allison.

Allison could deliver the provenance to Charles!

Veri texted Tate: Hey can you give me CW's contact. Someone came into the gallery today asking for a dealer of antiquities. Assuming he does that?

Veri bit her lip while she waited for Tate's response. She didn't feel great about her Allison plan, but it seemed like her best option. Her phone pinged with Charles Winthrop's contact number, but no address. Veri paused. Asking for his home address might sound too sketchy, so she texted Tate back: Thanks.

Tate: NP. Our penny's fine, btw.

Veri: Great xo

No! She groaned at her text. *Xo?* What was she thinking? "No, no, no." She watched his three dots blink off to nowhere, hoping he might think the "xo" was for the penny and not him, until the dots disappeared altogether.

SEVENTEEN

In the morning, Veri put her coffee down on the dresser and dabbed at the cat painting. Dry enough. She'd placed the painting inside an old wooden frame and was starting out the door when her phone rang. "Allison!"

"'Too important to text' is not a thing," she said. Opera music was playing in her background.

"I know, sorry. Thank you for calling me back. I'm sure you have stuff to do—"

"Rich people, of which I will soon be one, do not have *stuff* to do. They have *errands*." Veri heard a thud. "No way. My purse strap just broke."

"Oh no, sorry."

"Ucch, it's fine, it was a fake anyway. If it was a real Gucci, I'd be freaking out. Okay. Lay it on me, girl. What do you need?"

She'd texted Allison last night asking for a favor that was too important to put in a text. "Okay. You know how you always wished you went to acting school instead of art school, even though you didn't get into any acting schools?"

"Rude. Go on."

Veri continued, "I have an undercover gig for you."

"For real?"

"I need you to be a serious baller, like old-school Vanderbilt, Carnegie type, and deliver an envelope to a man, and be super aloof about it."

"Like on Broadway?"

"What? No."

Allison grumbled. "Fine. Can I wear a wig?"

"If it's not tacky."

"Yay. When?"

"I'm sending you his contact, and all you need to do is text that you have the information he wants, and ask if he can meet you this afternoon in the park, let's say like the entrance off Sixty-Ninth. Okay? Can you do that? It will be out in public, and he's not scary or anything. I'll be waiting nearby."

"Wait, so you know him? Why can't you just give it to him, then?"

Veri paused. "Look, Al. I can't tell you right now. But it's not dangerous; it's literally just handing him an envelope."

"I won't be breaking the law in any way, will I? I can't go to jail and miss out on my upcoming life of luxury."

"Ummm . . . you know what . . . forget it." It *might* be breaking the law, and Veri couldn't stand the thought of implicating Allison.

"Whoa, hey, hold on there, girlfriend. I'll do it. You had me at 'wig.'"

"Okay . . . but remember, wear a *nice* wig. Don't go all Hunger Games Effie. Look normal."

After they hung up, Veri printed out the photo she'd taken of Myra's computer screen with the ArtsData information and put it inside a plain envelope. Her coffee was getting cold, and she needed to get a move on. Mildred was expecting her at noon, and it was already eleven.

On the sidewalk, an older man stopped her at the bottom of their stairs and said, "I'm sorry to see this." It was Mr. Brenner, who lived across the street, and he meant the FOR SALE sign. She used to dog-sit his bulldog, Frisky, before she died, and when she graduated high school, he gave her a Target gift card for twenty-five dollars. "Thanks, Mr. Brenner. Me too. But my mom's opening an interior design store in Cape May."

"Congratulations, then."

"Have a good one." Veri waved and started for the train.

It was even more cluttered inside the Middle Street Gallery than the last time she'd been there. "Veri!" Mildred waved from behind a row of old floor lamps. "Let me see what you have." Veri held it up for her. "Will you look at that?" Mildred shook her head. "Those are handsome cats. Come with me." Mildred led Veri around more tables and chairs and grandfather clocks to the other side of the room, where she shut the office door, took the painting, and hung it up under a gold mirror that hadn't been there before. "Good. Still fits."

"Nice." Veri nodded enthusiastically and took a photo of it for her Instagram page. At least her work was finally hanging somewhere. "Sorry it took so long to get to you, Mildred."

"Don't even worry, doll," she said. "What did we decide, thirty bucks? Forty?"

"It's really up to you." It was already past noon, and Veri needed to meet Allison at the park by one o'clock. Charles had responded right away to Allison's text.

"Let's do forty," Mildred decided. "I'll give you a jingle if it sells. Oh, hey, how's your mother? Did she like the candlesticks?"

"Loved," Veri lied. She'd forgotten to tell her mother about them. "She wanted me to thank you. She's opening a store down in Cape May, so she's been super busy; otherwise she would have come in herself."

Mildred seemed slightly hurt. "I bet she wanted to keep these cats for herself, though."

"She definitely did." That seemed to cheer Mildred up a little. "I'm so sorry, I have to get to a doctor's appointment."

"Off you go, doll." Mildred waved. "We'll try our darn *darn*dest to keep the office door closed. My husband forgets, but I'll keep watch."

Veri thanked Mildred again and hurried out.

~

A group of middle schoolers coming from the opposite direction looked like they were heading for the same bench. Veri picked up her pace and got to it first. The middle schoolers settled for the next empty bench and immediately looked down at their phones.

A few minutes later, Veri spotted Allison walking toward her in black knee-high boots, dark sunglasses, and a blonde wig. She was a striking figure in her white fur coat. Too striking. She looked like Lady Gaga.

"Hey, queen." Allison sat and slid down her dark glasses. She had a full face of makeup, complete with fake eyelashes and glitter eyeshadow.

"Really? This is your version of OG wealthy?"

"I look amazing." She crossed her legs. "Oh my God, I googled this guy. He's a total DILF. Why aren't you hitting that?"

Veri rolled her eyes and handed Allison the plain envelope. "Okay, so remember, you're going to meet him at the twelfth bench. That's what he said, right?" Veri felt her stomach sour. She still had time to back out, but that finder's fee was only nine benches away.

"Yep." Allison pulled out her phone and double-checked the text. "'Hello Rachel Ritchie.'" Allison beamed. "Great name, right?" She continued, "'I will meet you today at one fifteen.'"

"You hid your real contact, though?"

"Uh, *yeah*, Veri. I'm a grown woman in the twenty-first century." Allison fluffed up her wig. "Why do you look like the barf emoji today, V? What's the matter?"

"I-I think this might be a mistake. I'll just figure out another way."

Allison clutched the envelope to her chest. "I didn't dress this fine for nothing. This bitch is getting delivered right now."

Allison wasn't going to change her mind; Veri had seen that look a thousand times. "Fine. But remember, he only gets to read what's inside, and then he has to hand it back to you. Don't let him take a photo of it or anything. Tell him if he wants to keep it, he'll need to hand over a check."

As she was saying it, she realized what a dumb plan it was. What if he didn't have his checkbook on him? People don't just carry $100,000 around in their wallet.

"Chill, I got this." Allison started walking away.

"Wait . . . ! Don't look surprised if he hands you like a super *lot of money* check. Just be cool. Like you're a Vanderbilt or something, and you eat checks like that for breakfast."

"Rachel Ritchie is used to money." Allison blew Veri a kiss and started down the curving path in her decidedly not stealth wealth outfit.

Five minutes later, Allison swaggered back to her. "I was amazing. He totally believed I was rich and British. I mean, *I* believed I was rich and British."

Veri stood. "So what happened, exactly?"

"He opened the envelope, looked at the paper in it, and handed it back."

"And?"

"He said he needs proof that it's real."

"Proof?" Veri's heart sank.

"Said you need to go see an authenticator. Rob Cole, maybe?" Allison handed Veri back the envelope.

"*Bob Cole?* Are you sure he said that?"

"Yeah. Look, I gotta go. I have a car waiting. But if you want me to deliver something to him again, I'm totally down. Hey"—she cocked her head and narrowed her eyes—"are you sure you're okay? You're not still bummed about Mr. Crypto Douchebag, are you? He *couldn't* still be with Phoebe."

"I'm totally over it," Veri answered, matter-of-factly.

"Good. You really need to come see my apartment. I've had two people want to sublet it, but I told them I'm waiting on you."

"Can you give me another week?"

"Sure. I'd rather have you sublet it over anyone else."

"Thank you again, Al . . ." Veri grinned at her. "I mean, sorry. Rachel Ritchie."

Allison sashayed away in her Lady Gaga outfit. The middle schoolers watched her for a moment before dropping their heads back down to their phones.

Bob Cole? Veri started for the train. Charles knew him too? But then again, Bob Cole had told her as much. *It's my job to know everyone in the art world, Miss Veridian. And at least until authenticators are replaced by those . . . crypto things . . .*"

Wait. That was it. Not only couldn't she get the original piece of paper to authenticate; she couldn't go see Bob Cole, either, because he already knew who she was, and he could easily reveal her identity to Charles Winthrop. But the *crypto things*, she repeated to herself. She stopped walking, remembering Pencil-Thin Man's words. *"NFTs, sir. Nonfungible tokens."* Maybe she could get one of those to prove the information was real. Except, where do people get those? There was only one person she could think of who could help.

She pulled out her phone and dialed.

"Veri! . . . Hello, Veri!" Derek screamed.

"Derek, why are you yelling?"

"Can you *hear* me? You've butt-dialed me five point two times since I saw you."

"Wait, really?" Veri searched through her recent calls. "Oh, sorry." He was right; she'd called him six times. "What's the 'point two'?"

"It only rang once that time. So is this a real call?"

"I need to know about NFTs. Like how you make them."

"Opensea.io."

"Words I don't understand when they're put together."

He sighed heavily. "Look, Veri. I'm working right now, *in* the office, so what do you need to know?"

Veri considered tracking him to see if he was telling the truth, until she remembered they'd revoked each other's access. "What are they, exactly?"

He lowered his voice. "Nonfungible tokens."

"Yeah, I know that. But what *are* they?"

"Is this for one of your paintings? I'm doing one for Phoebe." He hesitated. "Wait, did you know that?"

"No, and so nice of you, but *what do they do?*" She couldn't be too rude. He might hang up on her.

"Pretty soon, birth certificates, licenses, passports, artwork, everything that's important will be an NFT. It's a way to keep information and IPs safe."

"By 'important,' can that also be a list of people who owned a certain painting?"

"You mean can a *provenance* be an NFT? Yes. Obviously. They all should be."

She moved out of the way of a trio of businessmen walking toward her and tried her best to maintain a casual tone. "I'm asking for my boss, in case you're wondering. She took a photo of a provenance and needs to prove that it's real." There was a time when Veri never lied, but that felt like years ago.

"Okay, but putting something like that into an NFT doesn't *make* it real. It just puts it on the blockchain so it can't be changed. It becomes written in stone, so to speak."

"So how can I—I mean, *she*—prove that it's real?"

"I dunno. Claim your source, I guess?"

"Yes." Veri nodded. "It was . . . I mean it came from the US government; that's the source. The US government." It seemed reasonable enough. Charles had told her ArtsData was a government site. "So can you make it for me?"

"What? No, I'm busy with work, sorry."

She paused. "You were cheating on me with Phoebe, weren't you?" His end went silent.

"I'll take that as a yes." She started toward the train again. "So the *least* you could do for me then—"

"*Okay.* Send it to me. I'll do it for you." He started to hang up.

"Wait! The thing is, though, it's top secret, Derek. You cannot tell anyone about it. Not a soul. Okay?"

"Why?"

"Because, Derek, my boss doesn't want anyone to know about it." She wasn't sounding convincing, and he wasn't sounding convinced. "Hey, remember how you used to think Phoebe was, wait, let me check the text you sent . . ." She stopped again to scroll through her messages. "Oh yeah, here it is. You said, and I'm quoting here, you said she was 'the biggest poseur at RISD. Why do you even hang out with that girl? She's got no talent and just ass-kisses her way through school because her dad's some rich prick.'"

She heard him exhale.

"You don't remember? It's okay. There. I just sent you a screenshot of it. Feel free to share it with Phoebe. Or I can?"

"Jesus, you're a bitch," Derek said finally. "Whatever. I won't tell anyone about the whatever your thing is, okay? But I *really* gotta go now, and if you send Phoebe that text, then I'll tell everyone about it." *Click.*

Veri dropped her phone back into her pocket and watched the traffic go by. A smile crept up on her face. She *was* kind of a bitch now, but as long as she got that finder's fee to pay back her loans so her mother could move to Cape May and live her dream, she didn't care what anyone thought about her.

EIGHTEEN

She knew it before she spotted the ticket: she'd forgotten to move her mother's car. Sixty-five dollars. "Ugh." Veri left the ticket on the window and stayed annoyed for the rest of the morning until she got to work. After she opened the gallery, swept the floor, looked through the mail, and listened to voicemails asking questions about the gallery that could have been answered with a Google search, it was still only eleven o'clock. Last night she'd sent the photo over to Derek and told him not to forget to add that the information had been sourced from the US government.

"You sure you don't want to put down anything a little more specific?" he'd asked. "That sounds kind of random."

"Okay, fine. The US Government Division of Art. How about that?"

"I didn't know they had that."

"Look, my boss will kill me if I say any more. And anyway, the information is completely solid, Derek. I've seen it with my own eyes." Also, she'd told him she needed it by noon. He hadn't responded, but Veri worried he might ask more questions, and he might even ask to see what the painting looked like, so this morning she'd started sketching out a few more ideas in case he did.

"Hello, Veri."

She jumped.

"My apologies." Charles took a step back from her desk. "I seem to do nothing but scare you." Today he wore a suit and tie under his camel coat.

Her hands were shaking when she closed her sketchbook. "Hi, Mr. Winthrop." Had he seen her with Allison yesterday? Was he about to tell her that he knew she'd stolen the information from ArtsData? "Myra isn't here right now."

"In fact," Charles said, "I'm here for you."

Veri grabbed the arm of her desk chair. Here it comes. Sirens would start blaring outside. Police dogs would probably be involved. "Mr. Winthrop, I don't know anything about—"

"I was wondering if I could steal you away for a few hours. There's a new piece I need to see, and I'd love your opinion on it."

Veri released the grip on her chair. He wanted her to look at a painting? "I totally would, but—" She paused. "I probably shouldn't leave."

"You said she's not in there?"

When Veri shook her head, Charles pulled out his phone and made a call. "Myra? Charles. I'm taking your assistant on a field trip. I'd like her opinion on something. Very good . . . indeed. Bye." He grinned at Veri. "There. All set. She said to lock it up for the rest of the morning. We'll get you back by this afternoon."

"Okay, great," Veri said cautiously. She slid her sketch pad into her backpack and gathered up her phone. Still worried it might be a trap, she smiled at Charles when he held the door open for her. Outside, Tate was waiting by the town car, dressed in his black suit and skinny tie and looking *gorgeous*. "Hello, Veri," he said formally. But then, one corner of his mouth twitched up, and he winked at her. Veri felt a *ping!* go off in her belly button.

"Hi, Tate." Heat flew up her cheeks. She grinned at him and slid into the back of the car. It smelled like fresh dollar bills sprinkled with lemon juice. After Charles slid in on the other side, Tate started the car.

"Excuse me, Veri, I have to address this. One moment." Charles tapped on his phone. Veri tried to catch Tate's eye, but he was focused only on the road.

"Tate," Charles Winthrop said. "I keep scaring Veri. Will you tell her I'm not as frightening as she thinks I am?"

Tate grinned. "He *is* a bit intimidating, though, I will admit."

Veri wasn't sure how to respond. If she acted too friendly with Tate, it might get him in trouble. "I just get scared really easily," she said. "I should give up coffee." She chuckled nervously, and Tate changed lanes.

While they drove toward lower Manhattan, Charles stayed on the phone, talking business. "Get me the information on it, then, would you? I'll need to see it first." And "I'll be in Geneva next month, and we can go over the terms then." Tate kept quiet up front, and with nothing else to do but stare at his profile, Veri put her phone on silent and scrolled through TikToks. Most of her TikToks were of makeup artists working on runway models. Usually watching TikToks was calming, but today it was excruciating. Police stations were littered all over the city, and who was to say Tate wouldn't pull up to one of them at any minute? He worked for Charles Winthrop, after all. Twenty minutes later, Tate turned into Pier 9 and parked in a lot next to a helicopter pad, where an idling helicopter waited.

A man wearing a baseball hat opened her door. She wanted to ask Tate what was going on but didn't want Charles to hear, so she mumbled a quick "thank you" and stepped out.

The man took her elbow and hurried her over to the helicopter, with her ears wobbling and her hair blowing into her mouth. He guided her into the back seat, next to Charles, who handed her a headset.

"Thank you!" she yelled.

"You're welcome," he said inside her ears. There were microphones on their headsets. "You're not afraid of flying, are you? I should have asked."

She pulled hair out of her mouth. "It's my first helicopter ride, though."

"Well then, it's a privilege," he said. The helicopter blades sped up. "We'll be in Boston in less than an hour." He pointed to an iPad with Spotify on it. She gave him a thumbs-up and a toothy smile and looked out her window. *Boston?*

The helicopter lifted, and her stomach dropped. Underneath her, rooftops slid out of view, and it crossed her mind that she might never see the city again. She glanced over at Charles while he texted on his phone. Fleetwood Mac radio would calm her, and she tried not to think about anything but Stevie Nicks's words while they flew over New England.

Less than an hour later, the helicopter touched down on a helipad on top of a skyscraper in Boston.

"Have you been to the Gardner Museum?" Charles asked. These were his first words to her since they'd left the city. Charles had been on and off his phone the entire flight, sometimes talking through his mic and sometimes texting. If she ended up in prison, she would remember this helicopter ride forever.

The Isabella Stewart Gardner Museum was where he was taking her. Veri relaxed a little. *"A long time ago!"* she shouted into her mic, which caused Charles to flinch. "Sorry," she whispered. "A long time ago, like when I was in fifth grade maybe."

"One of its charms is that it hasn't changed since it was first built. Except for the famous heist, of course."

The helicopter door opened, and another, equally attractive man in a baseball hat helped her out and led her across the rooftop to an elevator. As soon as Charles reached the elevator, the attractive baseball hat–wearing man spoke. "Forty-five minutes, sir?"

"Make it an hour and a half, John. We have to walk a few blocks."

"Yes, sir." He pushed the elevator button and stood watching while the doors closed.

The sound of the helicopter blades disappeared, but the ringing in Veri's ears did not. Charles said, "Takes a few minutes," and he pointed to his own ear.

"That was amazing, Mr. Winthrop." Her voice rattled around in her head. "Thank you."

"You don't mind walking a few blocks?"

"Not at all." When Charles turned away, she straightened down her hair.

Outside, college students with backpacks and Simmons sweatshirts passed them on the sidewalk. She must have looked as worried as she was, because Charles said, "I won't let you get fired, Veri. I promise."

"Oh . . . um." She flipped her face up into a smile. "Actually, I was just thinking about my mom. She's afraid of flying, but maybe she wouldn't be, in a helicopter."

"We'll have to get her on one, then."

The thought of her mother and Charles on a spur-of-the-moment cross-state helicopter trip to a museum was hilarious. The most exciting thing her mom ever did was drink coffee after 5:00 p.m. "She'd never do that."

Charles grinned. "One thing I've learned in my advanced years is that people never fail to surprise."

"You don't know my mom."

"Mr. Winthrop!" A professional-looking, well-dressed Black woman greeted them in the middle of the sidewalk, just outside the museum entrance.

"Connie. This is Veri Sterling."

She held out her hand. "Connie Wright. Pleasure."

Charles Winthrop bid them farewell, leaving Veri to wonder exactly what she was doing here. Connie led her around the main entrance to a smaller entrance closed off to the public. "Is this . . . ?" Veri asked.

"Where the thieves entered," Connie confirmed. "Mr. Winthrop thought you'd like to go in and visit the scene of the crime, so to speak."

"He did?" Her voice caught. Was he setting her up for her own arrest?

The entrance door itself was unremarkable, and the entryway was cramped. "I wonder, have you seen the latest documentary about the stolen works?" Connie asked, without waiting for Veri's answer. "I'm sure Mr. Winthrop told you that he was interviewed as one of our experts."

Instead of telling her the truth—that no, she hadn't seen the latest documentary (and that, *wait, what*, did she mean Charles Winthrop was an expert on *art crime?*)—she only bobbed her head vaguely and smiled.

"We'll go right up to the Dutch Room, shall we?" Connie led her up the wide staircase built from dark oak and through a gallery filled with Renaissance art. "Stop me if you already know this," she said, walking a few steps ahead, unaware of how wide Veri's eyes had grown. She should never have gotten on that helicopter. Exactly what kind of art crime was he an expert on, *and might it have anything to do with stolen information on lost paintings by famous artists?* "On March 18, 1990, in the early morning, two thieves dressed as Boston police talked their way inside the museum by claiming an alarm had been tripped. They then tied the two security guards up in the basement and stole thirteen pieces of art, including a Vermeer and a Rembrandt." Connie glanced back to see if Veri was still following.

"The artwork is still missing, right?"

"Sadly, the artwork is still missing, yes." Connie continued: "Fortunately, we have much better security these days, so at least it can't happen again. Of course, art theft is different now anyway. It's harder to steal directly from museums, but that said, some previous crimes may never be solved. We're still trying to figure out original ownership of some of the works stolen by the Nazis. After those provenances were destroyed or tampered with, it left us with little way to tell where the pieces came from, who owned them before, or even if they're authentic or not."

Veri cleared her throat. "Has anyone ever found a provenance on a lost painting *before* they found the painting?" Feeling like that was too on the nose, Veri panicked and quickly added, "I mean, can a list of previous owners be used to help find a painting?"

"Of course. Provenances can be as important as the works themselves."

Inside the Dutch Room, Connie led her up to a wall where two gold frames sat empty in the center of it. "The thieves pulled the paintings off the wall, placed them on the floor right here, and cut both canvases out of their frames." She cringed. "It was a vicious way to steal the work. They then left these frames abandoned on the ground. Rembrandt was the mission." She nodded to one of the empty frames. "This is where *The Storm on the Sea of Galilee* was hanging. You'd be familiar with it, yes?"

"Rembrandt's only seascape." Veri nodded. "He put himself in the painting. I'm kind of a Rembrandt geek," she added sheepishly.

Connie was silent for a beat. "The real crime here isn't just the loss for the museum, or the people of Boston, or even art lovers. The real crime is the loss to humanity. These great artists are a part of our history as humans. Those thieves stole from all of us."

Veri thought about this all the way back down the stairs to where Charles was waiting for them. "A good visit?" he asked, then smiled at Connie. "Connie's a true believer that the stolen pieces will make their way back here someday and that the perpetrators will be revealed."

Connie nodded. "And brought to justice. Like you always say, Mr. Winthrop, no crime goes unpunished."

Like you always say, Veri repeated to herself. *No crime goes unpunished?*

Her cell phone rang in her bag. Without looking at who was calling, she clicked it off.

"Well, thanks again, Connie." Charles shook her hand.

"You're very welcome. Come back any time."

It wasn't until they were inside the elevator heading back up to the rooftop that Veri asked, "How was the painting?"

"I didn't need a second opinion on it, as it turned out." Charles smiled. "Wesleyan Frankel. Have you ever heard of him?" He opened his phone to a photo of an abstract painting, black-and-white squiggles and splotches.

"Nice," she lied.

"The truth is, I just made up an excuse for you to come along, Veri. I thought you might enjoy getting out of Myra's gallery once in a while. Her foot traffic isn't what it used to be." He grinned. "I hope it was a pleasant tour with Connie. The Gardner Heist is endlessly intriguing to me. The thieves stole a part of our collective history, and we need to do whatever we can to get those paintings back. Wouldn't you agree?"

"Definitely." Veri swallowed. "That's what Connie said too."

After liftoff, Charles slipped on his headset, and Veri looked at the brochure Connie had given her. Édouard Manet's *Chez Tortoni* was the last painting stolen in the heist. It was of a dapper young man wearing a top hat while writing in a café. His glass of wine, the reflection on the left side of his face, and his left hand all glowed with the same shade of bronze. The top hatted man appeared kind enough, but his expression was impossible to read, like he was trying to hide something from the viewer. He reminded her of Charles Winthrop.

NINETEEN

She hadn't been back at the gallery for five minutes before Myra stepped through the front door wearing a black fur coat that didn't look faux. "The only reason I'm not docking your pay today is because it's not entirely your fault. Charles is very persuasive, but next time tell him no: you can't leave your desk to go see a new artist." She sounded almost like she was jealous. "You work for *me*, Veridian, not Charles. Honest to God, that man."

It wasn't a question, but Veri nodded anyway.

"So how *was* the artist?"

"Nice. A Wesleyan Frankel."

"No idea." Myra clucked. "But I'm sure he'll turn him into the newest sensation and put him on the cover of *Artforum*." She headed into her office.

Veri checked her phone again. Still nothing from Derek. She was starting to text him when two people stepped into the gallery. "Hello," she said. "Welcome to the Hattfield Gallery."

The middle-aged couple nodded back pleasantly, and Veri could tell they were sorry they'd stumbled in. The man hovered by the door, looking down at his phone, while the woman, in Hunter rain boots and a Canada Goose puffer coat, stepped over to FAKES. "Babe, what do you think of this?"

The guy shrugged, never looking up. Veri could hear the faint noise of a sporting event coming from his phone. "They're words."

Veri hid her grin with a cough.

The woman looked over and spun around on her rain boots. "Thank you very much," she mumbled, pulling on the man's sleeve as they hurried out the door.

By four fifteen, Veri was starting to get apoplectic. Derek still hadn't responded, and she'd texted him seven times already. She'd stood up to straighten FEROCIOUS, which was constantly slipping down on one side and hanging crooked on the wall, when the door opened.

"Hello, honey."

"Mom? What are you doing here?"

"I called your cell this morning, but you didn't answer, so I called here and got—"

Myra's door opened. "Belinda!" She rushed forward with her arms wide.

"Myra!"

The two hugged. Myra was back in her fur coat, and Veri's mother was in jeans and a hot-pink jacket. Her cheeks were naturally flushed, and if she had any makeup on at all, it was mascara. Myra had a full face of makeup, including cheek highlighter.

"You're looking as amazing as ever," Myra said. "How's your job out there in Hoboken?"

It was a location dig, but her mother didn't look bothered by it. "Very creative and fulfilling at the same time." She glanced around. "Your gallery looks nice."

"Beck Becker is one of the most innovative artists right now. We're so lucky to have him."

Veri rolled her eyes as she remembered the $25,000 in cash he'd given her for such luckiness.

Her mother was still nodding. "It's very original."

"We must do coffee, Bell." Myra squeezed her arm. *Bell?* "I've got to run now, though. My car's waiting."

"Of course. Great to see you."

"You too. Ciao ciao."

Myra gave Veri a half wave. "Don't forget to lock up when you leave, Veridian."

After she was gone, Veri turned to her mother. "Why didn't you tell me you'd be back early?" It was only Tuesday, and she was supposed to be in Cape May for the week.

"It turns out I didn't need to be down there that long, so I told the Janets my eye doctor got COVID, so surgery was canceled. No sense using up my sick days." Her mother hesitated before saying, "Let's go get some iced tea."

"I don't get an *iced tea* break, Mom. I don't even get a lunch break."

"That's illegal. So I'm sure she'll be okay with a quick tea."

Veri looked at her doubtfully.

At the café around the corner, they ordered their drinks and chose the seating in front of the window. "So," her mother said, "Myra tells me you went on some sort of gallery visit with Charles Winthrop."

Was that what this was about? "I went to check out a new artist with him." If her mother knew that a helicopter ride had been involved, she would have said so already.

"Myra doesn't seem too happy about it. She doesn't think you should be advising him on art."

"It was literally no big deal, Mom."

Her mother shrugged and whispered, "I think she might be a little worried that he has the hots for you."

"'The hots,'" Veri said, genuinely surprised. "That's gross. He's *old.*"

"That's what I told her. There are plenty of men your age in New York."

"The hots?" she repeated. "Ew. I would never." Though, Allison most certainly would. Veri frowned. "Why would Charles Winthrop have even *dated* Myra? He seems too, like, classy for her."

Her mother took a sip of her iced tea. "They started dating right before I dropped out." Her voice always got quiet when she said "dropped out." "But I believe it was because of her grandfather. At least that's what I heard. He was a big art dealer in London with connections everywhere, and I think he gave Charles his start."

"Oh." Maybe that was how he'd known that Myra had access to ArtsData.

"Now." Her mother changed her tone. "What I came to tell you is that Carol called me. She got an offer."

Veri sat up, suddenly hopeful. "Okay?"

"It's a good one, but still not enough for me to buy into Divine, so I'm going to take the brownstone off the market."

"Wait, Mom, no. You can't give up yet."

"It's fine, honey. Like I said, nothing needs to change—"

"*Please*," Veri said louder than she meant to. "Can't you just wait a few more days?"

Her mother looked confused. "I don't think waiting a few more days will get us a better offer, honey. It was a good one, like I said." She played with her bottle top, and Veri felt her heart crack. To anyone else, Belinda Sterling might look like she was perfectly content, sitting across from her daughter, enjoying her drink. But Veri recognized that tight smile and intense stare; her mother was trying not to cry. Once again, she'd sacrificed everything for her.

"Mom." Veri sat forward. "What if I can get us a hundred thousand dollars? It will take care of my loans, and then you can buy into the store, right?"

Her mother's patience had clearly run out. "Veri."

"Look, Mom. Just *please* don't say no to the store yet, okay? Please?"

Her mother didn't nod, but she didn't shake her head either.

"I better get back." Veri stood. "Myra might be nice to you, but she is snarky as hell to me."

Her mother collected her purse. "Nothing would surprise me about Myra Hattfield. I once saw her put a slug on a girl's face when she was asleep in the quad."

Outside, Veri hailed her mother a cab, even though she protested. She'd taken an extra-long lunch break to come all the way into the city, which meant she'd have to stay later than usual tonight. The Janets didn't give paid time off for tea breaks either.

"I might be home a little late tonight. I have to go to the bank. I think I got hacked. I'm missing five thousand dollars."

Veri's stomach capsized. "Oh no." She couldn't look at her mother when they hugged goodbye.

As soon as she stepped back into the gallery, Derek finally texted her. It's done. This is the link to the NFT. He went on to explain that he'd created an account for her on a crypto wallet where it would be stored. Log-in is your Gmail. Password is: . . . Veri tried to read it, but the password was longer than a toothpick with random letters and numbers. Do Not Lose It! Do Not Show It To Anyone! Anyone can get into your account if they get the password.

Veri called Derek. "What's a crypto wallet? I have to send this to someone anonymously, so it can't be in my name."

She heard hardcore rap music in his background. "You want me to change the username? What do you want it to be?" Derek asked.

"I don't know . . . what sounds like *not* me?"

"Hotgirl69?"

"Thanks. Cute." She felt like telling him Phoebe was only using him for his crypto capabilities, except at this exact moment, so was she.

"Fine. I'll change it to a random username instead. I'm warning you, though, Veri: if you lose access to this account, you'll never recover it. Make sure you take a picture of your log-in."

"What if I—*we* don't want to keep the NFT, though. Like we want to sell it to someone?"

"They can buy it from your crypto wallet. Give them the new username that I'll make for you, and they can send you the money in crypto or cash. If they pay you in crypto, you can convert it to cash. It's real money either way."

"And you're *sure* they won't know it's from me . . . or my boss?"

"I mean like, there's always a trace of a digital fingerprint in any username, but it would take a full government or something to track it back to you. Hey, I never heard of this van Gogh painting. What does it look like?"

"Derek, you promised."

He didn't say anything for a moment, or if he did, she couldn't hear it. "I'll change the username," he said finally. "And I added the source, like you said. The US Government Division of Art."

Here was her chance to forget the whole thing. She could keep the NFT on her phone and forget all about the finder's fee. But her mother's sad face was still haunting her. So instead she said, "Thanks, Derek."

"You're not welcome. And if you show Phoebe that text, I'll tell everyone about this thing."

After they hung up, Veri sat at her desk and waited for Derek's next text with the new username, feeling increasingly anxious about it. Charles Winthrop had been nothing but nice to her, and now she was going to thank him by taking his $100,000, when Myra could have given him the same information for free.

Her phone pinged. It was the text from Derek with the new link. Instead of clicking it, she opened her phone and dialed.

"Hello?"

"Hello, is Rachel Ritchie there?"

"Hell yes she is," Allison said.

They planned to meet in the morning.

TWENTY

The morning sky was dark on the trip over to Manhattan. Veri decided to take the ferry to midtown and walk up to the Pie Place from there. It was Halloween. On the ferry, she sat across from a dad Spider-Man with his kid, Groot. Groot kept staring at Veri until eventually she heard Spider-Man tell the kid to stop.

There was a 70 percent chance of rain, according to her weather app, and it was too cold to eat on the patio. Inside, the restaurant smelled like caramel and coffee, and Veri was glad she'd skipped breakfast at home. She spotted the blonde wig right away. Allison was sitting at a four-top in the middle of the restaurant. "Hey, Al." Veri pulled off her beanie and leaned down to give her a hug. "I've been obsessed thinking about that mocha pie."

"So good it's a crime." She smiled. It read the same across the back wall: THE PIE PLACE: SO GOOD IT'S A CRIME. "Plus, Jeremy still gives me a discount."

"You talk like an Allison, yet you look like a Rachel Ritchie."

Today she was wearing black leather pants and a black asymmetric cold shoulder top. Large chandelier faux-diamond earrings swung from each ear. On the back of her chair, Veri spotted a black fur coat. "That's not real, right?" She sat down across from her.

"Hell no. I'd never wear a murdered whatever animal this is supposed to be."

"Phew. I thought maybe Shrivel Dick gave you a real one."

Allison didn't laugh.

"Sorry, I shouldn't have said that; I'm sure his dick is fine."

Allison wiped at her heavily made-up eye. "We might have broken up."

"What? Why?"

"He's got two dumbass kids who suck and don't want him to marry me."

"A story as old as time."

"They're grown *men*. Both of them are bald. I've seen pictures. So I might not be able to sublet my apartment to you."

"It's fine." Veri shrugged. She unbuttoned her army coat and decided to stay quiet about her mother's plans not to move now. "I'll figure something out." She grabbed the envelope out of her backpack and slid it across the table. "Rachel Ritchie hardly has to say anything this time. Just tell him everything he needs to know is in there. He doesn't even need to open it in front of you."

Inside the envelope were instructions on how to find the NFT on opensea.io. The NFT contained the information on the painting, which had been sourced by the "US Government Division of Art," and was listed as private. It required a password, so Charles would be the only one who could access it, but first he'd need to open his own crypto wallet and send the finder's fee to the anonymous crypto account (the new username that Derek made was filled with random numbers and symbols). Then, he would receive the NFT.

Derek had been surprisingly patient with Veri and her questions, and she guessed he must have been drinking. He was always nicer after he'd had a beer or two. Finally, after twenty minutes on the phone, she'd decided that if Charles Winthrop didn't know how to do all the crypto stuff himself, he was rich enough to know someone who did.

Now, Allison slipped the envelope into her purse. "Seems like a lot of trouble for a diamond tiara. The guy looks like he can buy ten thousand tiaras at Harry Winston's, to be honest."

"It's an heirloom, though," Veri explained. "You can't sell those in stores."

Earlier, Allison had wanted to know what exactly she'd be delivering to the DILF, so Veri had texted her back that it was an appraisal for a tiara that she and her mother wanted to sell. They didn't want to let him see the real thing until he'd paid them for half of it. Allison had begged her to see a photo of the jewelry, so Veri had sent her a screenshot of a diamond tiara out of the queen's jewels and told her it was her grandmother's and that they wanted to keep the transaction anonymous.

"You're smart, Veri," Allison said now, twisting her ring. "If those dickhead kids won't let us get married, maybe I'll sell this ring. You think the DILF would want to buy it?"

"Maybe."

When Jeremy came over, Allison whispered, "Has anyone noticed it's me?"

Jeremy shook his head without making eye contact. "Ready to order?"

After Jeremy walked away, Veri went through the plan again. Allison was to meet Charles Winthrop at one o'clock, same park bench. This time, Veri wouldn't be waiting around the corner, though, because Myra was making her clean out their storage closet today, and there was no way she could ask to take a two-hour lunch break to monitor the situation. But it was imperative that Allison get this information to Charles *today*. "Any questions?"

"Chill, girl. Rachel Ritchie's got this." Allison showed her the text she'd received from Charles, confirming their meeting time. "Easypeasy. I mean, no worries, mate." She garbled out an Australian accent.

"How about you just speak normal American this time?"

"Lesson number one in acting, V: stay consistent."

"Let me know what happens with Shrivel Dick too."

"Thanks, mate," Allison said.

After she left the Pie Place, Veri headed to the gallery. It was a simple plan. What could possibly go wrong?

~

127

At one thirty, Allison texted her. Myra was in her office, but just to be safe, Veri stopped what she was doing (organizing boxes by date in the storage closet) and stepped out onto the sidewalk to read it.

Allison: Damn, that DILF is fine.

Veri: Did he read the note?

Allison: All good. Said he'd follow directions. I was perfect.

Veri: Thank you so much Allison. Love you.

Veri exhaled a huge sigh of relief, which swirled around in a white mist in front of her before dissipating into the cold air. A number that she didn't recognize pinged her phone. It was a notice from the crypto wallet account that Derek had set up for her. She clicked on it and felt her brain melt. $100,000 has been sent to your account.

A post office worker was leaning against the building next door, watching her. He took a long drag off his cigarette without breaking his stare. She turned away from him and felt dizzy. She was a full-blown criminal now. Everything was going to be okay, she tried to convince herself. The worst was over. All that mattered was that she had the money to pay off her loans and help her mother start the new life that she deserved. Besides, if she hadn't sold Charles the information on the painting, someone else would have eventually. Probably. Anyway, all she needed to do was go back to living her unexciting and mostly honest life, and no one would suspect a thing. That was all she needed to do.

Instead, she dry heaved once and then threw up on the sidewalk.

The post office worker saw it all.

TWENTY ONE

For the rest of the afternoon, Veri alternated between staring at her crypto account and watching the front door. Every minute that the police did not come through with guns drawn was a surprise. Myra slipped out of her office around three, barked a few more orders at her, and announced she was gone for the day, leaving Veri to finish writing out addresses on the brochures for the artist Janis Pole's upcoming show and to wonder what prison would be like.

And Tate texted her asking if she was free tonight. I can come get you.

Veri's heart electrocuted itself. But then she hesitated. How was she going to maintain calm on a date with him after what she'd done to his boss? If she acted too distant from Tate now, though, she decided, it might seem suspicious. She texted that she didn't have any plans, felt her heart do that thing again, and went back to staring at her crypto wallet. She had another problem to solve. A sudden deposit of $100,000 into her mother's account would be ridiculous. Her student loan documents had to be somewhere in the brownstone, though. She needed to find them and pay them off herself without her mother knowing about it. After that, she'd ask Carol Pellowith to set up another open house. She'd explain that her mother was crazy busy in Cape May, but she was sure now that she wanted it back on the market.

At six o'clock, Veri locked the gallery and walked up to the town car double-parked in front of it. The passenger window rolled down.

"Sorry, I can't get out," Tate said. "There's a cop back there waiting to give me a ticket if I do." He opened her door from the inside, and Veri slid in.

"Hello," he said.

"Hello." He should have been an actor, or a model for toothpaste or something, he was that handsome.

They hugged over the middle console. He smelled like someone who hadn't committed a crime.

"Everything all right?" he asked. Most people only said that to make small talk, but he seemed to really want to know. The accent probably helped.

"Of course." She swallowed the bile in her throat. She hadn't eaten anything since the pie this morning, except for a Diet Coke that Myra kept stocked in the small refrigerator, and her stomach lining felt like someone was in there sandpapering it.

A car blared its horn behind them. Veri jumped. "It never bothers you, all the honking?"

"What honking?"

Veri punched him in the shoulder before strapping on her seat belt. "So where are we going?"

"Somewhere fun." Tate grinned at her. For the first time all day, she felt her shoulders drop. They drove out of Manhattan to Brooklyn, and Tate kept her guessing for the entire trip. Instead of dying over his looks and wondering what he was doing with a questionable dresser like her (today she was wearing her usual black jeans and white button-down under the army coat that she always wore), Veri started actually enjoying herself. He genuinely seemed like a nice person. After a gaggle of high schoolers crossed the street in front of them, they compared middle schools, or primary school for Tate. He'd wanted to be a footballer, the soccer kind, until he developed allergies to grass. "I wasn't that good either," he joked. But Veri could only think of him wearing soccer shorts and whipping sweat off his forehead after that.

Finally, they drove down streets full of nothing but abandoned-looking warehouses and parked in front of a particularly run-down one.

"I didn't know there was this much street parking in all of New York."

Tate laughed, and Veri noticed that whenever he did, his head tipped back slightly. Just another adorable thing about him.

"This is the final destination?" she asked. Trash piles were lined up on the sidewalks, and the buildings were covered with swirling, dripping graffiti.

"Yep."

"I've heard about these secret warehouse ragers, but I didn't know they started at six thirty."

"There won't be a lot of alcohol at this one, I can promise you that." Tate held the warehouse door open for her and then followed her into a dark hallway. Something moved, and it took a moment for Veri to recognize that the shadow was a boy.

"Hey, mate, what's up?" Tate asked.

"My mom's late," the boy, maybe ten, answered softly.

"Does Mrs. Storey know you're out here?" Tate sounded sincerely worried. The boy didn't respond. "Okay, tell you what. Let's go back in and find her."

Tate turned the boy around and walked him through another doorway. After making sure Veri was following, he said "Be right back" and led the boy over to a group of women.

The warehouse was buzzing. Dozens of kids were standing around a sea of giant inflated beach balls, at least eight feet in diameter, most of which were halfway painted in bright greens and yellows. Two or three kids, wearing oversize T-shirts with paint splotches on them, stood around each ball with brushes. On the wall, Veri spotted a photograph of the same beach balls filling an entire city reservoir.

When Tate returned, he nodded to the photo. "These are going into a reservoir in Brooklyn."

"I've seen this before, this same design somewhere."

"The A trains," Tate said. "This group painted the exteriors of them for last year's project."

"Tate!" A woman hurried over and pulled him into a hug. "You should have told us you were coming tonight."

"Cheers, Mrs. Storey. It looks amazing in here."

"Keeps the kids busy—that's what we want. We're finishing up tomorrow, though. It might be a long night." She laughed warmly.

Tate looked at Veri. "This is Veri, Mrs. Storey."

"I've seen the subway trains you did," Veri told her. "They're so cool."

The woman gestured toward the kids. "They're hardworking little fellows. Some of them, anyway." Two of the boys were painting each other's shirts instead of the balls. "We're down to the wire. We have to get these into the reservoir before it gets too cold and they bounce off the ice." She laughed at the thought. "I assume that's why you're here. To help out?"

Tate turned to Veri. "What's your fancy, then?"

"Sure," Veri said.

"Put your coats over there. We can sign off on volunteer credit if you need it. I should go stop them." Mrs. Storey hurried away to the two boys, and Tate led her over to a table with open boxes on it.

"I'd suggest putting one of these on," Tate said, handing her a T-shirt with *The Winthrop Project* written across the front of it.

"Hold on. Is this—?"

"Yes." Tate slid off his jacket and pulled the shirt over his white button-down. "Mr. Winthrop funds this project for high-risk kids."

Veri felt something slip through her toes: her soul. "That's really cool," she said, glancing around at all the young kids Charles was helping. The money she'd just swindled out of him could have been used to fund more projects like this one.

Tate followed her gaze across the room. "Sorry, did I say something wrong . . . wait—do you know one of these kids?"

"No." Veri pulled the T-shirt on over her shirt. "I was just thinking—people can be completely different than who you think they are. You know what I mean?"

Tate grabbed a few brushes and paper cups filled with paint. "Let's get to it."

By the time they'd finished painting their beach ball, it was eight o'clock. Veri had painted most of her side bright green. "You're fast," Tate joked. "You definitely know your way around a paintbrush." He was dismal at painting. He'd only filled in one quarter of his side.

"Don't be so worried about making a mistake," Veri teased. "You can always cover it up later."

"The great cover-up technique." Tate handed her his brush. "Maybe you should show me how it's done. You're the master."

He stood shoulder to shoulder with her while she finished up his side, making it impossible for her to focus on anything else but his warm body.

"Everyone, huddle up!" Mrs. Storey said from the first rung of a step ladder in the front of the room. "Time for the final photo." The kids smooshed together while Veri and Tate continued painting. "Hey, you two, get in here," Mrs. Storey called over to them. "You represent Team Winthrop too."

They stood in the back of the group. Tate had a smudge of yellow paint on his chin, but Veri didn't have the heart to tell him. She spotted a clump of green paint at the end of her hair. It was already dry and would take an actual wash to get out.

"All right, smile, everyone." Mrs. Storey held up her phone. "We're doing a . . . what is it called, Sharon?" She looked over at another volunteer.

"It's called an NFT," the woman said.

Veri's chest stung.

"Well, whatever it is," Mrs. Storey said, "this is the final photo for the project. Smile big for whoever buys it. Say cheese, everyone."

Someone pushed Tate closer to Veri, and she wondered if he was going to put his arm around her. Instead, he hit her in the head by mistake with his elbow while attempting to hold up a peace sign. "Sorry!" he said, cringing. "Are you all right?"

She shrugged off the knock and yelled "Cheese!" with everyone else.

Back in the town car, Tate said, "You inspired me to tell Mr. Winthrop he should consider giving out scholarships for art students."

"Actually . . ." Veri deflated. Of all the lies she'd been telling, she could at least clear this one up. "I never got the scholarship I told you about. My mom kind of made it up."

"Why would she do that?"

"She meant well; she just didn't want me to know that she'd paid for it all herself. She took out a huge loan, and now I'm trying to pay it back."

"Oh no, Veri. I'm so sorry."

"It's okay. I mean, hey, it happens, right? People get loans. You have them."

"Hell yeah I do. Welcome to the club." He held out his fist for her. She hit it back.

"Hey, can I ask you a question?"

"Gemini," Tate answered with a half smile.

"I mean, that's *interesting*," she teased. "But that's not my question."

"Do I think we need another penny for our penny so we don't feel guilty leaving him at home alone? And by the way, here you go." He dug his hand into his pocket and pulled out the penny.

"How do I know this is even the same one?"

"Look at the date: 2014."

"There's a lot of pennies with 2014 on them, Tate."

"But those are not *ours*. *That* one is ours."

"You're a little weird," she said, putting the penny in her pants pocket.

"So what's your question?" Tate asked.

"Did you see Mr. Winthrop in the documentary about the Gardner Museum heist?"

"Oh." He sounded disappointed that it wasn't a more interesting question. "Um, no, I haven't, but I heard him telling someone about it once when I was driving. Is it good?"

"Yeah, I don't know. I haven't seen it." She hesitated, but it had been gnawing at her ever since the helicopter trip. "Is he like an expert on art crime or something?"

Tate looked over at her. "Why would you ask that?"

"The woman at the Gardner Museum said that he was."

Tate nodded like he finally understood the question. "Oh, right. I think he just knows a lot about paintings and masterpieces and stuff. He's been in some other films too. A few for the BBC, I think. Was there a Rembrandt stolen from there?"

"Yup. It's so sad. And creepy, the way they left the empty frames on the ground."

"Okay, yeah. CW's an expert in Rembrandts. That's probably what the woman meant." Tate changed lanes, and Veri turned to her window and silently exhaled. Charles Winthrop was an expert in Rembrandts, not art crimes.

Tate asked, "Isn't there something about a fake Rembrandt at the Met?"

"What?" Veri turned back to him.

Tate looked embarrassed. "Uh-oh. Did I say something stupid? I swear, I thought CW told me there was a problem with a Rembrandt painting there. I think it was *The Auction*, maybe?"

"*The Auctioneer*." Veri nodded, remembering the controversy now. "One was done by Rembrandt's apprentice. Not Rembrandt himself."

"Good. I mean *not* good, but I feel less like a stupid arse now."

"You seem nothing like a stupid arse, Tate."

He looked over at her and grabbed her hand. "Thank you."

"You're welcome." *Ping.* Belly button *explosion.* His hand was warm, and it was holding hers. For a few seconds she forgot about her crime.

All she could think about was that Tate was holding her hand. They drove on like that for a few blocks until he eventually dropped her hand to turn on the music.

In front of the brownstone, Tate put the car in neutral and twisted his torso around to face her. "Thank you for letting me take you to the warehouse."

"Are you kidding? Thank *you*. I should be doing some charity work too. Like teaching little kids or something."

"You'd be a jolly fun teacher."

Veri blushed, and the next thing she knew, Tate was leaning over and kissing her. He pulled his cotton candy–sweet lips off hers and started to apologize, but Veri wouldn't let him. She grabbed his coat collar and pressed her lips back into his. Every few seconds they paused and made eye contact before Tate gently started kissing her again. He cupped the back of her neck with his warm hand, and Veri thought for sure she had to be dreaming. Never had she been kissed so sweetly. They kissed like that, with the middle console in between them, long enough for Veri to wish he would park the car and come inside the house. Finally, she pulled herself away. "I'd invite you in, but—"

"Please, I'm sorry if I—"

"My mom's in there, and she'd ask a million questions and get all smiley, and I'm not sure I should put you through that yet." Oh my God, how presumptuous! "Or at all, ever, I mean."

Tate did his half smile. "Mums love me." Right then, as if her mother had been listening, she knocked on Veri's window.

Veri rolled it down, trying not to look as annoyed as she felt. "Hey, Mom. This is my friend Tate."

"Tate Donovan." He waved. "Pleasure to meet you, ma'am."

"Belinda Sterling," she answered, with a sly smile that probably only Veri could recognize. "And it's a pleasure to meet you, Tate. How do you two know each other?"

"The gallery," Veri answered at the same time that Tate said, "Mr. Winthrop."

Her mother raised her eyebrows. "Charles Winthrop?"

"Yes, ma'am. I'm his driver," Tate said.

"Tate goes to business school," Veri added quickly and then turned to Tate. "I better go." She opened her car door before Tate could get out and open it for her.

"Hope to see you again, Tate," her mother said, waving.

"I hope so too, Mrs. Sterling." Neither of them were about to tell him that it was *Ms.* Sterling.

After Tate drove away, her mother said, "He seems sweet."

Veri groaned dramatically while secretly trying to collect herself. "Were you spying out the window or something?"

"No, honey. I was walking home from the train." She was. She had her purse on her shoulder and gloves on her hands.

"Sorry," Veri said sheepishly. But come on: Tate had just *kissed her*!

"He seems nice," her mother said, opening the front door. "Have you been seeing him for a while?" She sounded hurt.

"Oh my God, Mom. I'm not *seeing* him. I was just saying goodbye. I literally hardly know him."

"Okay." Her mother threw her hands up. "I'm just glad you're making new friends."

In the kitchen, when Veri finally felt her heart rate settle back down to normal, she said, "Remember earlier, when I told you that I was going to get the money to pay back my loan?"

"Uh-huh." Her mother opened a cabinet and pulled out a pan.

"'K, well, let's say I get it—"

Her mother turned around. "Ver—"

"*Some*day. I get it *someday*, like after I have my first show or whatever. I just want to know, like, where in general do I find the loan information?"

"What are you up to?"

"Nothing."

"Look, honey. Paying the loan off now isn't necessary anymore." Her mother put the pan on the stove and sat down across from her.

"I've been trying to make it work . . . all these different ideas . . . but the truth is that I just can't afford to stay here any longer. The taxes are too high, first and foremost. I saw the writing on the wall a long time ago. So even though I won't get enough to buy into Divine, I've decided I'm still going to sell the brownstone and move to Cape May. The ladies are going to hire me as their manager."

Veri shook her head. "Wait, *what?*" Had she just heard that correctly? She'd just committed a crime for no reason? "You'll . . . that means you'll just be working for more Janets, Mom!"

Her mother went back to the stove. "Truthfully, I think I might *be* the Janet this time. And it's fine. They've offered me a good salary."

Veri stood. "But—Mom. I just—"

Her mother turned around. "You just what?"

She'd just committed a real-life crime for no reason. "Want you to *own* the store, Mom." Veri sat again. "You can't keep getting pushed around by mean ladies for the rest of your life."

Her mother's expression grew darker. "I've made up my mind, Veri. End of discussion. I mean it." She did. She always did when her voice sounded like she'd drunk a glass of gravel. "So you'll go see Allison's apartment? Maybe I can meet you there sometime, if you can go around noon."

"Sure." Veri opened her phone. Her mind was racing. Instead of texting Allison, she clicked on her crypto wallet. Maybe she could give Charles Winthrop his money back and forget the whole thing. Her mom had already told her the loans were manageable. Maybe she could take over the payments instead. Charles could keep the NFT, as long as no one ever knew who'd sent it to him, and she could go back to being a normal twenty-three-year-old failure, instead of a criminal.

Except Veri had a feeling that erasing her crime wouldn't be quite that easy.

TWENTY TWO

On Sunday morning, Veri woke up to the sound of voices. Carol Pellowith. It was definitely her; she could tell from the cackle. Even before she checked her phone, she knew she'd overslept. Blinking out the sleep in her eyes, she threw off her covers, pulled on her sweats, and hurried into the bathroom. Her face looked puffy in all the wrong places. The same years didn't look this haggard on Allison or Derek. *Derek.* As much as she didn't want to ask for his help again, Derek was the only one she could trust to return Charles's money.

She went back to her room, grabbed her phone, and started down the stairs.

"Hi, honey." Her mother met her at the bottom. "Sorry, I didn't want to wake you, but Carol's giving a quick tour to someone. Is your bed made?"

"I mean, kind of. Can I get coffee?"

Carol and a bald man stepped around the corner. "Sampson, this is Belinda's very talented daughter. We were just admiring the ceiling." Today, Carol was wearing an all-pink pantsuit. The bald man was in jeans and a hoodie. A techie or crypto bro, for sure.

"That's so rad," the man said.

"Thanks. Sorry, if you'll excuse me." Veri slid past them into the kitchen. She heard her mother say, "I better get going too. Nice to meet you, Sampson. Good luck with your start-up."

Veri pressed the Keurig as her mother walked in. "What the hell, Mom?"

She shushed her. "I didn't know either. They'll be gone soon. Did you hear back from Allison?"

"Nope." It was true. Allison seemed to be ghosting her all of a sudden.

"Okay. But could you at least *please* start packing? The studio at least."

Veri nodded, but the idea of packing up her studio was overwhelming. She wanted to put it off for as long as possible.

"Good. Let's hope that dude out there makes an offer." She kissed Veri and hurried out again. Carol cackled upstairs while Veri took a sip of her coffee and moved over to the table. Hey, can you call me? It's about the crypto thing. She sent the text to Derek as another text slid into her screen.

It was from Tate. Good morning! Wondering if u want to go see that Rembrandt at the Met? totally cool if no.

"Yeee!" she cheered out loud. I'm down. She texted him back right away—so much for playing it cool.

They decided to meet at noon.

The stairs leading up to the entrance of the museum were sprinkled with small clusters of people hanging out. It had taken Veri the entire commute into the city to recognize the strange feeling she was having. It was hope. Like her mother had said, maybe it was time to change things up. Sing a new tune. Maybe she'd spend all day with Tate, start a relationship with him, and they'd move in together—assuming Derek could undo her life of crime.

She climbed halfway up the stairs and sat down to wait for Tate. Her stomach was swirling with anticipation. She smiled at a group of little kids playing with toy trucks while their moms, or maybe nannies, sat to the side, gossiping and laughing. Her phone pinged.

Tate: CW needs me today. 😖 Thot I had day off. Are you there yet?

Veri: Not yet. No worries. Totally understand.

Tate: Srry. I'll text later. 💀

Veri gave his text a thumbs-up, clicked off her phone, and sighed at the little kids, feeling her new tune of hope flip over onto its B-side of bummer. She started down the stairs until she remembered that Carol was doing more showings today—she'd told her as much before Veri left for the museum. More techies and parents trudging through her house. She might as well go see the Rembrandt alone.

The painting was worth the trip. *The Auctioneer* was as brilliant as she remembered it was. Veri stood as close to the painting as she dared, scanned the QR code next to the frame, and listened to the curator's words:

"*The Auctioneer*, painted sometime between 1658 and 1662, is one of Rembrandt's most popular pieces. However, questions about its authenticity have kept scholars wondering if the work may have been authored by an apprentice. In 1982, it was decided that this work was indeed painted by someone other than Rembrandt. Yet without conclusive evidence, questions still remain today over whether this is an original by the great master himself, or an excellent reproduction."

So *this* was the fake: the version done by one of his students. Veri studied it more closely, imagining how it must have felt to copy Rembrandt's style so perfectly. Painting with thick impasto and turpentine would have been challenging. The toxic fumes alone probably lessened the painter's life expectancy. Veri stared at the painting long enough for her feet to start hurting. When a bench opened up behind her, she hurried to it, just barely beating out a kid wearing light-up sneakers, probably dragged into the museum by his parents. He plunked down next to her anyway. "Why are you smoking a pipe?"

"It's not lit."

"You're not a man," the kid continued.

"You're not either."

The kid crossed his arms and kicked his feet against the bench.

"So what do you think of that painting?" She nodded to the Rembrandt.

"Bad," he said after a few more kicks. "He looks mean."

Veri nodded. "Yeah. He probably had gout."

He wrinkled his nose at her.

"They all did back then. Also, it's plagartism—Rembrandt didn't even do it."

"I gotta go." The little boy kicked his feet hard enough to swing up to standing and sprinted away without looking back.

Her phone rang. She scrambled to get to it before it went off again. At least four people sneered at her. "Hello?" she whispered, hurrying out of the gallery.

"Hey, doll." It was Mildred from Middle Street Gallery. "So, good news. Your cat painting sold."

"Oh wow, cool."

"I told you it was good! So, listen, I'm gonna leave an envelope here with your twenty bucks in it. Come anytime. Sound good, doll?"

"Sounds amazing," Veri said, dodging the clusters of people coming and going.

"If you want to do another cat painting, we'll keep the spot open for you. Say hello to your momma."

"Wait, sorry, Mildred, do you know who bought it? Like, was it a man or a woman, older or like my age?" If her art was going to be on someone's wall, it would be fun to imagine who was going to be looking at it. "The viewer plays an important role in your work," one of her professors had always said. "Different eyes see different things."

"Hold on, I'll ask. *Fraaaaaaannnnnnk!*" she yelled. "Who bought the cats?"

Veri watched two gorgeous men hurrying past the Met holding hands and carrying Eataly bags. She wished that they were Tate and her. Maybe she should tell him the truth about what she'd done. Come clean about the finder's fee. Or maybe—she dropped her head and looked up at the sky—she should just tell Charles Winthrop himself.

Mildred returned to the line. "He says 'a man' bought the cats. That's all I got for you, doll."

"Okay. Thanks again." They hung up, and Veri dialed Tate. "Hey, can you talk?" she asked as soon as he answered.

"Yeah, sure. Sorry about the Met."

"It's okay. But . . . I need to talk to Mr. Winthrop about something. Do you know where he'll be today?"

"I'm about to pick him up to take him to the Hamptons." He lowered his voice. "To see a lady friend, if you know what I mean. But tomorrow morning he's back in the city. Want me to give him a message?"

"No thanks, that's okay. I need to see him in person, though. Something to do with Myra. Do you know where he'll be tomorrow?"

"Probably at the New York Men's Club. He takes meetings there. How about I text you in the morning and let you know."

"Okay."

"And maybe, if you're free, we can see each other after?"

She smiled down at the sidewalk. "That sounds great."

"Great."

"Bye," she said and hung up.

TWENTY THREE

The lobby of the New York Men's Club was on the third floor of the building. "Good morning, miss. Can I help you?" A middle-aged man wearing a watered-down version of a tux greeted her as soon as she stepped out of the elevator. A deer head with enormous antlers took up most of the wall behind him.

"Hi good morning, yes, thank you, I'm here to see Charles Winthrop." She knew she would be nervous, but she hadn't expected to lose her grammar. All night she'd tossed and turned deciding whether or not to come clean. In the end, she'd decided to lie. She'd happened to see the information about the missing van Gogh on Myra's computer and showed it to her ex-boyfriend, and he was the one behind the crypto account. She was here to ask how to return the money on his behalf. It was pretty low of her, but she'd never give Derek's identity away.

"Is he expecting you, miss?"

"Yes." She nodded, relieved that he was. If she'd shown up uninvited, she would have been quickly turned away. "Veri Sterling."

"One moment." The host picked up his phone. No one else was in the lobby, but she felt someone's eyes on her. It was a distinguished-looking gray-haired gentleman with bifocals, wearing a bow tie. The figure was staring down at her from inside a gold frame. Veri considered the painting. Early 1900s, most likely. Oil paint. Heavy brushstrokes. The man's pasty-white face looked puffy from alcohol.

"Very good, sir." The host placed the phone back into the receiver and walked around his mahogany desk to another elevator. He pressed the button, then stood back with his hands clasped. The doors opened before they needed to make any small talk.

"My colleague will take you to Mr. Winthrop." He nodded to the man standing in the elevator, who wore roughly the same outfit but looked two decades younger. "The Reading Room," he ordered the younger version of himself.

On the fourth floor, she followed the younger host down another dark hallway with more photos of men from days gone by lining the walls. He led her into a room with leather couches and club chairs separated into small groups. It smelled like soap and cigars. "Mr. Winthrop, your visitor," he announced.

Charles Winthrop peeked his head around a chair and closed the *Wall Street Journal* he'd been reading. "Thank you, Anton." He stood, quickly buttoned his sports coat, and walked up to her. "Hello, Veri." He held out his hand.

"Hello, Mr. Winthrop." She grabbed his hand too tightly. "Thank you for seeing me."

"Charles, please. And it's my absolute pleasure. Anton, bring us some coffee, would you? Unless"—he smiled at Veri—"you care for something stronger?"

"N-no," Veri stuttered. "Coffee's great." It was eight thirty in the morning.

Charles gestured to the club chair across from him. Veri was relieved she'd worn a skirt. All the men were in coats and ties—and there were no other women as far as she could see. Charles waited for her to sit before he took his seat again.

"I hope everything is okay. Tate made it seem like it was urgent."

"Yeah." She was losing her nerve. She shouldn't have come. "I wanted to talk to you about something, um, but not in the gallery."

"Of course." He sat back and crossed his arms and legs.

She crossed her legs and uncrossed them again. She thought she might throw up. "It's about"—she paused again and lowered her voice—"a certain thing that Myra . . ." Her voice got caught.

Charles sat forward. "Is this about Estrella?"

"Est—?"

"As I told Myra, and please know this is not for lack of effort, but I am still going to pass on one of her pieces."

"On an Estrella?" *Estrella with the soda cans and dental floss? The kindergarten project, interrupted?*

He nodded. "I'm sure her work will find a better representative." Charles sat back again with an easy confidence on his face, the one that made him the DILF that he was. "You know, Veri, after you mentioned it, I looked up your mother. Now I recall her being a very talented artist." Veri blinked at him, thrown off course, again. "I hope she's still painting."

"Ah . . . not really, but she's working hard and stuff and also probably—well, I guess now definitely—moving to Cape May. There's a store she's opening—or I mean working in—down there, so she's leaving our place in Hoboken where we live now." Charles nodded along politely, like he was listening to the details of someone's uninteresting dream, until Anton returned with the coffees. "Your car is here, sir."

"Ah, very good." He looked at Veri. "I was just about to leave for a private auction at the Frick. Would you care to join me?"

"Uhhh . . ." She was supposed to be begging for Charles Winthrop's forgiveness on behalf of Derek, and instead she was deciding whether to go on another art trip with him. *Which Myra wouldn't like,* she thought with a grin.

Last night, she'd called Derek to ask how she could return Charles's money and delete the NFT. "You can't delete an NFT," he'd told her. "It's his now. All you can do is get him to sell it back to you. And by the way, his address was encrypted. This guy might be smarter than you think."

"Veri?" Charles asked now. "It will be quick. Of course I understand if you have other plans today. It's your day off, I presume."

"No I mean, yeah, I'd love to go. I'm wearing a skirt." She shook her head. "Forget I said that last part."

"Excellent." Charles stood, so Veri did too.

"Tate is busy with other matters this morning. You know he's in business school?"

"Yes, I know."

"He's an impressive young man. I'm glad you're becoming friends. I got a call that you both stopped in to help with the Winthrop Project. Now let me get my coat, and I'll meet you at the elevator."

Veri exhaled as soon as Charles left the room. She'd expected to be back on the train headed for home by now. Or arrested. One of the two. Definitely not going to the Frick with Charles Winthrop.

TWENTY FOUR

It was a Klimt, *Portrait of a Lady*, that was being auctioned.

"They're auctioning off a *Klimt*?" Veri asked as soon as they'd sat down in the front row. She'd been to the museum a few times before, but never to a private event inside. *Portrait of a Lady*, one of Klimt's most well-known paintings, was showing on the flat-screen behind the lectern. Anyone could recognize a Klimt from the gold leaf and colorful blocked robes that his subjects wore. But while the bidders in the small courtyard looked wealthy, these kinds of works were usually auctioned off in Sotheby's and Christie's, with proxies standing in for Saudi princes and oligarchs, and not normally in small museums like the Frick.

"This Klimt painting was stolen a few years back," Charles whispered.

"From Piacenza." Veri remembered learning about it in school. "We discussed this in one of my classes."

"Did they tell you that the gallery had a fake version ready to put in its place even before the theft?"

Veri shook her head. "Why?"

"In an effort to drum up press for their upcoming Klimt exhibit." Charles crossed his legs and arms and settled back into his chair. "The gallery owner decided to stage a fake heist. Ironically, just before the fake heist would have occurred, the real painting was *actually* stolen. This was in 1997. The thief would eventually return the original painting to the gallery some twenty-odd years later."

Veri nodded. "My professor said it was all over the news when he returned it."

Charles Winthrop lowered his voice and grinned at Veri: "But what most people *don't* know is that the thief *himself* had been planning on replacing the real painting with *another* fake when he stole it. He chickened out at the last minute, though, took the real one, and left *his* fake hidden in a church wall not far from the gallery. And this"—he nodded to the image of the painting in front of them—"is *that* fake."

"Wait." Veri took a moment to review this in her head. "So there are actually *two* fakes of the same painting. What happened to the first fake that the gallery owner was going to use to get all the press?"

Charles leaned in close enough for their shoulders to touch, making Veri feel suddenly important. She hoped the art patrons in the room were taking note; maybe *she* was his next great artist discovery who would soon be on the cover of *Artforum*. "This is a great question, Veri. *That* painting was sold to a private collector a long time ago, but this version is also genius. In fact, the artist who painted this version has a hugely successful career. He lives here in New York. Wonderful man."

Veri frowned. "Was he arrested too?"

"Well, of course, it could never be proven that this wonderful artist intended to do anything criminal with his copy of the painting, so there was nothing to arrest him on. Does this surprise you? That an artist who painted a fake can still have a lucrative career?"

Before she could answer, the room went quiet, and a man stepped up to the lectern. Veri's breath caught. It was Bob Cole. Today he was in a suit and tie instead of his jiujitsu outfit, but it was definitely him. She looked down at her lap. What if he recognized her?

"Good day, everyone." Bob Cole nodded to Charles and paused on Veri for a split second before looking out at the rest of the room. Off to the side, Veri spotted Pencil-Thin Man standing with his hands clasped in front of him. She slid lower in her seat.

"We are auctioning off *Portrait of a Lady*, one of two renditions of the original painting. Is Major Cohen here?" Bob Cole looked directly at Charles. Veri coughed into her hand and opened the brochure she'd been given. *Bob Cole, Authenticator* was listed inside.

"I guess not," Bob Cole continued. "Now let's get going, ladies and gentlemen."

Two men wearing white gloves rolled the framed Klimt into the space. The audience oohed and aahed quietly. It was stunning. The gold leaf details, the beautiful face of Adele, the rich colors of her clothes—it looked like an authentic Klimt.

Bob Cole shushed everyone. "Let's start with one hundred thousand; do I hear one hundred thousand dollars?"

Someone must have raised their hand behind her, because Bob Cole pointed his gavel and said, "One hundred thousand . . . how about one hundred and fifty thousand?" He nodded at someone else directly. "I'll tell you what, ladies and gentlemen, I can see you're all eager, so let's get to two hundred thousand right away. Do I see two hundred thousand dollars?" Veri glanced back. At least eight people had their hands raised.

"Three hundred thousand, Bob!" someone called out.

Bob Cole looked slightly annoyed by the outburst. "All right, we'll go right to three hundred thousand dollars . . ."

It continued on like this for another few minutes. When the price reached $500,000, Charles raised his hand, and Veri tried not to look shocked.

"Five hundred thousand . . . do I hear five hundred and twenty-five thousand . . . ah, I see you, ma'am. Going once . . . twice . . . five hundred and twenty-five thousand dollars, sold to Mrs. Allen."

There was light clapping, and a few people (including Veri) turned to see who the winner was. Mrs. Allen had a helmet of dark hair and sat next to a younger version of herself with the same heavy hairdo. She looked neither pleased nor displeased at having just spent over half a million dollars for a fake Klimt.

"I may regret not bidding higher," Charles whispered. "Ready to go? The car is pulling up."

Outside, Tate's replacement, the same blonde female driver who'd driven them earlier, opened their door.

"I hope you don't mind, but I need to make a quick stop to check in on a client before we drop you off," Charles said.

"Yeah no, that's no problem," Veri said, sliding into the car. "That was amazing, Mr. Winthrop. Thank you for bringing me." She felt genuinely flattered that he had.

"You're very welcome, Veri." He looked a little embarrassed about the double *very*. "Oops, I bet you must get that a lot, don't you?"

"*Very* often," she said with a smile. "But I like it." She wasn't sure if she'd ever admitted that to anyone before.

A few minutes later, the driver stopped at an apartment building on Park Avenue.

"Actually, I'd love for you to come in with me," Charles said. "She's quite an important client of mine."

"Of course." Veri slid out of the car and followed Charles into the nicest apartment building she'd ever seen. A gigantic arrangement of white lilies was centered on a glass console table in the center of the foyer. It smelled like heaven. "Hello, Mr. Winthrop," the doorman greeted him, then pressed the private elevator button.

One floor later, the doors opened into another, even grander, entrance. Veri had only seen entrances like this on TV. Whoever this woman was, she was *rich* rich.

The butler led them into a drawing room with high ceilings and long olive green drapes. Next, a frail woman was wheeled into the room by a maid. Two gray cats sat on her lap. Another cat pounced in and sprang up onto one of the windowsills. "Henrietta." Charles leaned down and kissed the back of the frail woman's hand.

"Charlie," the woman said. Her voice was shaky.

"This is Veridian Sterling. An amazing young talent."

Veri stepped forward, unsure if she should shake the woman's hand or curtsy. Before she could do either, the maid wheeled the woman past both of them and into another small living room, where three more cats were lounging on the dark velour couches.

"I had them place it here," the woman said in her trembling voice. They all followed her bony finger to the wall where she was pointing.

Veri stopped breathing. She closed her eyes and opened them again, but it was still there.

Her cat painting.

"Th-that's mine," she said quietly.

Charles didn't react. Maybe he hadn't heard her. Maybe she was wrong.

"It looks perfect there, Henrietta." Charles stepped closer to the painting and crossed his arms. "Lovely."

"It does, doesn't it?" the woman said. One of the cats jumped off her lap and went to join another cat on the windowsill. "You see there?" She pointed and giggled, or hiccuped; it wasn't obvious which. "Looks just like them. My Felicity and Stan."

It was *definitely* her cat painting. There was the gray cat with one white paw lying in the windowsill and two cats on the floor licking their paws. And finally, there was the cat to the left side, walking out of the frame. *It was her painting.* She felt cold sweat start to form on the small of her back. "Excuse me, Mr. Winthrop . . . Um, excuse me . . . ," she said a little louder this time. "I think that's mine. Like, I'm pretty sure."

Charles ignored her again and stepped inches away from the painting this time. "Of course, these are slightly brighter colors than we're used to seeing him work with, but I quite like it. And you see here how he put his initials in the cat's face? That's how we knew it was a Herman Craine." He pointed to the cat with the white paw while Henrietta was wheeled closer to him. "You see? Right here. The H and the C?"

Veri was thunderstruck. She saw it too: an H shape made up the cat's nose, and the mouth could be interpreted as an upside-down C. It wasn't just a little cat smile that she'd copied from her mom's sketches; it was the *artist's signature.* HC. *Herman Craine.* She'd copied her mother's cats, and her mother must have copied Herman Craine's cats.

"We believe this is another painting in his series called *Lazy Day Cats*." Charles seemed genuinely delighted by the painting. Veri felt like she was listening to him from underwater. His mouth was moving, but the words that came out made no sense. "Naturally when I saw this, I knew you would love it. I knew you would have to have it, Henrietta."

The woman clasped her hands together and bobbed her head. "Thank you, Charlie."

"Shall I settle with Bobo, then?"

The woman petted the remaining cat on her lap and nodded again. The housekeeper spun her around and pushed her back into the living room. Charles followed without saying a word. The two cats on the windowsill jumped down and pounced out of the room, leaving Veri alone.

She walked up to the painting and googled *Herman Craine paintings*. Most of his work was currently in a gallery in Sweden. She looked back up at her own copy. How could this be real life? Her painting had been set in an elaborate gold frame. The last time she'd seen it, it was behind Mildred's office door. This was a gigantic mistake. She had to stop this. She hurried back through the living room, tripping on one of the antique Persian rugs along the way. Charles was talking to the same butler standing by the open elevator. "Thank you again, Bobo. Let's go, Veri."

"Thank you, bye." Veri waved before stepping inside the elevator. As soon as the doors closed, she turned to Charles. "What is going on? Why aren't you listening to me?"

Charles stared straight ahead. "We will discuss this in a minute, Veri."

A chill went up her spine. His monotone voice was terrifying.

Once they were on the sidewalk, Veri threw her arms out. "What is happening here, Mr. Winthrop? That's *mine*. *I* painted that. It's not real. It's not a real Herman Craine. I didn't know about the initial things in the cat face when I did it."

"Charles," he corrected her calmly.

"What?"

"Call me Charles," he said in the same ice-cold tone.

"Charles. I am *one hundred percent certain* that that painting is mine. I painted it for a thrift store . . . for this woman, Mildred. She put it behind a door. How did you even find it?"

The blonde driver hopped out of the town car and opened their door.

"You're a real talent, Veri. I wouldn't have let anyone else buy that painting. You should know that." Charles's face grew softer. "I'm giving you the forty-one thousand dollars, of course. Exactly what she paid for it."

"Forty-one . . . *what?*"

"That should help pay back your school loans."

She took a step back. "Wait a minute, h-how did you know about my *loans?*"

Charles tried to usher her into the car first. "Shall we get you home?"

But Veri stayed where she was. Something was very wrong here. "I'm not going anywhere with you."

Charles Winthrop looked disappointed. "We're happy to drop you off."

"No. Thank. You." She crossed her arms and shook her head.

"Very well." Charles leaned into the car and handed her her backpack. He started to slide into his seat but paused. "Oh, and Veri, I'll send the money directly to your crypto wallet account. Again."

She died right there standing up. Dead people can't talk. She could not form words.

"It's chilly," he said, tying his scarf under his neck. "You sure you don't want a ride?"

All along, he'd *known* it was her. He didn't wait for an answer this time. The blonde driver shut his door, hurried around to the other side, and drove away.

When she could finally move again, Veri pulled out her phone.

It took ten rings before Mildred picked up. "Middle Street Gallery?"

"It's Veri Sterling. I was hoping you could tell me a little more about what the man looked like who bought my painting? I-I know it's weird, but I need to know."

"Okay, doll. Let me ask Frank, again. Hold on." Veri heard Mildred put the receiver down. Maybe she was hallucinating. That would make sense. Also, she felt like she had no feet. Or she was invisible. The wind howled through her. That was her painting.

Mildred returned on the other line. "Hey, doll, he says 'a man' again. That's all."

"Sorry, but can you ask . . . was he super handsome and medium old, wearing a camel overcoat?"

"Lemme ask." The phone dropped again. Veri kicked up her leg and pressed the walk button with her foot. Mildred returned on the other end. "No, doll. He says young, like you. Your age. He doesn't know about handsome."

"Are you sure?" The crosswalk sign lit up, and she started across Park Avenue.

"He's sure. And an accent. He had that too."

She stopped in the middle of the street.

"Hey, doll, have you thought about a new cat painting?"

Veri nodded and hung up.

Tate.

TWENTY FIVE

Tate called thirty-two times. It started as soon as she got back to Hoboken and continued for the rest of the day, while she stared at *Interesting Builds*, reliving what had happened over and over again in her mind and trying to figure out what to do next. She deleted the voicemails as they came in, and all of his texts—most of which read one of three things: I can explain, give me a chance, or can you just PLEASE call me back.

His last text was seven minutes ago. Veri lay back on the couch and stared up at *The Creation of an Artist* on their ceiling. She remembered painting every stroke of it. Her mother had painted most of the surrounding details, while Veri focused on the two floating figures: the young artist reaching up toward the ethereal goddess handing down the paintbrush. Although everyone commented on how much the figures looked like Veri and her mother, she disagreed. To Veri, it was obvious that they looked nothing like them. The viewer only *wanted* them to look like them.

Tate called again.

She let it go to voicemail for the thirty-third time and tried to persuade herself to sit up and take a bite of her burrito. She DoorDashed Chipotle, and right after she did, she got a text from Jamie Spring. The Climate Crew was growing. We're going to Washington you should totally come with! Veri texted back that she'd think about it, and then she actually *did* think about it. Leaving the last year of her life behind seemed like the perfect move at this point. Besides her mother and Allison, she wouldn't miss anyone she'd met since graduation. Everyone she'd thought she knew was turning out to be someone she didn't.

One look at her burrito and she flopped back on the couch again. A chill kept going up her spine whenever she remembered Charles Winthrop's expression in the elevator. *We will discuss this in a minute, Veri.* The chill was turning into a full case of frostbite. She couldn't get warm, even under two blankets, and as soon as she closed her eyes, all she could see was Charles's face again. He had made her feel so special today, like he was actually invested in her career. *"This is Veridian Sterling. An amazing young talent."* She should never have trusted him. Or Tate. No wonder he felt too good to be true. He was. There was one thing that didn't add up, though. Why would Charles want to help her pay back her loans? Even *after* he knew it was Veri who'd sold him the information on the van Gogh? He had to have known the provenance came from Myra's ArtsData account. At least he knew the truth now.

The doorbell rang.

Veri sat up. It was dark outside but still before six thirty, when her mother usually got home. It rang again. This time, Veri got up and stood by the door.

"Veri?" It was Tate. He knocked. "Veri? Are you in there?"

Her pulse quickened. She stared at the door. She wanted to open it so she could call him a traitor to his face, but at the same time she didn't want to give him the satisfaction of telling his side of the story.

"Veri, if you can hear me, please, I just want to talk to you. Mr. Winthrop told me what happened today. I know you're angry with me, but I need to tell you . . . ah, bollocks," he groaned. It sounded like he was about to leave.

Veri stepped closer to the door. "Tell me what?"

"Veri! Hey. Can we talk a moment . . . please?"

"I'm listening."

He paused. "Okay . . . Mr. Winthrop had me go buy your painting at that shop, but I didn't know why."

"You were the only person besides my mom who knew it was even there, Tate, which means *you* were the one to tell Mr. Winthrop about it."

"I showed him your Instagram post. That's all I did. He thinks you're really talented, Veri, which you are, and he wanted to see your work in person."

Veri stared at the door. She *had* posted the cat painting on both her Instagram page and her website. "Why didn't you tell me that you bought it from Mildred? Seems like something you would mention, Tate."

"Look. People are walking by and wondering why I'm chatting to a door."

"Is Mr. Winthrop out there?"

"No. I took one of the cars, though."

Veri flipped the lock and pulled open the door. Tate was wearing a black bomber jacket over his white button-down. His forehead was wrinkled in worry. "Thanks. I don't want to interrupt supper or anything." A black town car was double-parked in the street with its hazards on.

"My mom's not home yet." Veri still hadn't invited him in. "Go ahead, explain."

"I thought it was going to be a nice surprise for you. Mr. Winthrop wanted one of your paintings, which means he must really think you're brilliantly talented. Right after I bought it for him, from Mildred I guess, I had finals to study for. I didn't even know you were *with* Mr. Winthrop today."

Veri softened, remembering that Charles had used a different driver to take them to the Frick. "How do you know about what happened, then? Why are you even here?"

"Mr. Winthrop called me about my driving schedule and asked if I had spoken with you. When I said that I couldn't get ahold of you, he told me what happened."

"Oh." Veri paused. Most of that added up, and Tate was starting to shiver. "It's freezing out there. You can come in."

Tate wiped his feet and stepped inside. "Thanks. It got chilly." He leaned in for a hug. "I wish you had just answered your phone."

He smelled amazing, like peppermint testosterone. Veri shut the door and wished she had just answered her phone now too. "I'm sorry, Tate. But this whole thing, it's so weird. Charles was so weird. He sold it for so much money, forty-one thousand dollars." She'd gotten the notice of the pending payment in her crypto wallet, but she hadn't accepted it yet.

Tate rubbed his hands together. "I get it. But it's not like that came out of his pocket. He has some über-wealthy clients, Veri, that don't think twice about paying that kind of money. Kind of a win-win, right?"

"I guess," Veri said. It didn't seem like Tate knew about the whole NFT thing, but she wasn't about to ask. "Did you tell him about my loans?"

"No. You did."

"I did?"

Tate frowned at her. "How else would he know?"

"Myra," she realized with a sinking feeling. Her mother must have told her about the loans when she told her about selling the brownstone. "I bet Myra told him." It made sense. Myra hadn't liked the idea of Charles taking Veri to look at artwork, but she couldn't say no to him either. In her eyes, Veri guessed, telling him about her loans belittled Veri just enough to make him feel sorry for her, like she was a charity case. Veri scrunched her face up at Tate. "I really should have answered my phone."

Tate smiled his perfect smile. "So we're all right?"

She nodded. "Do you want . . . can I get you a beer or something?"

"I'd be totally down for hanging, but I have another final tomorrow." He groaned. "I *have* to get home and study for it, even though I would really, really rather stay here with you." He stepped forward and pulled her into another hug. This time when they started to pull apart, he kissed her. He paused to check on her reaction and then kissed her again. Veri grabbed onto his biceps and kissed him back. Not a friend zone kiss either. "You sure you have to go?" Veri mumbled onto his soft lips.

He bit her lip gently and nodded her face along with his. "But ask me again sometime."

"Deal," she said. They started kissing again. Her insides felt like they were at an EDM concert, every cell having a party. Veri Sterling, the art freak who chewed on a tobacco pipe and lived in Hoboken, was getting kissed by a *legit* hot guy. *For the second time.*

Her phone rang midmash. It was her mother's ring: "Purple Rain." Tate grinned. "That's quite funny."

"My mom's a Prince freak. Sorry. I can just ignore it."

"I ought to get going anyway. I don't want to be Mr. Winthrop's driver forever, do I?" He opened the door. "So this weekend? An actual dinner together?"

She nodded. Tate did his half smile and stepped outside.

"Good luck with finals." Veri waved before he got back into the town car. After she closed the front door, she backed up and sat on the staircase. She was swooning, like the way it was described in novels. *Swooning.* Derek kissed like a street rat compared to Tate.

"Oh, you scared me," her mom said, stepping inside and pulling off her white beanie.

"Hey, Mom."

As soon as her mother closed the door, her expression changed. "Come into the kitchen."

"Um, okay?"

Veri followed her in and stopped at the sink.

"Does Myra know you were off with Charles Winthrop again?"

"What—?" How did she know about that? Did she know about the cat painting too?

"I just saw a town car drive away, honey." She frowned.

"Mom," Veri said, relieved. "No. That was Tate. His driver. You met him before. Charles wasn't even in there."

Her mother backed off. "Oh, that's right. I'm sorry," she mumbled, getting down a wineglass. "Would you like one?"

"Sure."

Her mother reached in for another glass. "I should have asked before assuming like that. I just know . . . well, Myra's not someone you want to make angry. She can ruin a reputation. I've seen it happen." She poured their wine and changed her tone. "So it's getting serious with Tate?"

"We're just friends, Mom."

"To Tate, then." She smirked. They clinked glasses. "Tell me about your day."

Considering how her mother had just reacted, Veri wasn't going to say anything about the Klimt auction or her cat painting, even though she was dying to ask why she'd made so many Herman Craine copies in her sketch pad. There was no way she could tell her mother she'd spent the morning with Charles Winthrop now. "Nothing exciting. How about you?"

"One of the teacups dropped and shattered, so Janet had me take them all down. I have to go back in before seven tomorrow to put in a new window design. She wants me to make it Christmas themed and it's not even Thanksgiving. Anyway, I just didn't have the energy to stay later tonight." She kicked off her platform ankle booties and took another sip of her wine. "I must have packed up thirty boxes of product today."

Before Veri could make her usual comment about the Janets and their cruel rule, her mother held up her palm and exhaled. "I shouldn't be complaining. I'm going to be giving them my notice soon anyway."

It took every bit of restraint for Veri not to ask her mother to reconsider buying into Divine Homes. It was so doable now! She had the money to pay back her loans and even more money from her cat painting. But there was no way to explain how she could have come up with the cash, and even if she did tell her the truth, her mom would make her give it all back to Charles Winthrop anyway.

They clinked their glasses again and sipped in silence, both too exhausted from their days to say much more.

TWENTY SIX

The next day, Myra waltzed into the gallery around noon, wearing some kind of bodycon hooded turtleneck dress under her fur coat, which she shook off immediately. "Jesus God, it's hot in here. What did you do?"

"Nothing—it was this hot when I got in. I thought you turned the temperature up, so I didn't want to touch it." Veri had been sweating in her cranberry velvet button-down shirt and black leggings ever since she'd arrived this morning, but she'd guessed Beck Becker had convinced Myra to keep the gallery hot for some reason. His dripping black letters might've been getting cracked from the cold.

"It's hotter than Hades in here." Myra went to the thermostat. "Seventy-nine degrees." She dialed it down. "Veridian. We need to talk." Myra stepped into her office and left the door open.

Veri braced herself. She was going to get fired. It was inevitable. Myra had to know by now that she'd stolen information off her computer. She might even know about her cat painting.

Myra dropped into her desk chair and took a swig from a Fiji water bottle, then swiveled around to look at Veri, still standing inside the doorway.

"All right. I might as well just come out and say it," Myra started. "And I don't need you telling the whole world." Veri nodded. She didn't want that either. What kind of maniac wants the whole world to know they're going to jail? "I'm having plastic surgery."

"Wh-what?"

"It's a very serious procedure. Dr. Fisher wants me to be completely rested beforehand."

"Of course, Myra. No problem."

Myra slid her dark glasses lower on her nose and leaned on her glass desk. "I don't want to hear a single word about this. Not to anyone. Including Charles Winthrop. And Beck . . . he's been a real pill lately . . . oh, and your mother. If you tell anyone, I will fire you."

Veri had to stop herself from smiling. This was great news. Myra, gone for weeks, maybe even months. It was even a little touching to see how insecure Myra was beneath all that cold, glossy veneer. "I won't say anything to anyone, Myra. I understand. When?"

She pulled off her glasses, sat back, and exhaled unhappily. "*That*, I don't know. I'm scheduled for May. However"—she sat up again and dabbed at her neck and lower face—"I'm on the cancellation list. It's practically a sure thing that someone cancels right before Thanksgiving. If that happens, I'm taking it. I don't even care if it's Dr. Fisher's last procedure of the day; I'm nabbing it." She seemed to suddenly notice that Veri was still there and stopped pressing on her jawline. "Oh, and one more thing, Veridian. I heard you went to the Frick with Charles. What did he get this time? Any new artists I should know about?"

"I don't think so," Veri said.

"Good." Myra pursed her enhanced lips and raised her microbladed eyebrows, then dropped them again. "You don't think . . ." She paused and looked at Veri. "You don't think I'll regret it, do you? I'd rather die than end up on one of those botched–plastic surgery shows. You won't let that happen to me, Veridian, right?"

For the first time since she'd met her, Myra looked scared. Her eyes were pleading as she waited for Veri to answer. It must be terrifying not to have anyone to depend on, Veri realized, and it didn't seem as though Myra did. "No. Not a chance. You're going to look great. Knowing you, you've picked the best doctor in the city."

Myra nodded with the beginning of relief on her face, until she looked like she remembered who she was talking to and turned back to her screen. "Damn right I picked the best doctor. He only does ten faces a year. Now, do *not* forget to mark my calendar for the Sotheby's auction this Thursday. Okay, out you go."

Veri pulled the door closed, then exhaled everything she wanted to scream—she *wasn't* getting fired and Charles *hadn't* told her about the ArtsData information. She half wished Charles had told her about her cat painting, though. She would have loved to see Myra's face when he told her that he'd sold it for $41,000.

~

It shouldn't have been a surprise when Charles walked into the gallery right after lunch, but it startled her anyway. Veri had been watching the door all morning, in between staring at her crypto wallet and the $41,000 that was still pending.

"Hello, Mr. Winthrop," Veri said in the coolest voice she could manage.

"Veri," he greeted her. "At least I didn't scare you this time." He slid off his leather gloves. "I trust Myra's here? We have an appointment."

"She's on a Zoom call. But I can tell her you're here if you want?"

"No, that's fine. I'm early." He smiled. "I hope you received the money?"

Veri lowered her voice. "I'm not accepting it, Mr. Winthrop."

"That's a shame. You earned it fair and square."

"You tricked an old lady. That painting wasn't real."

"'Real' can be relative, Veri. Your painting brought Henrietta real joy. So it's very real to her." Charles glanced over at Myra's door. "My appointment with Myra will last through the afternoon, upon which time, I will be taking her to dinner." He twisted the signet ring on his pinkie. "I'm going to send you an address; it's not far from here. It's an artist friend of mine. I think it would explain a great deal about my interest in you if you would visit him at his studio."

"No thanks. I can't leave anyway."

"Veridian!" Myra shouted from her office. Veri slipped around her desk and cracked open Myra's door. "Let me know when Charles is here!" she screamed. She was wearing AirPods and staring at her screen.

"Yup." Veri closed the door again. Charles was still hovering by her desk, so she stayed against the wall and straightened out the FEROCIOUS painting, which was, once again, and somehow always, crooked.

"I have to admit: I wasn't all that familiar with NFTs," Charles said. "I knew they were going to become a big part of the art world, though." He pulled his gloves out of his pocket again. "I recently learned that once an NFT is on the blockchain, it's on there *forever*. Are you aware of this? If a provenance, or *any* information for that matter, becomes an NFT, it can never be tampered with again."

Veri didn't answer.

"All to say, Veri, that anyone who *creates* an NFT has, whether they like it or not, forever left their fingerprints on it. Digitally, of course."

Veri felt like she'd been sucker punched. *Forever left their fingerprints on it.* Derek had told her the same thing; the NFT he'd made for her could never be changed, and even if Veri hid behind a string of random digits and never shared her password with a single soul, with enough "corrupt" searching, eventually, the trail would lead back to her. "Why are you telling me this, Mr. Winthrop?"

He smiled. "I need a sketch of *Girl in Yellow on Beach*."

This was not what she was expecting. She crossed her arms. "That's too bad, because no one knows what it looks like."

She waited for him to backpedal, except he didn't even blink.

"Which is why it could be anything at all. Until we find the real one, who could argue? Plus, 'girl,' in 'yellow,' on 'beach' is a fairly thorough description, wouldn't you agree?" He paused. "Don't tell me *you* haven't thought about what it might look like, Veri. A van Gogh fan like yourself? I certainly have. But in order for me to try and get my buyers interested, I need to show them something. Not everyone has imaginations like us."

"Veridian!" Myra called out again. This time, Charles breezed past her and poked his head through the door. "Hello, Myra."

"Charles. I didn't realize . . . is Veridian out there?"

"There's no rush, Myra. I'll be in the car." Charles closed her door again and stepped over to Veri, still pinned against the wall, where FEROCIOUS was already *impossibly* uneven again. "The center must be off," Charles said, nodding to the frame.

"Okay," Veridian said, feeling the same way about Charles. Something about him was off too.

"I'm hoping you can get me the sketch by tomorrow afternoon."

She shook her head. "Mr. Winthrop . . . that's not possible. I'm moving—my mom and I have to pack up an entire house."

"You are a superior talent, Veridian Sterling." He glanced around at Beck Becker's word bombs on the wall. "A *rare* talent in a sea of mediocrity. I'll look forward to seeing what you come up with. Let's say the Men's Club, tomorrow around four?" He started to head out but stopped. "The friend I mentioned will be expecting you later today. I'll text you his address."

"I can't just leave," Veri said, her voice wobbling.

"As I mentioned, I will have Myra fully occupied for the rest of the afternoon. We have a meeting and dinner." He lowered his voice. "I doubt you'll miss any sales if you close up early for the day."

As soon as he stepped out, Myra blew past her, back in her fur coat and sunglasses. "I'm out for the day, Veridian. If Beck comes in, tell him I'm with Charles." The way she said it made it clear she was trying to make Beck Becker jealous.

"Sure."

"And keep the heat down!"

Veri watched the female driver open the door for Myra, and after they drove off, Veri collapsed in her chair. *That* was a threat. A *definite* threat. Charles could, and would, trace the stolen provenance back to Veri unless she did a sketch of the van Gogh. Unless she *made up* a sketch of the van Gogh. It didn't seem right for her to do, but then again, it made sense that Charles needed something to show his clients.

She needed to ask Tate. He would know what to do. She dialed and started pacing.

It's Tate. I can't answer, but leave a message.

"Hey, it's Veri. I need to ask you something, so can you call me when you get this . . . sorry, I know you're in finals . . . okay, thanks, bye."

A text pinged while she was leaving the voicemail. It was the address from Charles, not far from where she was on the Upper East Side. *"It's an artist friend of mine. I think it would explain a great deal about my interest in you if you would visit him at his studio."*

She found the address on NYCityMap and took a screenshot of it, then sent it to her mother with a note: if murdered, look here. Her mother wouldn't check her phone until after work, and by then Veri would be home. Or murdered.

TWENTY SEVEN

The Upper East Side was like a different corner of the universe from the rest of New York City. Most of the buildings had elaborate details with gargoyles on them. Hedge fund managers, celebrities, sports heroes—all lived in the area. Whoever this friend of Charles was must have been rich. Her heart skipped a beat. Maybe he was sending her to someone who might buy her art. Maybe he'd looked up her *Walk Out* series on her website. Maybe he really *was* only trying to help her get started in her career.

Unlike the rest of the buildings in the neighborhood, the address Veri stood in front of had only a doorbell, not a doorman.

An old man pulled the door open. He was disheveled to the point of worry. His cream-colored polo shirt was covered in paint and other questionable splotches. His khaki pants were baggy and ripped, and one pant leg was rolled up to his knee, exposing a hairy white chicken leg. He wore Converse sneakers, black, low-top, which redeemed him slightly in Veri's eyes, but it was his facial hair that was the most off putting. Gray matted chaos sprang out from his chin and sideburns. Curiously, though, his mustache looked trimmed.

"We don't want any," he grumbled before shutting the door on her.

Turn and walk away, she told herself. *Turn around and walk away.* This guy was obviously deranged. But he did have paint splotches on his clothes, which made her curious. An artist, living in this area?

She knocked again.

The door opened right away this time.

"What?" the man asked. She caught a glimpse of canvases leaning against the walls and cans of paint on the ground.

Veri forced a smile. "I'm a friend of Charles Winthrop's?"

He looked at her cleavage. "Christ in heaven, they're getting younger."

"I'm not . . . like a girlfriend."

"Just a hookup, then." He stepped back. "Enter." He closed the door after her and walked to a stool, where, presumably, he'd just been sitting in front of an easel. Veri stepped over an abandoned half-painted canvas of a woman wearing dark-rimmed glasses. "Is that a Katz?"

"Very good," the man said, bending over to rinse a paintbrush out in an old Chobani greek yogurt container.

His paintings were very good too. Looking around, Veri spotted replicas of some of the greatest contemporary artists in the world. A copy of David Hockney's *A Bigger Splash* was leaning against the wall. She knew it was a copy because the real one lived at the Getty in Los Angeles. But it was incredible. Perfect, even. The frozen splash of water in the bright-blue pool quintessential Hockney. And almost impossible to replicate. A copy of Georgia O'Keeffe's *Ram's Head* hung on the wall above it. Also perfect. The original one was at the Met; she'd just seen it there.

Veri continued scanning the studio. A copy of Jasper Johns's *American Flag*, painted on a thick slab of wood, was hanging on the back wall. "That's an incredible Jasper Johns. They're all amazing." When she spotted the small *Adele*, which looked to be a study of the bigger Klimt, *Portrait of a Lady*, it dawned on her. "Wait, are you Corporal—?" The name was on the tip of her tongue.

"*Major*. Major Cohen." He flipped the painting he was working on upside down, or maybe right side up. "Am I supposed to know *your* name?" he asked with a grunt.

"Veri. Veridian Sterling."

He stepped back to consider his work. Veri considered it too.

"Wait, is that a Deibenkorn?" It had to be. Deibenkorn's *Ocean Park* pieces were painted in serene blues and yellows: some of the most beautiful colors ever put on canvas. Deibenkorn's ability to fold colors into one another was unparalleled. One of her classes in college had focused entirely on his color schemes. If she were to paint anything even remotely abstract, she would paint something similar.

When Major Cohen coughed, his belly shook. He crossed his arms and studied his work. "*Number Six.* Taken me three goddamn years to match the blue."

"It's perfect. You're really, really good. I mean, you don't need me to tell you that, obviously."

"So you like Deibenkorn. I never really understood the appeal, to be frank. I mean, the colors are a pain in the ass. You know what he said the secret ingredient to his blues is?"

"Yellow?"

"No." Major Cohen scoffed. "Quiet. He adds a few drops of 'quiet,'" he said with air quotes. "Pretentious asshole."

This old guy was as quirky as he was gruff. "If you don't like the artist's work, why do you make copies of them?"

Major Cohen turned around and sniffed at her. The gray chaos of his lower face lifted as one unit when his nose wrinkled. "I smell an art grad."

"Rhode Island School of Design." Veri nodded. "Just graduated a year—"

Something banged against the other side of the wall. Major Cohen stepped over to the spot and pounded his fist against it, twice. "Shut the hell up in there!"

Another bang. Major Cohen pointed his paintbrush at Veri and said, "Don't steal anything. Cameras." He pointed up to the corner of the room. There was no camera there, or anywhere else along the ceiling, but Veri nodded anyway. Major Cohen took his paintbrush with him over to a door, pulled it open, and disappeared.

Not sure what to do now, Veri sidestepped over to the Georgia O'Keeffe to get a closer look. "Amazing," she mumbled. It was beautiful. She knew this painting well. Georgia O'Keeffe was any female artist's idol, whether you liked her genre or not. Ironically, she thought, Georgia O'Keeffe would never have copied another artist's work. She'd spent her final years living on a ranch in New Mexico to get away from materialism and people. *That* was what being a true artist was.

"Help!" Three young children tore in through the door where Major Cohen had disappeared. Veri wasn't good with ages, but these kids were all shorter than her waist. Two of them ran directly past her, and one grabbed onto Veri's army jacket and hid behind her. "Don't let him see us," she whispered.

Major Cohen waddled back in. He walked like a prima ballerina, turning his arches out with each step. It was a strange sight, a disheveled old man taking graceful ballerina steps toward her, but so was the entire scenario.

The kid behind Veri dropped hold of her sleeve and ran back to where the other two kids were hiding behind an easel. "There you are, you little monsters!" Major Cohen sprang into action and tackled them onto the floor. Gray beards and pink sandals collided. "Your mother is going to be so mad!" he warned. The girls giggled and tried to squirm out from under him.

"Who's that?" One of them pointed to Veri.

"No idea. Now go back to your mother and tell her you tried to escape, but I found you."

"Okay!"

The smallest one waved to Veri when she ran by. Before stepping through the side door again, the little girl pressed a button on the wall. Right away, the entire wall began to lift like an oversize garage door. Even the sketches tacked onto it slid up and disappeared. Behind the phony wall was a gourmet kitchen and family room. Copper pots and pans hung over a crisp white rectangular island. Two enormous stainless steel refrigerators were against the back wall, and a shiny goosenecked faucet glistened over a large apron sink. Next to the kitchen, a boho chic great room was filled with white couches and block print pillows. A giant plasma screen was tucked inside the middle of an enormous bookshelf.

"Minor! Keep these kids out of my studio!" Major Cohen grumbled.

"Sorry, Dad." A brunette woman, around thirty or forty, hurried out from around the corner. She had the same turned-out ballerina walk. "Come here, you little thugs. Say goodbye to Grandpa. Time for swim lessons."

The little girls waved back to Major Cohen and followed their mother out of the room.

It was impossible to stop staring at the apartment. The art studio was only the front room of the rest of the flat, which had to be worth millions. Upper East Side millions.

Major Cohen walked over to the side door and pressed the button again. The giant wall lowered, and Major Cohen went back to his easel. "Painting copies doesn't look so bad anymore now, does it, art grad?"

"You paint fakes for a *living?*" she asked. It came out as rude as it was surprising.

"You know"—he paused—"I had the same attitude when I was a young artist. Painting copies was for hacks and bottom-feeders. I was going to blow the world away with my own work." He dabbed at the canvas. "And now I live on the Upper East Side. My neighbor's Elton John. Course, he's never here."

Elton John? Veri pulled out her phone, made sure the sound was off, and snapped a picture.

"Hey, no posting that, art grad. And tell Charles to stop sending spies to check up on me. Tell him I will be done when I'm done. Now go."

"Yes, sir, I will," Veri said. "I'm not a spy, though. I don't know why he sent me here, to tell you the truth."

"Maybe I do." He turned around to consider her. "Are you talented, art grad?"

"I-I won the most prestigious award at school, and everyone who's ever won it went on to have a giant lucrative career and become really famous. I won it for a series of paintings called the *Walk Out*. Basically it's a study of what's left behind after someone or something steps out of the—"

"*Making copies*, art grad. Are you good at *making copies* of other artists' work?" He kept his eyes on her and coughed again without covering his mouth.

She thought about denying it, but Major Cohen seemed like the kind of guy who would get it out of her anyway. "Yeah," she said. "Really good. The only painting any gallery has been interested in is a copy of a van Gogh that I did."

"Van Gogh, huh? Has he sold it yet?"

"No . . . ?" It hit her then why Charles Winthrop had sent her here. He wanted Major Cohen to convince her to do the van Gogh sketch. *"I think it would explain a great deal about my interest in you if you would visit him at his studio."*

He studied her. "So you're here for my advice, then. Okay. Do what he wants, art grad. It's easier, trust me."

Was Charles Winthrop blackmailing this guy too?

"Mr. Cohen." Veri cleared her throat. "Is Mr. Winthrop *making* you do these?"

He chuckled, which turned into another cough before he turned back to his canvas. "No one makes me do anything, anymore."

"So why do you keep making these copies instead of doing real art?"

Major Cohen dropped his brush into the Chobani container again, crossed his arms on top of his belly, and spun around to face her. "Let me guess: You think that every painting you see in a museum or a fancy gallery is authentic. You never consider that sometimes the original painting might be kept hidden so it can't be stolen or damaged. You *expect* that you're looking at the real potato because you spent thirty-five bucks to see it. But here's the thing—sometimes you're not."

He shuffled over to the Alex Katz painting on the floor and leaned it up against the wall.

"Sometimes, even the richest people like my neighbors can't afford an O'Keeffe or a Hockney, or a Twombly or de Kooning, but they still *want* one. *They must have one on their wall!*" He shook his fist for emphasis. "*Those* people who want a perfect replica come to me."

He went back to his stool. "And then there's Hollywood too." He plucked his brush out of the yogurt container. "Those fellows do a film on Picasso or Pollock and need *authentic-looking* copies of their work. They come to me too. I paint the damn paintings for the film." He started dabbing at his Diebenkorn again. "*That's* why I do what I do. That's why I'm rich, art grad."

His words sunk in while Veri watched his brush flitter over the canvas, barely touching it but leaving its mark nonetheless. Rich people, Hollywood, hidden paintings. She'd never considered any of this before. She'd only ever considered painting fakes to be plagartism. "Are you trying to convince me to do these too, Mr. Cohen? Is that why Mr. Winthrop sent me here?"

"The question isn't whether or not Winthrop wants you to paint fakes, art grad. The question is, What are you going to do now that you know painting your own stuff won't pay as much?"

He leaned over to rinse his brush in the Chobani container again.

"It's not always about the money, Mr. Cohen. Some people paint just to create more beauty in the world."

"But not you, art grad. You want the fame, and the money that comes with it too."

Veri was taken aback. Who was this guy to tell her what she wanted? "No, I don't. You don't even know me." She stopped just short of swearing at him.

"Yeah, I do. I do, because the first thing you told me was that you won a prestigious award and then bragged that it'd made everyone rich and famous." He chuckled lightly, and she could see the back of his body shake. "When I only asked if you were good."

This man had no idea what he was talking about, and she needed to leave. "Thank you for letting me come see your studio." She headed for the door.

"I didn't." He leaned back to study his work again. "But you should know, Winthrop doesn't just send anyone here. I think you might be the only other artist he's ever sent. Don't let that get to your head now, art grad."

"It won't," Veri said. She let herself out.

~

Back at home in their kitchen, she looked up *Diebenkorn Ocean Park #6* on her laptop. She compared it to the photo she'd taken of Major Cohen's Diebenkorn. They were identical. If Veri had not seen Major Cohen working on it with her own eyes, she would never have believed that his was a fake. She looked up Major Cohen's address again and put it into Zillow. His apartment was worth $17 million. Seventeen million dollars was more than most of the artists whose work he was copying had been paid in their lifetimes.

She looked up at Bunny Bonheur's portrait on the wall and then to the photo of her mother on the refrigerator. The truth was that as talented as these artists were, neither of them had ever made a dime off their artwork. And as much as she didn't want it to be true, the way things were going, the same might be said about her someday too.

She closed her laptop and went into the garage studio. She found the sketches of *Girl in Yellow on Beach* that she'd already done. They were good, but she could do better. She took out a fresh piece of canvas paper (twenty-four by eighteen) and a charcoal pencil, propped it on her easel, and started sketching.

She started with the girl; she sat on her right hip, with her long dress flowing out to the left. There was always movement to consider in a van Gogh. Like *Wheatfield with Crows*, which she googled again on her phone. In the painting, van Gogh's crows were midflight, most of them heading off the canvas to the right, while the wheat tillers blew in different directions below them. The single path leading through the wheatfield was where the eye landed. Veri looked at her sketch. Surely, van Gogh would have done the same kind of movement in *Girl in Yellow on Beach*. She started sketching the ocean in the background, with the currents moving to the right. The clouds, too, should be blowing right. On the left side of the canvas, she sketched out rocky cliffs. This way the eye would be drawn to the center of the painting, to the girl. Maybe the sun was coming up . . . or maybe it was going down. Which would van Gogh have chosen? Sunrise seemed too optimistic for the artist. It was probably sunset.

Pretty soon, Veri lost track of time. She was so deep into her sketching that she didn't hear the front door open until her mother was calling out her name. "Veri? Are you here? What's with the murder text?"

"In here," Veri called back, flipping over the canvas paper and covering it with her sketchbook. She'd have to work on it later.

After they'd ordered dinner, Thai food again, Veri said, "Hey, Mom, do you think you've ever seen a fake instead of the real thing at a museum?"

"I don't think museums could get away with that kind of thing."

"What if they were keeping the real one somewhere for safety reasons or something?"

Her mother poured herself a glass of wine. "That sounds like something you'd see in the movies, honey. There are authenticators and expert historians when a painting is put into a museum. I'm exhausted. How about a *Build* while we wait for dinner?"

They watched three episodes of *Interesting Builds* while they ate their Thai food. After her mother had finally gone up to bed, Veri went back to work on the sketch. And just in case her mother surprised her again, she filled a box with her supplies to make it look like she was packing. It was a good thing she had, because at midnight her mother poked her head into the studio. "Hey, honey. You're still up—everything okay?" She held a mug of steaming hot tea in one hand.

"Yeah, fine," Veri said as she knelt in front of the box, having heard her mother in the kitchen. "Just packing up. Why are you awake?"

"I'm just tossing and turning up there. Figured I might as well get some tea and find something productive to do. Want some help?"

"I'm almost done. But thanks."

"Don't stay up too late."

As soon as she was gone, Veri got back to work on the sketch. The girl was wearing a bonnet now, tied with a long flowing ribbon. Veri sketched the ribbon twice. Fabric was much more difficult to draw than she remembered.

When the sketch finally felt done, she sat back to consider it. She felt a jolt of pride rush through her. If she didn't know it was a fake, she might even think it was real.

TWENTY EIGHT

The post office worker puffed on his cigarette and watched Veri struggle with the gallery door. Myra's freshly pressed black Gucci velvet pantsuit was hanging over her arm. "My closet by Wednesday morning, Veridian," Myra had ordered that morning. "The auction is on Thursday."

Inside the gallery, Veri knocked on Myra's door just in case. She hadn't mentioned yesterday's afternoon getaway with Charles in her text this morning, but it didn't look like Myra had come back to the gallery last night either.

After hanging Myra's pantsuit in the closet, she felt the room spin a little. She'd worked on the sketch until four in the morning. After only three hours of sleep, she'd woken up to a sore jaw. The pain was still reverberating down the back of her neck.

At her desk, she took the poster tube out of her backpack and carefully unrolled the sketch. She wondered if Major Cohen could have done any better himself. She'd even added van Gogh's signature in the bottom-right corner.

"The dry cleaning, Veridian?" Myra asked, walking into the gallery. She had a blue scarf wrapped around her head, Jackie O–style, and wore oversize Valentino sunglasses.

"In your closet," Veri answered, careful to hide the sketch. Myra walked straight into her office like she always did, and Veri checked the time. She had to be at the Men's Club at four o'clock with sketch in hand, and that meant leaving early. She knocked on Myra's door and peeked her head inside. "Hey, Myra, sorry to interrupt." Myra was in the middle of putting on lipstick and looking at herself in a hand mirror. "I have a dentist appointment this afternoon, so I need to leave around three, if that's okay?"

"Reschedule." Myra popped her lips. "I need you here."

"I would, totally, but I *have* to go. Dentist's orders. I broke part of my tooth." It had happened to her mom once; she'd cracked a tooth eating granola. She'd had to work weeks of overtime to cover the cost.

"I don't pay you to have dental emergencies, Veridian."

I mean, *duh*. Veri didn't know how to answer that, so she didn't.

After a few more lip pops, Myra looked over at her. "Fine. Go. Now shut my door. Oh—and look at the email I sent you. You'll need to send Janis Pole the contract."

"Again?" She'd sent her one days ago.

"I've decided to give her another week at the gallery. Her work is excellent." Myra gauged Veri's reaction. "Don't get your feathers all ruffled up, Veridian. Send her the contract. Out you go."

"Sure." Veri shut the door and went back to her desk. Myra was purposely taunting her, but she refused to give her the reaction she was expecting. For the first time, Veri felt zero guilt for breaking into her ArtsData account.

Janis Pole was getting a monthlong show, starting next week, according to Myra's email. The artist needed to put down a $50,000 "deposit." The only good news was that it was *bad* news for Beck Becker. The thought of watching him drive away with all his *f*s banging around in the back of his van made her feel better. At least Janis Pole had some decent art to stare at all day.

As soon as she'd sent the new contract off to Janis Pole, Beck Becker stormed into the gallery.

"She here?" he asked without stopping. He looked terrible. His cheeks hung low on his sharp face, and his eyes looked sunken. Even his white pants and T-shirt were wrinkled and unkempt. He looked like a housepainter who'd fallen asleep under a bridge for a few days. He knocked once and stepped inside Myra's office.

"Beck, you should have called," she heard Myra say before he shut the door.

Ten minutes later, Beck stepped out again. He looked the same amount of disheveled, so it was impossible to know if sex had been involved. His mood was slightly better, though.

"Hey, Veri," he said, stopping at her desk—unfortunately. "I'm thinking of doing a *V* series next. You mind if I use 'Veridian'? You won't sue me, will you?"

"No," she answered, feeling strangely flattered. "Totally cool with me."

"Hey, great, thanks. See you around, then."

"You too." She wanted to add that she was sorry nothing of his had sold, but he was out the door before she could.

Myra stepped out of her office. "I'll be gone for the day."

"Okay. I'll close the gallery around three," Veri reminded her.

"Why would you do that?"

Veri pointed to her teeth. "Dental emergency?"

Myra rolled her eyes and slipped on her dark glasses. "Fine. Anyway, Veridian, you're fired. Beck's taking over for you. I'll pay you through the end of next week. Leave the desk clean." She paused for a moment, then pushed open the door and stepped outside.

Veri hadn't moved. *Fired?* That couldn't be what Myra had just said. Except it *could* be, and she *had*. Maybe it was her lack of sleep or just her overworked anxiety, but Veri felt nothing at all. She sat back in her chair and stared at her computer. The wallpaper on her screen was a floating Hattfield Gallery logo that disappeared off to the right every few seconds before returning on the left side and starting all over again.

Allison texted while Veri was still staring at her screen.

Allison: Have news. Need to meet. Pie Place tmrrw 8am?

Veri: What's going on? Why haven't you texted?

Allison: Tell u tmrrw.

At three o'clock, Veri locked the gallery and started for the Men's Club with the poster tube under her arm. She ignored her sore jaw and chewed on her pipe. It was frigid outside. Winter was imminent. Most of the trees had lost their leaves. It had rained earlier, and now there were puddles on the road that would be frozen later tonight.

By the time she got to the Men's Club, her black Converse were soaking. She dropped the tobacco pipe into her pocket before walking up to the front door. A different doorman, looking about Tate's age, opened the door this time. "Can I help you, miss?"

"I'm here to see Charles Winthrop."

"Very good. Dimitri will take you up." He ushered Veri inside and into the elevator, where Dimitri stood waiting to man the buttons. Veri leaned against the back wall and tried to slow her heart rate, which was beating in her ears.

"You're here to see Mr. Winthrop?" a much older man wearing more or less the same outfit—black suit with a black tie and a purple handkerchief peeking out of his breast pocket—asked when she stepped out of the elevator. Veri nodded. "Right this way," he said, leading her into the same reading room as before.

Charles Winthrop was sitting on one of the leather couches with his legs crossed and a newspaper covering his face.

"There's a young lady here to see you, sir."

The paper came down. "Hello, Veri. Thank you, Bill."

"Hello," Veri said.

"Bill, get us two hot teas, if you will."

"Right away, sir."

Bill hurried away, and Charles Winthrop stood. "Please have a seat." He motioned once again to the seat she'd sat in only days ago, before she'd known that *he knew* she was a criminal, and before he'd sold her cat painting for more money than her mother made in half a year.

"I don't have a lot of time, Mr. Winthrop." On the way over, she'd decided not to tell him that she'd just been fired. "I had to tell Myra I cracked a tooth."

"I hope you didn't, though."

The room was almost empty today. After shrugging off her backpack, Veri sat. "The truth is, while I appreciate you trying to help me out—you know, financially—I called the police three times."

Charles Winthrop raised his eyebrows. "Oh?"

"But I hung up every time."

"Hard to explain," he sympathized, without looking like he believed her. "My reselling of an excellent reproduction in the likeness of a Herman Craine, done by you, and then giving *you* all the proceeds, without even taking a commission for myself. I am an art dealer, Veri."

She looked over his shoulder. That was exactly why she hadn't called the police. She'd googled it. A real Herman Craine went for low six figures, and she guessed Henrietta might not have cared that it was a copy as long as it was a good one.

"In any case, police don't generally deal with art crime. It's the FBI," Charles said. Two men walked by puffing on cigars, and he waited until they'd passed before continuing: "So. I'm assuming that's the sketch?" He nodded to the poster tube sticking out of her backpack.

Veri crossed her arms. "What are you going to do with it?"

"I told you. It's hard to get buyers excited about the *idea* of a painting. Clients need to *see* something, even if it ends up being a wrong interpretation of what that painting will eventually turn out to be. I will be presenting your sketch to my clients as a possibility of what the painting might look like. And by the way, I have some scouts looking in the Netherlands now. I should have remembered that van Gogh's sister might have kept some of his paintings."

Veri glanced around the stuffy room—there were two lone men reading newspapers—and whispered, "I could be completely wrong about this. The real one might look totally different, you know."

"True," Charles Winthrop agreed. "Although we know he modeled it after Gauguin's piece, so I imagine you're not too far off. Did you enjoy meeting Major Cohen?"

Obviously, Major Cohen must have reported back to him. "He's definitely talented."

"I believe you to be equally as talented," Charles said, with what sounded like pride. "Now," he added with a nod to the poster tube, "I should probably wait and take a look at that back in my office."

Without handing it to him, Veri shifted in her seat. "You're not going to go sell this to some old lady and pretend it's real, though, right?"

He looked amused. "I can promise you that if I did, I'd give you the money, Veri. And it wouldn't be five figures; it would be seven."

It wasn't exactly the answer she was looking for, but she pulled the tube out of her backpack. "In exchange, Mr. Winthrop, I'd like to ask that the 'digital fingerprints' on the NFT that I—that *was made*—remain anonymous. Forever."

He smiled. "Yes, about that. It turns out that I'm not sure *who* got me the information for *Girl in Yellow*, but I've decided that, in fact, I'll never know. It was a random address on a random crypto account, as far as I'm concerned. In the end, it doesn't matter where I got it, just *that* we got it, and now we're one step closer to finding a new painting from a true master artist." He looked directly into her eyes when he said, "The case is closed, as far as I'm concerned."

Her jaw relaxed for the first time in days. She held her hand out, and they shook on it. He took the poster tube from her and placed it on the couch next to him.

"I should get going." Veri stood with her backpack.

Charles stood too. "Thank you for coming. I hope that tooth feels better," he said with a grin.

Veri nodded. "It does. Thanks." She headed to the elevators, and Dimitri escorted her all the way outside.

Around the corner from the NYMC, Veri stopped to lean against the side of the building and catch her breath. Her entire body was shaking.

But she was, finally, free.

TWENTY NINE

The next morning, her phone woke her up with a text. It was 6:00 a.m., and her eyes were blurry. She reread the text.

> I need you at Sotheby's today. 11am. Name at check-in.

Before she could text back, her phone rang.

"Veridian, I need you to go in for me. Hattfield Gallery *never* misses a Sotheby's auction. Or a Christie's, for that matter. Twenty-five straight years. Dealers don't take galleries seriously unless you show up."

"You fired me," Veri reminded her. Her voice was groggy.

"You have something to wear, right?"

"No offense, Myra, but I don't have to do anything for you anymore." The other end of the line went silent for a long moment. Maybe she'd hung up. "Are you there?"

"I'll show you."

"What?"

"Your own show. In my gallery. Next week. Tomorrow. Whenever you want it. You can have the whole space."

Veri threw her legs over the side of the bed. "What about Janis Pole?"

"Who cares. You can take her place."

Her head was spinning. *Her. Own. Show.* She'd be written up in *Artforum.* She'd be discovered by curators all over the city. She'd be a professional artist. Something was sounding too good to be true, though. "Wait, why can't *you* go?"

"I got off the wait list. I go in at two o'clock this afternoon. Last appointment of the day, but I took it. I haven't missed a Sotheby's auction *ever*, but my face can't wait any longer. You'll know what I mean when you're my age. We can't all look like your mother."

Veri held back her chuckle. Myra could have baby skin transferred directly onto her face, and she still wouldn't be in the same zip code of pretty as her mother. She didn't owe Myra a single thing. She could easily say no and hang up. Myra was a terrible boss, a terrible frenemy to her mother, and a terrible human. "Why should I believe that you'll keep your word? And oh yeah, I don't have *fifty thousand dollars* to pay you."

"I'll waive my fee." Hearing Myra sound so desperate was giving Veri serious pause for concern. Going to a Sotheby's auction sounded totally amazing too. "And I'll put it in writing. A two-week show, no cost to you."

"I mean . . . I *guess* I can go."

"You'll thank me, Veridian. People like you never get in. Oh, but for the love of God, do *not* bid on anything." Her voice was back to normal snarky. "Wear a dress, or at least a pantsuit. And no pipe." There was a loud honk in the background. "I'm going to get labs done now. I'll call to put your name in at check-in." She hung up.

Veri went to her window, opened it, and yelled, "I'm getting my own show!"

Mrs. Reiner from across the street was walking her cat on a leash. She stopped to see who was doing all the screaming. When she spotted Veri, she pulled on the leash and walked on.

~

At the Pie Place, Veri picked a table by the back wall and scrolled through photos of Sotheby's auctions. After a show at the Hattfield

Gallery, who *knew* how famous she could get. Maybe she'd even have one of her paintings, like *Night Appointment*, auctioned off at Sotheby's one day. Or maybe Christie's.

A few minutes later, Allison hurried in. She looked like she'd been crying. Her eyes were puffy, and she had zero makeup on. "Uh-oh," Veri said. "What's wrong?"

"Saggy Dick got someone pregnant, and it wasn't me."

"No way."

Allison ripped off her scarf and her jacket and sat across from Veri. "His Pilates instructor."

"Old guys do Pilates?"

"And screw their instructor afterward. You look great—why?"

Veri looked down at her outfit. Black wide-leg pants and a fitted black velvet suit jacket with her different days of the week doughnut T-shirt underneath. Myra hadn't said anything about wearing graphic tees. "Thanks."

Allison sniffled and looked around. A waitress across the room noticed them. "Did you order?"

"No. So what are you going to do about Saggy Dick?"

"That's what I wanted to talk to you about. Since you hate your job and I hate my life now, I was wondering . . . I mean hoping . . . maybe you'd want to move to Chicago with me."

"Chicago?"

"Yeah, look. I know you probably don't want to leave your mom and stuff, but I met someone there who said she needed a few assistant art teachers."

"For like college level?" Allison looked terrible. Veri felt sad for her. Whoever the guy was, she could tell that Allison genuinely liked him.

"Younger, I think. Like middle school, which is horrid, but I think I'm going to take it. Second City is there, too, so I can keep up my acting." There was a glint of hope in her eyes when she said that. "But I don't know anyone else there, and I don't want to go alone. I'm not good at alone."

The waitress came over and handed her a T-shirt. "Hey, Allison. They wanted me to give you a new one."

"Thanks." Allison threw the T-shirt on the table. "We're gonna get two coffees and the maple chip pie à la mode."

"Sure thing." The waitress scribbled on her pad and walked away.

Allison nodded to the shirt. "I told them I'm coming back. Supposed to start tomorrow. I think I'd rather die, though."

Veri leaned into the table. "I got fired."

"What the fart?" Allison perked up.

"Last night. Yup."

"Shit."

"And my mom's moving to Cape May."

Allison banged the table. "It's fate, then." She pulled out her phone. "I'll text that lady and tell her we're interested. What about that DILF money you got for the tiara? Can you use it for an apartment? I think it's a pretty good salary, but Saggy Dick let me have one of his credit cards, so I already took ten thousand cash out and transferred it into my savings. We could get a sick apartment, a penthouse maybe. Like this one." She flipped her phone around and showed her a Zillow page. "If you don't like it, I have like twenty other places saved."

Veri took the phone and scrolled through her saved pages. "Totally cool." The waitress brought their coffees and the maple chip pie à la mode, and Veri handed Allison back her phone. "The thing is, Al . . . Myra's going to give me a show."

"Say what?" Allison put her phone down on the table. "You just said you got fired?"

"In exchange for going to a Sotheby's auction this afternoon. She can't go because she's getting a facelift."

"Ew. I mean I'll probably get one, too, though." Allison pinched her cheeks, not registering Veri's words.

"So that's the only thing. And if it goes well, maybe I won't even need a job, and I can just keep, you know, painting . . ." Veri's words hung in the air for a moment until Allison's expression finally changed.

"Wait. Oh my God. V! A show? *Omigod*. Don't even worry about the Chicago thing." She looked disappointed enough to cry but high-fived Veri anyway.

Veri felt her gut pinch. Allison was the best friend she'd ever had. She'd never been flaky, and she'd never let her down. Even when Veri dressed like Gustave Courbet for an entire month—long gray beard and all—to try to get into the artist's frame of mind so she could do her final project on him, Allison would walk around campus ready to fight anyone who made fun of her.

"But truthfully, Al . . . I kind of hate it here too. And I don't even know if Myra will actually keep her word. She's the worst." It was true, Veri realized as she stirred her coffee. Why would she believe anything Myra told her? She was probably just lying anyway. Allison looked tentatively hopeful again. "And I mean, *come on*. We could rent a studio together too." She paused. "You're an incredible sculptor, Allison Parker. I don't believe for a second that you really wanted to give it all up. What about the sculpture you did of your little stepbrother, when you made him look like King Louis, the bratty one?"

Allison looked at her sheepishly. "You mean when I put Chasey's face on Louis XIV's head? That *was* pretty funny."

"It wasn't just funny. It was totally brilliant. You were going to start a whole website doing that."

Allison nodded. "Bust-A-Move."

Veri made a face. "Still not the best name, but yeah. That."

"Okay . . . so it's a maybe?"

Veri nodded. "A total maybe."

They agreed to wait until Monday to decide about the job.

Allison grabbed her hand from across the table. "I love you, even if you still chew on that gross pipe."

"I love you too. Even though you're not that great with accents."

After they got the bill—the waitress only charged them for the coffees—Allison's phone rang. When she saw who it was, her mood changed. "I gotta get this. It's ass-wad Saggy Dick. Talk later." She hugged Veri and hurried out the door.

"Wait, Allison!" Veri called after her, but she was already gone. She swiped the Pie Place T-shirt up from the table. She'd give it to Allison later. Now, she needed to get uptown. The auction was in an hour. She gulped a final swig of her coffee and felt liquid dribble down both sides of her mouth. "*God, Veri,*" she mumbled, looking down at her shirt. The doughnuts were splattered with coffee.

THIRTY

Sotheby's. She'd been inside twice on field trips, but never to an auction. She hurried across the street and under the five nations' flags flying over the entrance. There was no doorman, but there was a security check in the middle of the lobby. A few men were in tuxedos, and it was only ten forty-five in the morning. The women were in business suits. Veri had replaced her stained doughnut T-shirt with the Pie Place shirt that Allison had forgotten. *So Good It's a Crime* was visible under the velvet jacket.

"Excuse me, we don't allow influencers." A woman with a Sotheby's badge stopped her before she reached the counter.

Veri tucked her loose hair behind her ear. She'd put her hair in an updo in the taxi. It looked chic-messy, and thanks to her dark eyeliner and bright-blue mascara, apparently she looked like an influencer. *Which was so cool.* "I'm representing the Hattfield Gallery, but thank you."

The woman looked bothered. She pointed to a table against the wall. "Gallery check-in is down there. You'll need to wear the lanyard."

"Thanks."

A few minutes later, Veri walked into the auction room. A jumbo screen was on the wall, with a sleek modern lectern placed in front of it. Most of the hundred or so chairs were already occupied. The woman at the gallery check-in had given her specific instructions to stand in the back of the room, where "all the other assistants line up. Sorry we don't have seating for you."

The dozen other relatively young people standing against the wall were wearing lanyards around their necks like Veri's. Most of the assistants were basic supermodel types, even the men. She reminded herself that she'd just been mistaken for an influencer and marched over to an empty spot against the wall, trying not to trip in her mother's platform booties.

"Hey." The assistant next to her, about Veri's age, wearing a mauve jumpsuit, leaned into her. "Do you know if we can FaceTime from back here?"

"I'm not sure," Veri answered. "First-timer." She pointed her thumb at herself, which she immediately regretted doing.

The stylish assistant nodded toward Veri's *Hattfield Gallery* name tag. "I heard Emma got fired."

"She did," Veri said, noticing that her lanyard read *528 Gallery*. It was the same assistant who'd turned her away all those weeks ago. She didn't look like she remembered. "I'm Veri."

"Kent," she said. "Nice to meet you."

A well-dressed man in a robin's-egg blue suit walked up to the lectern and waited until the crowd got quiet. "Welcome, all, to Sotheby's today. We have a nearly three-hundred-year tradition of bringing you the very finest artwork from all over the world. We thank those of you tuned in from elsewhere, and those of you here in the auction house, for joining us. Let's begin."

A framed painting was rolled out from the left side of the room, and two men in white gloves and navy blue Sotheby's aprons stood on either side of it. The houselights went down, and a painting of a white clapboard house with a yellow Lab sprawled out on the lawn appeared on the jumbo screen. It was a Fairfield Porter. A thrill went up Veri's spine. Maybe, someday, her painting would be rolled out to an adoring crowd too.

The auctioneer leaned on the lectern and scanned the room. "Fairfield Porter, ladies and gentlemen. 1907 to 1975. American painter of abstract expressionism with a remarkable ability to elevate images of mundane life and make them beautiful. This painting is from the later works of his home on the coast of Maine. Opening bid is one million dollars. Let's begin. One million . . . do I see one million dollars . . . ?"

Dozens of green paddles sprouted up. The auctioneer continued upping the bid while Veri took in the scene. Twenty or so proxies standing to the right kept their hands in front of their mouths to prevent any lipreading while they spoke into their cell phones. These were the heavy hitters: billionaires who sent their people to do the bidding for them while they cruised on their yachts and flew in their private jets. Veri wondered how many of these billionaires already owned a van Gogh and which of them would eventually bid on *Girl in Yellow on Beach* once it was found.

The auctioneer chanted on, and the tension rose as fewer paddles did the same, until eventually only a scattering of paddles could be seen. "Two million . . . do I see two million dollars . . . yes, for the gentleman over here." The auctioneer banged his hammer.

"That was quick," Veri said, attempting to make small talk with the 528 assistant, Kent.

"Morning auctions are usually pretty lame," she said. "Most of these people are art critics, not bidders."

"Yeah, of course." The platform booties were uncomfortable. There were a few open seats in the audience, but none of the other assistants had gone to sit in them, so Veri stayed where she was, shuffling her weight from foot to foot.

The next painting was auctioned off quickly too: an abstract in watercolor.

As soon as the hammer struck, the crowd started to leave. "If you'd be kind enough to wait a moment, ladies and gentlemen," the auctioneer said with a wave. "We have one more item to auction this morning, so if you'll all stay seated, I promise it will be worth it." The room quieted down again, and the jumbo screen changed to a new image.

Veri blinked at it.

Girl in Yellow on Beach was on the screen.

Her sketch.

"No. No no no no . . . ," she mumbled loud enough for Kent to frown at her. "Not happening." *This was not happening.*

"We have a wonderful surprise today, as only Sotheby's is wont to do. *Girl in Yellow on Beach* is *a never-before-seen* drawing by Vincent van Gogh." The crowd oohed and aahed as Veri's sketch, now framed in gold, was rolled out. "Recently discovered from the basement of an old hospital in the Netherlands." He shook his head, delighted. "What an absolute treasure of a discovery. I should note before the bidding begins that the sketch has been authenticated by Robert Cole."

Bob Cole. Fake passport, jiujitsu, *Bob Cole.* Veri shook her head. *This could not be happening.*

The audience whispered excitedly while Veri stared at the jumbo screen. For a moment, she wondered if maybe it wasn't hers—maybe it *was* the real van Gogh. She closed her eyes and opened them again, but the image on the screen was definitely hers: the water and clouds moving to the right, the rocks to the left, the girl's back facing the viewer. She started sliding down the wall, groaning "*Nooo*," until a hand grabbed her elbow. "Are you okay?" Kent asked, fanning her with a brochure. "You're not pregnant, are you?"

Veri shook her head. "Just . . . hot."

"Ladies and gentlemen, we will start the bidding at two million."

Green paddles bloomed over heads again, and cell phones began ringing in the proxy section.

"Do I see two million dollars for this sublime van Gogh sketch?"

Veri ripped off the velvet. Her T-shirt was sticking to her now.

"Two million, five hundred thousand . . . ," the auctioneer continued while Veri scanned the seated audience. Charles Winthrop had to be in there somewhere, and as if the auctioneer had just read her mind, he pointed to the left: "Yes, Mr. Winthrop, I see you there . . . three million dollars . . ."

Veri spotted the back of his head, and fury filled her body. He was seated in a middle row. A blonde woman sat to his right, and to his left, a dark-haired man. Charles lowered his paddle.

"Three million, two hundred and twenty-five . . . ," the auctioneer continued. *She had to stop this.* Her sketch wasn't worth *three dollars.* She had to tell them *right now.*

"Sir . . . excuse me, sir?" Veri waved her hand and stepped forward.

The auctioneer spotted her. "Yes . . . I see someone in the back there . . . three million, two hundred and fifty thousand dollars . . ."

Kent grabbed her arm and pulled her back. "Oh my God, girl. Are you really bidding?"

"That's . . . mine." Veri didn't dare move. The auctioneer kept looking back at her.

"Do I see three and a half million . . . ladies and gentlemen, this is a once-in-a-lifetime opportunity . . . yes, there." He pointed to Charles Winthrop again.

"*Come on,*" Veri grumbled. What was he going to do, buy the sketch and give her $3.5 million? That was too insane to be real. This *whole thing* was too insane to be real. Charles Winthrop was a liar. A con artist. A thief. He was *selling fakes.* She could prove it . . . except she couldn't. No one else had seen her van Gogh sketch. Not even Tate. She'd handed it directly to Charles in the Men's Club. She felt a herd of elephants drop into her stomach. What a fool she was. *This whole time,* he'd planned to auction off her sketch. His words kept repeating in her head: *"The case is closed, as far as I'm concerned."* But it was all lies. The NFT could be traced back to her, and he knew it. Which meant that if she said anything right now, she'd be incriminating herself.

"Four million dollars . . . do I see four million dollars . . . ?"

Please, no one bid. Please, no one—

"There we are, Mr. Brochard! Four million dollars . . . going once, going twice . . . for four million dollars to Mr. Brochard!" The auction-eer slammed the hammer.

The jumbo screen changed back to the Sotheby's logo, and the sketch, *her* sketch, was wheeled out of the room.

"Ladies and gentlemen, this concludes the auction. Thank you all for coming today. We do hope we will see you again soon."

There was light clapping before everyone stood. Veri lost sight of Charles. She tied her jacket around her waist, hiked up her backpack, and started walking against the crowd. "Excuse me, sorry, excuse me." Charles was taller than most men. Her eyes passed over anyone shorter than her.

Finally, she found him. He was standing in the same spot where he'd been sitting, talking to the blonde woman. Veri stood at the end of the row, keeping a laser-eye focus on him. The woman acknowledged her first, and Charles must have sensed something. He turned around and smiled. "Hello, Veri. What a surprise. I didn't see Myra here."

"I need to talk to you." She hardly recognized her own voice.

"I see," he said, looking, or pretending to look, delighted. He turned back to the woman. "Again, call me if I can be of any help with the issue we discussed." They shook hands, and the woman hurried out of the row on the other side.

"Now." Charles stepped over to Veri. "What can I help—?"

"This time, I *am* calling the police."

"Oh." He clasped his hands together. "What for?"

"*What for?* Are you—*really?*"

"Veri. Please be more clear. What for?"

She blinked at him. Was he insane? He had to be insane.

Someone squeezed his shoulder as they passed him. Charles lit up when he saw who it was and kept the same smile on his face while he waited for Veri to answer his question.

"You just auctioned off my sketch for four million dollars." She slapped her forehead. "Four million dollars for a sketch I did in my garage. That *you* asked me to do."

Charles calmly picked up a brochure left abandoned on a chair. "I have no idea what you're talking about, Veri. But if you'll excuse me, I have a car waiting."

Orange danger cones fell from the sky and hit her on the head. The world had gone into the upside down. "You have no idea what I'm *talking about? You* have *no* idea what I'm *talking* about?"

"Please send my regards to Myra." He started to slip past her, but she grabbed his arm. He glanced around to see if anyone noticed, looking a little worried for the first time.

"Why are you doing this to me, Mr. Winthrop? I don't understand." Her voice was shaking now. She dropped his arm.

Charles softened for an instant, but a nanosecond later, he was back to his same old disarming smile. "Try to get some rest, Veri. I can see that Myra is working you too hard."

"I got fired, Mr. Winthrop." Her delivery of the news was cold as ice.

He looked genuinely surprised. "Oh no. I'm sorry to hear it. If you need a reference, please reach out. Now I really must get going; my driver is waiting." He seemed to remember something. "Tate's out for the week, as you already know."

He slipped past a group of people still milling around in the back of the room and disappeared out the door.

"Hey, I like your shirt," one of the Sotheby's employees said, gathering up the rest of the brochures. "'So good it's a crime.' Ha ha. That's awesome."

THIRTY ONE

The lobby was still crowded by the time Veri made her way out of the auction room. She spotted Kent laughing with a group of people her age. She should've been one of those twenty-year-olds headed to brunch or going to a yoga class. Instead she was probably going down for drawing a fake van Gogh that had been sold for $4 million at Sotheby's. She didn't need to be a lawyer to know that *someone* would be going to jail, and unless she could prove it should be Charles, it would be her.

There was no sign of Charles anywhere now. She wanted to call her mother; maybe she would know what to do. Except she couldn't risk getting her involved. She couldn't know about any of it. She had to tell someone, though. *Someone* had to know what she should do. The only someone she could think of was Tate.

Yellow taxis and black town cars were waiting under the line of national flags. Charles could be in any one of them. Instead of crossing the street, Veri decided to hug the building until she could get around the corner. It was much less crowded on the other side, and Veri pulled out her phone. She felt bad about disturbing him during finals, but he would understand. This was an emergency.

The phone rang straight through to voicemail. She hung up without leaving a message, threw her head back, and stared up at the colorless sky. Who else could she call? Myra was a hard pass. She considered Major Cohen, but she didn't have his contact. A father figure would have been nice right about now, but of course, that ship had sailed.

She'd started to text Tate this time when he called.

"Tate?"

"Yeah, hi. I saw you called. I was just starting a review session."

"I know you're in finals, but I didn't know who else to tell."

"Tell what?"

"The sketch, the one I did for Mr. Winthrop, it just sold at auction for *four million dollars*." She whispered the last part and looked around to make sure no one had heard.

"Wait, *what* happened?"

Her mouth felt like it had never known water. Her tongue was so thick with panic that it was hard to form words. "He's a crook, or like a grifter or a con man or something. I don't know what to do."

"Whoa. All right, hold on." She heard a door open and shut behind him. "Sorry, I can't talk in there. Can you start over, please?"

She pulled some air into her lungs, which felt like they had been boarded up with wood. "He sold the van Gogh sketch that I did for him—"

"What van Gogh sketch?"

"*Girl in Yellow on Beach.* The van Gogh painting he's trying to find. I sketched it out for him so he could try to sell it, or find it, or I don't know why."

"That makes no sense."

"Tate, please just listen, okay!" There was silence on the other end. "Sorry, I know I'm not making sense. He told me he just needed it so he could get an idea of what it might look like. He wasn't supposed to sell it. And then I got to Sotheby's . . . and it was here. It's my sketch."

That finally seemed to be clear enough for Tate. "Bloody hell. Are you still there?"

"I'm around the corner."

"Did you call anyone? Are you in danger?"

"I don't think so. He's gone already."

"Listen, Veri. I'd come down there, but I have this review session in three minutes and then right after that, the final exam . . ." He sounded truly sorry about it. "I could see if I can reschedule, tell them I have COVID or something."

"No, it's okay." Veri shook her head. Hearing his voice brought her to tears. "Don't leave the exam, Tate. I'm fine." She wasn't, though. She felt like every car that passed by had someone inside who was about to jump out and grab her.

"Don't bother with the police . . ." He must have stepped into the classroom again because she heard loud voices in the background. "Call the FBI. There's a guy there. Mea—" A car blared its horn, making Veri jump. "Mr. Winthrop's met with him before. He's in the Art Crime Division. And then leave me a message so I can get it right after this session's over. I have an hour in between the review and the final."

"Okay. Thanks, Tate. I just . . . I can't believe he did this to me."

"It's going to be all right, Veri."

"Maybe." She didn't tell him the part about Charles pretending he'd never seen the sketch before. The psychotic part.

As soon as they hung up, Veri googled the FBI Art Crime Division. She was surprised when an actual number came up. She waited until a few people had walked by, then called the number. After a menu of mundane options, a male voice finally answered: "FBI."

"Yes, hello, hi." Veri covered the phone with her hand and turned her body toward the building. "I'm calling to report a crime, I mean kind of a crime, an art crime."

"So you want the Art Crime Division, ma'am?"

"Yes, thank you."

She was put on hold.

"Art Crime," a woman answered.

"*Yes*, hi, I'd like to report one—an art crime."

"Okay. Let's see here. Sorry, just a moment while I find my book . . . Is this an active crime?"

"It happened maybe fifteen minutes ago. I'm not like in danger or anything."

Another pause. "You'll have to come in and fill out some forms, then. Oops, just a sec." It sounded like she'd put the phone down. "So yes, you'll need to come into the office and make a report in person. Anything else I can help you with?"

"Your address?"

After she'd given Veri the address, the woman said "Have a good day" and clicked off.

~

The FBI Art Crime Division was in a nondescript building around the corner from Museum Mile. Millions of people every day, sometimes including Veri, passed by it without realizing it. There was no sign out front, only the address. No doorman either. Veri pushed the heavy door open and stepped into a dingy foyer with a small directory on the wall. Art Crime was on the third floor. There was an elevator, but it looked sketchy enough that Veri chose the stairs instead.

There was no reception, but the woman at the desk on the third floor was probably the person to speak to.

"Help you?" The woman didn't really want to ask; she could tell.

"Yes, I called earlier about an art crime?"

"A lot of people call about art crime, ma'am. Do you want to fill out a report?"

"I guess, but it was just like an hour ago, so it's kind of still active?" Now that she knew "active" was code for *I need help now*, she would use it.

The woman looked Veri up and down. "How active exactly?"

Before Veri could answer, the woman's landline rang. "Yes, Mr. Meaker."

Meaker! "I'm here to see Mr. Meaker," Veri whispered while the woman glared at her. *Mr. Meaker.* That was who Tate had told her to see.

The woman nodded to whatever Mr. Meaker was saying while she jotted something down and ignored Veri's wave. "Also, sir, there's a woman out here who would like to see you." She paused, nodded once, and hung up. She looked at Veri. "Sorry, he's busy. You'll have to make an appointment."

"No, but you don't understand—this is an *active* situation."

"I'm sorry." She went back to her paperwork.

"Please. Can you tell him it's about an art dealer named Charles Winthrop . . . he just committed an *active* crime."

The woman looked up at her. "Charles Winthrop?"

"Yes!"

"Hold on." She picked up the phone again. "It's regarding Charles Winthrop. Yes, sir. Okay." She hung up and pointed her pen at the door. "Go back out that door, around the corner to 303."

Veri said a quick thank-you and followed the woman's direction down a dark hallway until she'd found the door with the number on it.

Mr. Meaker, or whoever it was, was short and round, with definitely dyed black hair. He was sitting behind a cluttered desk. "Mr. Meaker?" Veri asked when she stepped in.

He looked up at her and chuckled. "'So good it's a crime,' huh?" He pointed his pencil at her T-shirt. "That's a good one."

Veri nodded. "Thanks."

"Have a seat. What you got for me? I heard something about Charles Winthrop."

Veri slid off her backpack and sat. "Do you know him?"

"He's got a prior." Mr. Meaker swiveled in his chair and pressed his fingertips together. "Which is the only reason you're sitting there. So go on."

Veri was still stuck on "prior." Her eyes bugged when he said it. "I sketched something. I'm an artist, and he sold it at an auction for four million dollars . . . just now . . . at Sotheby's."

Mr. Meaker raised his eyebrows. "So congratulations, then."

"No." Veri shifted forward in her seat. "I didn't know he was going to sell it. I . . . he said he wouldn't . . . but then he just *did*."

Mr. Meaker started taking notes. "So he owes you the money, you're saying. Has he paid you anything?"

"Only in my crypto wallet."

Mr. Meaker looked up. "Crypto wallet?"

"I haven't touched it yet, but it's there, in my wallet. I can show you . . ." She started to pull out her phone, but Mr. Meaker held up his palm.

"So he paid you four million in a crypto wallet."

"*No.* Just like a hundred and forty-one thousand. But I haven't accepted all of it. And most of it was for the NFT I made." He frowned, and she slowed her words down before he could ask. "The NFT is just *about* it, the sketch—who owned it before and stuff."

"You sold him a provenance? That's illegal." He put down his pencil and sat back.

Veri felt the room close in. "I know that. But it's still sitting in my wallet. So no crime was committed, right?" Her voice got thin. Mr. Meaker sat forward again.

"What crime are you alleging Mr. Winthrop did, young lady?"

"*He knowingly sold a fake van Gogh.*" That made sense. Mr. Meaker raised his eyebrows and grabbed his pencil again.

"That you painted?"

"Sketched."

"Okay." Mr. Meaker picked up the phone on his desk. "Mike, get in here." He hung up. The door opened, and another man, younger, same heavy build, brown hair, stepped inside. "This young lady's here about Winthrop. Apparently he sold a van Gogh fake."

The younger man scanned Veri. "When?"

"Like an hour ago. At Sotheby's. Can you arrest him?" She looked back and forth between the two.

Mr. Meaker said, "Dunno yet. We'll need to go talk to him."

"Now?" Veri asked.

The two men looked at each other and must have passed on silent information because Mr. Meaker stood. "All right, young lady. We'll take it from here. You leave your number with Patti out there. You said Sotheby's?"

"Yes, sir." Veri stood. "He already left, though—I'm pretty sure. I don't know where his office is, but he goes to the New York Men's Club a lot."

The two exchanged another knowing look, and Mr. Meaker nodded. "Sounds good. We'll go have a chat with him and let you know if we find anything."

The younger man opened the door for her.

Veri hesitated. "Wait . . . that's all? Don't you need me to identify him?"

"We know who he is, miss," the younger man said. "We'll take it from here."

After giving Patti her cell phone number, Veri went back outside and texted Tate. Sorry to bother u I just wanted to tell u Mr. Meaker is going to talk to him.

Standing on the sidewalk, Veri didn't know what to do now. She didn't need to go in to the gallery. She hadn't heard anything from Myra yet today, and anyway, she guessed she wouldn't. Facelift drugs were probably strong enough to keep her down for a while. The only thing she really wanted to do was make sure that Charles Winthrop was going to get arrested. And the only way she could think to do that was to go to the Men's Club and see for herself.

So she hailed a cab.

～

Veri waited across the street and around the corner from the Men's Club for twenty minutes, and still, there was no sign of Charles or the detectives. It was almost four o'clock, and she was dying of thirst. Her stomach felt like it was clawing to get out. According to her app, there was a Chipotle two blocks away. She peeked around the corner again. Nothing. No one was coming or going through the front door of the NYMC. She tucked back around the corner and ordered a burrito with chicken and extra guacamole. She'd run to Chipotle, pick up her order, and bring it back to the same corner to stay on watch. She felt like every private investigator she'd ever seen on TV but without a car. Or a gun. Or a trench coat.

She gave the Men's Club a final glance before starting for Chipotle— and saw them. Charles, flanked by Mr. Meaker and Mike, was stepping out of the front door and into a black Ford Explorer.

Veri watched them drive away. That was it! Charles was toast. Locked up. Arrested.

"Oh my God." She stood on the corner, not knowing what else to do except go and get her burrito.

THIRTY TWO

Her adrenaline rush was still going strong when Veri got back to the brownstone. She paused before opening the front door to make sure no one had followed her. No one had, of course. She was only being paranoid.

In the kitchen, she guzzled down a few chugs of her mother's white wine and sat down at the table. Tate still hadn't returned her text, which she'd sent in all caps. HAVE NEWS! CALL ME WHEN YOU CAN! HOPE FINALS OK!!!

The white wine hit her immediately, and harder than she wanted it to, but she needed to calm her nerves. She needed to do something. Anything. She couldn't just sit and stare at her phone for the rest of the night. She'd just gotten a man arrested. She should pack. Her studio and her bedroom. She was going to Chicago, she'd decided on the PATH back to Hoboken. That was it. She needed to get the hell out of New York City. Charles was going to jail, and she would never set foot inside the Hattfield Gallery again. Not even having her own gallery show was worth staying in New York. Not even Tate—although they could try long distance, maybe, whatever. She was out of here.

After a few more chugs of wine, her head felt like it was getting heavy with expired adrenaline, and suddenly she was exhausted. She grabbed the wine bottle and a bag of chips and headed upstairs.

After ripping off her velvet jacket, she fell into bed and texted Allison. Totally in for Chicago girl. Call me.

The thought of living with Allison made her smile, and she imagined the two of them setting up their art studio together. They'd need a town house, for sure. She picked up her phone and started scrolling through Pinterest for decor ideas.

~

A doorbell woke her up. It was dark in her room, but there was the doorbell again. Her phone was lying on top of her chest, where it must have landed when she fell asleep. Her clock read seven o'clock. "What the hell?" She pulled herself up to sitting and checked for a text from Tate. For a moment, she wondered if she'd had the most visceral dream of her life. In it, she'd gotten Charles Winthrop arrested. But then she read through the texts that she'd sent to Tate earlier. Her wine buzz was long gone now, and everything that had happened today was real.

The doorbell buzzed again.

Veri pulled herself together and made it down the stairs. Out the window, a black town car was double-parked in front of their brownstone. Terror ran through her veins. What if it was Charles coming for her? The doorbell buzzed again. "Who is it?" she asked in the deepest voice she could muster.

"It's Charles."

Veri's skin prickled. She knew she should call 911, but her phone was upstairs, where she'd left it.

"Veri?" Charles knocked this time.

"What, um, do you want?" Her voice was shaking.

"I need to talk to you."

"No thank you." He was going to strangle her. There was no doubt about it. This was a death visit.

"Veri, please. I'll have my driver wait outside the car so you know I don't have any ulterior motives. I'm sorry for our last interaction, and I'd like to explain."

Veri's mouth went dry. "My mom's here," she lied. If her mom *were* home, her purse would be on the table where it always was.

"That's fine. We can talk inside your house, if it makes you feel better."

Veri pulled the door open an inch. Charles smiled his same stupid smile at her. "Shall I come in?"

"No. I'll talk to you outside."

She opened the door. She was still wearing the *So Good It's a Crime* T-shirt and black pants. She must have taken the platform booties off at some point because she was currently wearing only socks. Charles seemed to notice this too. "Would you like to get some shoes? It's cold outside."

Veri gave him the stink eye, opened the coat closet, and grabbed her mother's puffer coat and rain boots.

The same blonde female driver opened the back door of the town car for her. Veri hesitated but slid in, and Charles slid in after her. The driver stayed outside on the sidewalk after she'd closed the door. The engine was running, and the atmosphere between Charles and Veri was heavy. She expected Charles to start talking, but he only stared at her for a few beats, making Veri even more nervous. Finally, he said, "Everything you did today was good. Perfect even." Veri felt her forehead fold together.

"You're unhinged."

He grinned. "I want you to work for me."

She narrowed her eyes at him. He *was* unhinged. "Ah-yuh. *That's* not going to happen. I'm going to Chicago, for one thing. And also, *oh yeah*, I'm not a criminal."

"You'd be a good one, though."

Veri threw her arms up. "Well, this was fun. So like, are you going to jail?" She tried to sound flippant, but it came out as serious.

Instead of answering, he slipped his hand inside his camel coat. Veri's hand flew up to her mouth. It was a gun. Mace. Pepper spray, at least.

It was a wallet, though. Charles opened it and held it up to her.

"I'm not a criminal, Veri. I'm—"

"FBI?" She read the gold badge and pushed herself back against the car door. "Did you—is Mr. Meaker dead?"

"Yes. And no."

He flipped his badge closed and slipped it back inside his coat pocket while Veri experienced her mind blowing open. "Wait, you're serious? *You're* FBI? You did bad things . . . you sold a fake van Gogh . . . you're going to jail . . ."

"I am an undercover detective for the Art Crime Division of the FBI. I work with the gentlemen you saw today, Meaker and Cooper."

"Cooper?"

"Mike Cooper. You met him too."

Veri nodded. "Younger."

"Yes. He's younger."

Veri stared at nothing.

"Do you need some air?" Charles asked. "I realize this must be overwhelming."

"What about Myra? Is she FBI?"

"Ah. Good question. No. She is not. Look, Veri, I know this is a shock. I'll answer all the questions you have, but I want you to know one thing, and that is that I would never *ever* hurt you or put you in danger. I think you are amazing—one of the most gifted artists I have ever seen."

"Thank you?"

"And I want you to come work for me. For us."

Now Veri grinned. "Like *in* the FBI?"

"Yes."

She sat up. "In the actual mother-effing FBI?"

"Yes. The actual mother-effing FBI."

He was serious. She was dumbfounded. "I don't want to, and I'm moving to Chicago."

Someone knocked on Charles's window. Charles and Veri both looked to see who it was.

"Oh my God."

"Let's keep this to ourselves."

"But you were going to come inside when I told you—"

"No, I wasn't."

Veri held her breath, and Charles rolled down his window. "Belinda," he said cheerfully. "Is that you?"

Veri could already see how mad she was. "Charles," her mother said calmly, but Veri knew that tone, and it wouldn't stay calm for long.

"Mom—hey, we were just—"

"That's my daughter, Charles," her mother said.

Charles seemed smaller all of a sudden compared to her mother, and not just because she was towering over them both on the other side of the window. "Yes, I know. And I'm very fond of her. She's quite a young lady." Charles sounded genuine when he said, "It's so good to see you."

Her mother pinched her lips together. Watch out. That was her version of a glare.

"I better go," Veri said. She opened her door without waiting for the driver, who was suddenly back in the driver's seat.

Charles turned to her with a fake smile. "Okay, Veri. We'll go take a look at that piece I was mentioning tomorrow. But I'd appreciate you not telling anyone about it yet. I hope you understand. Pick you up at the gallery at what, ten o'clock?"

Veri was out of the car when he said this—and she'd already told him she'd been fired, so she simply nodded. Charles turned back to her mother. "I hope to get the chance to catch up soon."

Veri hurried around the back of the car and stood next to her mother. The anger emanating off her could have been bottled.

"Goodbye, Charles," her mother said. Her words froze in the air as she spoke them.

Charles waved. "Have a good evening." He added a tight smile before rolling up his window. Her mother's message was delivered loud and clear. That was a beatdown.

As soon as the car started moving, her mother turned to her with her lips still tight. "Inside. Now."

"Mom. What the hell?" Veri could tell she was about to blow her stack.

Inside the front door, her mother let loose. *"What the hell have I been telling you, Veri!"* she yelled louder than Veri had expected. "I told you not to get involved with that man. *I told you!"* Her anger was turning into a cry. "And now—"

Veri held up her hands. "Mom. Calm down, please. He's—"

"Your father."

"Mom, just *please—*"

He's . . .

"Mom—"

Your . . .

"What . . . ?" Veri cocked her head. *"What did you just say?"*

Her mother dropped her head into her hands. "Tell me you didn't sleep with him . . . please tell me that did not happen." She was crying now.

"Holy . . . whatever *this* is." Veri backed away. "Jesus God, *what?*"

Her mother looked up at her with the most desperate eyes she had ever seen on a human face. "Tell me, Veri."

"Mom." Veri stepped forward and grabbed her wrists. "Mom. Nothing happened. Not even like a kiss. Like probably maybe the most is even a handshake."

Her mother threw her arms around her. Veri could feel her shaking as she wept. "Thank God," she repeated.

With her mother still squeezing the life out of her, Veri said, "Also, PS: *What the hell?* That guy is *The Sperm?* That guy is *not* The Sperm."

Her mom finally released her. She inhaled deeply and nodded. "Yup. He's The Sperm."

~

Veri and her mother talked for another hour. More like, her mother talked, and Veri listened. By the end of it, Veri was in no less shock.

Everything her mother had always told her about her father was a lie. Her mom had been pregnant with her *before* leaving on the winter trip to Florence, but she didn't know it until she got there. She and Charles had had their one-night stand a few days before she left, and he'd cheated on Myra when they did. "Makes sense why she and I aren't exactly besties now, right?" Her mother rubbed her eyes. She looked as drained as Veri.

"Does Myra know about him being, uh, the dad thing now?"

"No, oh God no." She grabbed Veri's hand. "Veri, I *promise* you, Charles doesn't know either." This was the first thing she'd told her after they'd sat down at the kitchen table. *Charles did not know.*

"But why didn't you tell him you got pregnant, Mom?"

"I did, honey." She looked sad again. "He refused to believe it and wouldn't take the DNA test. He was in London. The part I told you about not being able to make someone take a DNA test if they are out of the country is true. He wouldn't do it."

"He still had to kind of guess about who got you pregnant." *Ew.* "The dates matched up."

Her mother shook her head. "I was so furious at him. I was just so scared. Obviously I know now that I shouldn't have, but I wrote him a letter—we didn't have email back then—and I lied. I told him that he was right. He wasn't the father. I told him someone from Italy was. Roberto Rossi." She paused. "I never slept with Roberto, to answer your next question. But I knew it would at least give me the story I needed. And then a few years later, way before you would have started asking about your father, Roberto conveniently died."

"Conveniently died?"

"Sorry, that sounds terrible." Her mother reached out to hold her hand, but Veri pulled it back.

"Mom, can I just, like, take a moment here. Jesus, there's a lot that just happened." Her mother had lied about the student loans, and now she'd lied about her father too? She felt like she didn't even know her mother at all.

"Have some water, honey."

Veri sipped on the sparkling water in front of her, but her head was hurting from her wine hangover, and her mind was melting, and her mother was talking in words and phrases that Veri could only vaguely understand. There was literally nothing that could have topped finding out that Charles was an undercover FBI agent, except finding out that he was her father. This day wasn't real. "This day isn't real," she repeated out loud.

Her mother nodded. "I'm just so sorry, Veri. I thought I was doing the right thing, but it turns out I did everything wrong."

"Yeah," Veri agreed. She could feel anger building in the back of her throat. "How could you lie to me for so long, about everything?"

Her mother looked devastated. "I kept telling myself that it wasn't the right time to tell you. But the truth is that once I started lying to you, it was easier to just *keep* lying."

Veri looked away, feigning disgust, but hadn't she done the same thing? Once Veri had started lying about stealing the ArtsData information, and the NFT, and the money she'd stolen from her mother, wasn't it just easier to keep lying?

Her mother wiped her tired-looking eyes. Even as furious with her mom as she was, Veri felt a pang of hurt for her.

"But, honey, now you know everything."

"Did you know Charles Winthrop was back in New York? Is that why you didn't want me to work for Myra?"

"I had no idea he was back until you told me he was. I called Myra to confirm it, and that's when I told her about selling our house and the move to Cape May. She's always been in love with Charles, and she's always suspected that the two of us had, you know."

"Ew, yeah, okay, I get it." Veri wanted to tell her mother the other mind-altering news about Charles, but she had the sense that her mother truly did not know he was anything other than an art dealer and . . . her father. "Wait," she said, suddenly legitimately wondering. "How did *I* get so unattractive? Two hot parents and I look like this?"

"Really, Veri. Don't be ridiculous." Her mother paused. "Listen, honey. Do you need to go to a therapist? I will find one for you. Money doesn't matter."

"Mom. Stop. Okay?" Veri tried not to get frustrated, but her mother was starting to really annoy her.

"Okay. Whatever you need."

"Actually, I need to keep packing," Veri said, back to being angry and overwhelmed again. "I'm moving to Chicago with Allison."

"Oh?"

"We got jobs. Assistant art teachers." Her mother looked sad about it, which made Veri angrier. "What, Mom? You're not even going to be in Hoboken anymore. It's a two-and-a-half-hour plane ride instead of a two-and-a-half-hour car ride to come see me."

Her mother looked like she was struggling not to cry. "You're right, Veri. It's a good decision, considering all of this . . . So, you'll get an apartment together?"

Veri nodded. Her head was flickering, like her brain was about to run out of battery. Charles Winthrop was her father. The guy who had tricked her into sketching a fake van Gogh. The guy who had been lying to her the whole time about who he really was. The guy who had randomly walked into her life one day at the Hattfield Gallery. *That* guy was the father she'd always secretly wanted. Charles Winthrop.

"Why don't you go take a hot bath? I'll order Thai. You must be exhausted."

You have no idea, Veri wanted to say. Instead, she simply stood and walked out the door.

Right before she got into the hot bath, Tate finally texted her back. Just out of the final what is going on?

Veri texted: All good now. Giant mistake by me. Talk tomorrow. She had to find out if Tate had known about Charles being in the FBI before she could say more. And in order to do that, she decided she would meet Charles at the gallery tomorrow morning at ten, like he had asked her to.

THIRTY THREE

In the morning, Veri waited for her mother to leave before getting out of bed. She'd told her she could be at work a little later this morning because Myra wasn't coming in—but nothing about how she didn't actually work at the gallery anymore. After Veri's bath last night, her mother ordered dinner and insisted she come down to eat. She then answered every one of Veri's questions: the ones she'd thought of when she was in the bath. Yes, Charles was an only child. No, her mother had never met his parents. And the big one: "Do you still love him?" It was a doozy of a question, but she had to know.

Her mother shook her head. "I could have still loved him. But when he refused the paternity test, it made me sick. I hated him, to tell you the truth. I'm sorry to admit that to you. But he's got a dark side, honey, that most people don't see." She threw her hands up and sat back on the couch. "Or maybe he's changed. I don't know. It's been twenty-five years."

"I'm pretty sure he's still got that dark side," Veri said.

"Obviously he's very fond of you, honey. It's probably time for him to know. We can tell him together, or I can tell him alone—whatever you want."

Veri was crushed for her mother. What kind of man would refuse a paternity test? It was one thing to think of an Italian man whom she knew nothing about, refusing to believe he'd gotten her mother pregnant. But it was a whole other thing to know that *Charles Winthrop* had refused to believe her. He was worse than what her mother remembered him being. He was blackmailing Veri into working for him. He was a con artist, or at the very least, a sketchy undercover FBI agent. And he was most certainly a liar. "Can I just think about it, Mom?"

"Of course. Take as long as you need. It's entirely up to you, honey."

Now, Veri expected Beck Becker to be sitting at her desk when she arrived at the gallery. Instead, it was closed. She used her key to get in, somewhat surprised Myra hadn't already switched the locks on her. Everything had changed in a single day. It was too ironic to be sad. She had finally gotten her own gallery show, and now she was going to move to Chicago and be an assistant art teacher instead. She'd already decided she was not going to tell Charles anything about the *father thing*. Not yet, anyway. Her mother had kept the secret from him for Veri's entire life; there wasn't exactly a rush to fill him in now.

The town car pulled up at exactly ten o'clock. After the blonde driver opened the door for her, Veri slid in next to Charles.

"Good morning," he said, as if the world were still rotating on the same axis.

"Hi." Suddenly she couldn't stop staring at every feature on Charles's face. She had the girl version of his large nose. And even though she thought she had a dimmer version of her mom's hazel eyes, she didn't. She had his blue eyes. Her dark hair could have come from either one of them. Her height too. She was tall for a girl, but so was her mother.

"Do I have egg on my face?" Charles asked.

Veri got back to the business of being furious with him. "Look, Mr. Winthrop, I'm only here because I need some answers."

"As promised, I will answer all of your questions in due time."

"Okay, but like when? I'm moving to Chicago, so I'm sorry, but I can't work for you, and I still don't know why you sold my"—she hesitated, unsure of what she could say in front of the driver—"artwork."

"In due time," he repeated.

"You know what, forget it." She started to open the door. If he wasn't going to tell her everything, she had nothing else to say.

"Veri, please. Indulge me. I have a piece I would like your advice on."

She chuckled. "Are you for real? You think I'm going to help you decide on a painting at this point?"

"It will only take a little of your time. It's not far. I insist."

The car started moving. She crossed her arms and legs and looked out her window without another word, until they stopped in front of the Guggenheim Museum.

"The piece is in here," Charles said. "I promise it won't take long."

After Charles had bought their tickets, they started walking up the spiral gallery a few feet apart from each other. She hadn't been to the Guggenheim in a long time, definitely not since the whole Sackler debacle and the "blizzard of prescriptions" protest had happened. Some of her professors had been at the protest, playing dead on the ground to represent all those who had died of OxyContin overdoses. She'd seen it on the news like everyone else.

"If the painting is already in here, why do you need my help?" Veri asked.

"Paintings in museums aren't always what we think they are." It was more or less what Major Cohen had said too.

On the fourth spiral, Charles finally stopped. To the right, off the main gallery, was a small hallway leading to a door that read *Employees Only*.

"The piece is in this alcove here," Charles said. Veri's danger antenna went up. She stayed where she was, refusing to follow him in.

"Veri, please," Charles said. "It's right here. This is the painting."

It was a sparse crowd at the Guggenheim today. Only a few solitary people and a handful of couples were walking around. There had to be cameras set up somewhere, though. If Charles tried to kidnap her or shove her over the railing, he'd at least be caught doing so. She stepped into the alcove and stopped at the painting Charles was looking at. It was of a single sailboat painted in an almost impressionist style. Veri looked closer at the signature. "It's a Dufy."

"Raoul Dufy," Charles said, nodding. He seemed mesmerized by the painting.

"One of your favorites or something?"

"Are you familiar with fauvism? The artists use pure, brilliant color aggressively applied straight from the paint tubes to create a sense of an explosion on the canvas. The colors exist as an individual element to the subject matter. It's a brave technique, don't you think?"

"Not a lot of room for error," Veri agreed. She was surprised by how touched he seemed to be over the painting. "It's pretty, but why do you need me to tell you that?"

He turned to face her. "You know I went to RISD to be a painter myself. At the time, I was trying to paint like Dufy. He was my favorite then. A friend of mine could paint just like him, but I was terrible. I'm a terrible artist." He chuckled to himself.

And person, she wanted to add. Instead she said, "So then you decided to sell fake art to unsuspecting people. I guess you found your true calling." It came out just as snarky as she wanted it to. She could tell it got to him because he turned away to sit on a small bench opposite it.

"Have a seat." He patted the space next to him. Veri sat as far away from him as possible without falling off the other side. "This painting"—he pointed to the Dufy—"is why I agreed to work for the FBI, Veri. Because it's a fake."

"It *is?*" She stood to get a closer look at it.

"Only a few people in the world know that."

"It's a Major Cohen, right?" She tried to remember if she'd seen a Dufy in his studio.

"That's clever of you to put together," Charles said. "He's one of the best forgers that I've ever known. As are you."

She turned around. "I told you already, Mr. Winthrop. I'm not going to do"—she lowered her voice and looked into the main gallery—"another painting for you."

He exhaled. "I hear you, but I'm an undercover agent for the Federal Bureau of Investigation, Veri." He meant it as a threat, and it worked. Veri felt her throat tighten.

"So what are you saying—you're going to arrest me or something if I don't?" She crossed her arms so he couldn't see her hands shaking. Maybe now *was* the time to tell him.

"I'm going to tell you a secret," he said, freaking Veri out even more.

"Fine. What?"

"This Dufy"—he lowered his voice—"wasn't done by Major Cohen." He paused. "Veri," he said, sounding suddenly sad about it. "It was done by your mother."

Veri dropped her arms. *"What?"*

Charles waited for a couple to pass by. "It got into the wrong hands and ended up at an auction."

"You're lying." But it hit her square in the head—the same smaller version of the Dufy was framed on her mother's wall.

He cocked his head. "Does that sound so impossible? It just happened to you."

Fear rippled through her. She started backing out of the alcove. "Why are you doing this to me—to us?" Her eyes were burning. "My mom is a good person." She spun around and slammed into a body. "Sorry—" Veri stepped back from the man. "Tate!" She felt a flood of relief. It was Tate. Except, he wasn't looking surprised to see her. Or happy either.

"Hey, Veri," he said without emotion.

She blinked at him and turned back to Charles. "What the actual hell is going on?"

"Agent Donovan is one of the only other people who know about this situation."

"What the *who*?" She turned back to Tate. "You're in business school."

"I'm sorry, Veri. I know this must be really confusing." He spoke with the same British accent but sounded like a completely different person. Veri felt like she was going to pass out. Tate must have known it, because he stepped closer and took her arm. Veri pulled it away.

"Tate works with me," Charles said.

She shook her head at both of them. Tate was fake. Charles was fake. Her mom was fake. Everyone in her life was turning out to be fake. "What do you want from me?" Her voice was small and shaky.

Charles cleared his throat. "When this painting went to auction, it was too late to stop it. I couldn't find a way to tell anyone the truth without starting a domino effect. If an authenticator tells the world a painting is real, and then it turns out not to be, everything he's ever authenticated before will come under question. Galleries, museums, collectors—they actively try *not* to know if a painting is a fake, to avoid having to prove that the rest of their artwork isn't fake either."

"Bob Cole," she mumbled. It was so obvious. He was turning out to be the only person who *wasn't* fake. He was just a straightforward criminal. A corrupt authenticator.

Charles nodded, clearly impressed. "Yes. Bob Cole did authenticate this painting. And—"

"My van Gogh sketch." She couldn't believe how everything was fitting together so easily. "Does"—she was afraid to ask—"does my mom know?"

"No," Charles said definitively. "Your mother *never* knew what happened to this Dufy after she painted it for me." He watched Veri's reaction carefully. "It was me, I'm afraid. I did something I should never have done, but I never meant to hurt her. I needed tuition money. I'd just been accepted to the London School of Economics, and I didn't have the money for it. I got caught, of course, and my choice was prison or helping the FBI with other art crimes. So I made a deal with them: Your mother's painting would never be questioned, and I wouldn't go to prison, as long as I agreed to work for them." He paused. "And now I'm offering you the same choice."

Veri looked over at Tate, who was staring at the ground. "Wait, so what you're saying is that I work for you, or I go *to prison?*"

"Well. The only crime you've committed is selling secret government information that you stole off the internet." Charles paused. "You
know, I never asked Myra what happened that day she got a call about
a fire in her building, but I can only imagine how stressful that must
have been for her. Myra has some expensive art. I know she dropped
everything she was doing, though, because she was talking to me on
the phone at the time, and as I recall, she was also logging in to her
ArtsData account. My guess"—he nodded to Tate—"or rather *the plan*
was that she would be too panicked to log *out* of her account before
running outside for a cab, thus leaving it open on her screen for anyone,
and by that I mean *you*, to see."

How did he *know* that? It was exactly what had happened. Myra
had left ArtsData open on her computer just before she ran out in a
panic about her apartment. The cameras. "Were you *spying* on me?"

Charles Winthrop tipped his head. "We're not spies, are we, Tate?"

"No," Tate said quietly.

"We're not spies. We *can*, however, add information *to* the ArtsData
site whenever we want. Not exactly kosher, but sometimes it's necessary.
We could even add, let's say, a fake provenance, a phony list of owners
for a made-up painting by a famous artist, for example. You'd have to
know the exact title of the painting to locate the information, though."

Charles paused, and Tate looked at his shoes. Veri thought out
loud. "The title of the painting. Myra didn't know what it was called."
The search line only read *van Gogh lost painting*. She didn't know it was
called *Girl in Yellow on Beach*. But Veri did. That entire page was put
there *for* her. And she'd fallen for it. She'd fallen for everything.

"And by the way . . . ," Charles said, brightening. "The whole NFT
addition—well, that was genius, something we were *not* planning for.
We just anticipated that you'd get the information authenticated by Bob
Cole, who you met at the Frick the day I brought you there. And, as
it turns out, you had met him earlier too." Bob Cole had told Charles
about her passport? "Instead, however, you had it put on the blockchain. You have quite the criminal mind, Veridian Sterling."

She shook her head. The NFT wasn't her idea. It was . . . she couldn't remember exactly. It was Bob Cole's . . . except no, he'd only told her they would eventually replace authenticators. It was Derek's . . . except no, that wasn't true either. *It was Veri's idea.* She looked at Charles. He was right. She felt a corner of her heart blink off. The NFT was her idea.

Charles sighed and uncrossed his legs. "So no, Veri, we can't put you in prison. But your mother, on the other hand . . ." He gestured at the Dufy. "I'd hate for it to happen, but anonymous tips can be called in to the FBI about potential fraud. And with forensics these days, there are ways to identify the forger."

"*Not* my mother," Veri said, feeling her adrenaline reignite. "You leave her alone." She looked at Tate. He made her stomach turn now. That ping in her belly that she used to feel for him was now a bullet. "And go to hell, Tate."

"Hold on, Veri. Tate was only doing his job. He wanted to tell you who we were right after the auction. But I needed you here, in front of the painting, to explain it all."

That might have been true—Tate *had* told her to go to the FBI right away—but Veri glared at him anyway. He looked miserable.

"Veri, we need you to do one painting for us," Tate said quietly. "That's all we're asking you to do, and then this can all be over."

"Obviously," Veri scoffed. "*Girl in Yellow on Beach.*" That's what this was all about. "You want me to paint it for you this time, so you can sell it at Sotheby's again."

She was surprised when they both shook their heads. Tate continued, "Your van Gogh sketch was just a setup. The sale wasn't real. From time to time, just to keep up his image as a heavy-hitting art dealer, we need the art world to witness Charles bidding for something large. And of course it's cheaper on us if what he bids on isn't real. But great reproductions are hard to come by. Which is why when we met you . . ."

"So you've been using me this whole time?" That wasn't the word, though. They weren't using her, they were . . . "*Grooming* me, actually?"

Charles looked offended at the word. He glazed over Veri's question without answering. "A Vigée Le Brun," Charles said. "We need you to re-create a portrait of Marie Antoinette."

"*Vigée Le Brun?*" Veri repeated. Élisabeth Vigée Le Brun was one of the only well-known female artists of the eighteenth century. Le Brun was Marie Antoinette's personal portrait painter. Veri had never even dared to *try* to re-create one of her masterpieces. They were magnificent. She wasn't going to do it. "Sorry. Ask Major Cohen."

"I would, but he doesn't do eighteenth-century art," Charles said. "You, however, do."

"You think I can re-create a Vigée Le Brun because you saw, what, *one* van Gogh sketch that I made up?"

"I saw more than that." Charles nodded to Tate, who pulled out his phone and held it up for Veri to see. It was a video of her garage studio and her old master copies she'd put on the walls. Tate must have taken it the night he picked her up at the house. "Gustave Courbet, Monet, Vermeer." Charles shook his head, looking genuinely impressed. "You're telling us you can't re-create a Le Brun?"

"Exactly." Except suddenly, in the smallest recess of her mind, she was wondering if maybe she could.

Charles grinned. "What if we told you that we're working with the Gardner Museum. We have an opportunity to get the stolen Rembrandt back."

"*The Storm on the Sea of Galilee?*" Veri was shocked.

Charles nodded. "We have intel that the thieves who took it will trade the Rembrandt for a Le Brun portrait of Marie Antoinette. If you do this for us, Veri, you'll be helping us recover a stolen piece of history."

Veri looked at Tate. "It's true," he said.

She looked back at Charles Winthrop. "So *that's* why you took me to Boston. To make sure I knew about the missing Rembrandt."

He didn't exactly nod. "We'll get you everything you need to re-create the portrait; then we'll make sure to 'smoke it' just enough for it to appear legitimate."

"Smoke it?"

"It took years for these artists to create some of their masterpieces, and tobacco smoke from them or their assistants would inevitably have made its way onto the canvas. Forensics would know to look for this."

"I never knew that," Veri said, quietly.

Charles shifted on the bench. "And we'll keep everything here just as it is. Nothing will change. No one else has to know about your mother's painting."

Veri's phone pinged. She pulled it out of her backpack, hoping it was her mother. She could blurt everything out before they could stop her—but it was a text from Allison. **Hey gurl. Saggy dick and me made up. Can't do Chicago. TTYL.**

Charles and Tate passed each other a look. Veri kept the phone in her hand. "So if I do this *one* painting, will you leave me alone? *My mom and me?* You'll never tell her about *any* of this?"

"That's our deal, Veri. Yes," Tate said.

"What about the hundred thousand dollars you sent me? And the cat-painting money. How do I send it back?"

"I'll tell you what," Charles said. "You paint the Le Brun for us, and we'll call the cat painting a fair payment. Henrietta loves the painting, as I already mentioned to you. That was a real sale. The hundred thousand dollars we'll take back, though."

Forty-one thousand dollars. He'd let her keep it? He had to be lying. But Charles looked pretty serious.

Charles stood. "Everything stays the same, Veri. You keep working at the gallery, and I keep coming in to take you to private viewings and such so we can check in, and Myra won't know any differently. And Tate"—he nodded over to him—"keeps driving."

"Myra fired me."

"We'll take care of it," Charles said without missing a beat.

"And there's another problem."

"What's that, Veri?"

"I'm going to need a place to live."

Charles hesitated. "We can manage that too."

"Actually, I already have a place in mind. It's for sale. You'll have to offer six hundred and fifty thousand dollars over the asking price, though. I can put you in touch with the Realtor."

Charles looked confused. He shifted his eyes to Tate for clarification.

"Is this place you're thinking of in Hoboken?" Tate asked.

Veri tipped her head slightly. "Very good, Tate. If that's even your real name."

Tate looked stricken, and Charles—if Veri could read it right—was looking impressed.

"Well, I think buying a place in Hoboken sounds like a good investment for us." He nodded to Tate. "And Tate's his real name."

Veri sneered.

"So we have a deal?"

"I'll think about it."

"Twenty-four hours," Charles said.

Tate stepped to the side, and Charles led Veri out of the small alcove. They started down the spiral gallery together, while Tate stayed a few paces behind them. To most people, Charles and Veri probably looked like father and daughter, enjoying a day at the Guggenheim together.

THIRTY FOUR

Harlem was cleaner than she remembered. She kicked a few drops off her boots from the puddle she'd just stepped in and buzzed apartment number four.

The door was open, though, and after she'd stepped inside, she clicked it shut behind her. The four flights of stairs in front of her were practically vertical, and by the time she'd reached the top, sweat had broken out on her forehead.

"It's me." Veri knocked, panting.

Allison opened the door, apparently with her elbows. Both her hands were covered in clay.

"Dude. Finally."

"You're right," Veri said. "It's pretty nice here."

Allison stepped back. "Lie much? Lock the door behind you. The lady at the corner market was robbed at gunpoint two nights ago."

The living room looked suspiciously like a pottery studio instead of an apartment. One large table took up the majority of the room, except for the tiny kitchenette to the right. Veri stepped up to the table and inspected a clay bust in midcreation.

"*Bust a Move*?" Allison started pounding on a pile of wet slimy clay. "Or, *I Bust U*?"

"*U*, like the letter?"

Allison used her wrist to wipe at her cheek. "Yeah. *U*. Is that tacky? Feels desperate."

"It's better than *Bust a Move*. That sounds like a boy band."

Allison motioned to the left with her elbow. "Under there."

Veri lifted a corner of the plastic tablecloth to find a book underneath it. *Antiquities through the Years*. "Thanks. I mean, I really didn't need this. Or, like, want it."

"'I am nothing if not a man who keeps his promise.' Benjamin Franklin said that. Probably." She shrugged. "And the museum insisted that I give it to you as part of the award you won at school."

There was a clay bust of the founding father at the end of the table. The face looked too young under the powdered wig on its head. "How's it going?"

During the two weeks since Charles Winthrop had destroyed her life, Allison had rekindled her affair with Saggy Dick, broken up with him again (for good this time!), and started her new business making personalized custom busts of famous figures. Together, they'd decided not to go to Chicago and instead move into this apartment. Maybe. That was what Veri was here to decide—and to get the book.

"It's going." Allison looked happier than Veri had seen her since RISD.

"How much are you charging per bust?"

Allison flicked her eyebrows. "Depends on the client. Like for Shrivel Dick's grandkids"—she nodded to the bust of Benjamin Franklin with a young boy's face instead of Ben's actual visage—"which, by the way, I *made* him order. For him, I'm charging two thousand. But like for the Italian guy down the street who wants me to make one with his kid as King George V, just free food forever, I guess." She tipped her head. "He's part of the Mafia, so it comes with perks like no one murdering me in my sleep."

"You should be charging more." Veri moved to the second bust drying on the table, this one with a bicorne and padded shoulders. "Wait, this face looks familiar." She'd seen this teenage boy somewhere.

"That's Jeremy, from the Pie Place. He let me practice my plaster technique on him."

"He's Napoleon?"

She nodded. "*Girl*, there's like *a lot* of crap that's happened over the years. I've had to brush up on my history."

Veri chuckled, but to be fair, RISD wasn't big on history classes, and who knew what Allison had learned in high school. She'd once admitted to skipping most of her senior year. "True. Okay, so, bedrooms?"

Allison blew a wisp of hair off her face. Her clay-caked apron read, *your anxiety causes me stress.* "Yeah, no. This is it. But I have a queen-size blow-up mattress under the table."

"Really?" Veri bent down to look. There was a deflated square of rubber with a brown blanket thrown on top of it. "Pretty . . . grim . . . Al—" She sneezed three times. There was clay dust everywhere.

"Bless you. Still sneezing in threes."

"Yeah, sorry," Veri said. "Anyway, it's a little small for two people, don't you think?"

"I know. But only until we find another place. Unless we can stay at yours?"

"There's just no way." Veri shook her head. "My mom's Realtor keeps showing up unannounced. She doesn't even want *me* there. She keeps complaining to my mom that she has to clean the kitchen before she lets her clients in. She's the worst." Veri was back to lying, and it was frightening how easy it was. The truth was, no one could come into the brownstone now because her studio was full of practice sketches for the Marie Antoinette portrait.

"Fine. Whatever. I'll just stay here with my weird friends. I swear, some of them are starting to talk to me." She nodded over to a draped bust on the floor. "I had to shut that guy up. Girl, actually."

Veri stepped over and peeked under the drape, then sucked back her breath.

"It's Marie Antoinette, if she were a girl from Connecticut named Chloe Farrington," Allison said.

Marie Antoinette. There was no way Allison could know about the portrait. Could she?

"Hey, by the way, thanks again for being Rachel Ritchie," Veri said nonchalantly.

"How *is* that DILF, anyway?" Allison smirked. "I'd deliver anything to him again, including my fine ass."

"I have no idea." *Phew.* It didn't seem like Allison had secretly met with him again, but calling Charles Winthrop a "DILF" was just creepy now. "What about Brooklyn? We could look there?"

Allison grimaced. "Do I look like I own a dog and a giant stroller?"

"Yeah. Hey, I gotta get going. Thanks for the heavy book I never wanted."

Allison dipped her hand in some clay soup and started brushing down Benjamin Franklin's shoulders. "If you know anyone with a podcast, I'm trying to get *I Bust U* on one. My TikTok's popping off right now. You should follow."

"I'm so proud of you."

"Thanks." Allison wrapped her elbows around Veri when they hugged goodbye. "Let me know the minute you get kicked out by the Realtor for good, okay? When it sells?"

Veri promised she would and hurried down the four flights of stairs, feeling slimy for pretending to be looking for apartments with her best friend.

As soon as she jumped off the PATH, she headed into Hoboken Art Supply. She wished she didn't, but she needed new supplies to start on the portrait. Her practice sketches were going okay, but actually *painting* it was going to be tricky. Vigée Le Brun worked with precise brushstrokes and used late-rococo tones and colors. Veri wasn't even sure she could replicate the same hues with modern oil paints. Drawing a presketch to a painting that no one had ever seen was one thing, but fooling people who knew what to look for was another.

The same creepy guy was at the register. It seemed like a lifetime ago that Veri had been eyeball assaulted by him. She shifted her backpack around, wishing she'd thrown the book Allison had given her into the trash already, then grabbed a cart that looked like it had been shrunk in the dryer by mistake. It only took her half an aisle to fill it completely, and she still needed to buy all the oil paints and turpentine and about a million brushes. She had no idea how Charles Winthrop planned to find a canvas that would trick anyone into thinking it was two hundred years old, or paints that could pass forensics. But that was his problem, she decided.

"Is that you, doll?"

In aisle three, Mildred was wearing more or less the same clothes as the last time Veri had seen her at the thrift store. "Oh hi, Mildred."

"I haven't spotted your mom around in a while. Nothing's wrong, is it?"

"She moved down to Cape May, actually. She's working at a new design store." Her mother seemed to have made peace with the fact that she was the manager at Divine Homes. She always sounded upbeat, although Veri was still upset about it.

"Cape May. The hubby and I honeymooned there, way before your time, but anyway, I'm glad I ran into you, doll. We have an opening on our back wall." She lowered her voice. "A very hard-to-find mirrored bookshelf—the kind you hang on the wall, not the floor kind—just sold, and I was thinking—well, it came to me just now—it would be a perfect spot for another cat painting. Easy money, am I right?"

"I'd love to, but I have my own show coming up soon, so I'm kind of focused on that."

"Very nice." She nodded. "The half-a-person painting?"

"Yes." Veri quickly convinced herself that wasn't an insult. "The *Walk Out* series."

"Think about it, doll. It sold in what, a week? Anytime you want to bring us another one, just stop on in." Mildred picked up a roll of painter's tape and turned for the register. "Hi to your mom. Don't forget."

"I won't." Except she probably would. There were so many things she wanted to tell her mother these days but couldn't. When they'd packed up her things for Cape May, her mother had asked at least five thousand times how she was feeling now that she knew about Charles.

Veri's answer had been the same every time—she needed some time to think about it. She didn't tell her that thinking about it made her feel first, angry, and second, sorry for herself. She could have been making macaroni necklaces on Father's Day like all the other kids in her school. She could have had *two* passports. She could have had a dad.

Sometimes she wondered if it wasn't even true. Maybe her mom had gotten it wrong. In the nicest way, maybe she'd hooked up with another guy around the same time, and *that* guy was her real father. She was literally nothing like Charles Winthrop.

After loading her cart to the tipping point, Veri headed to the register.

"Hey," the creeper said.

Veri avoided eye contact. "Hey."

"I know you," he said, after beeping through a few paint tubes. "Didn't you go to Hoboken Middle? We were in the same class."

She looked up at him. "Oh yeah. Hey, how's it going. Sorry, I didn't recognize you." She still didn't, though.

"You were like the cool, hot artist."

"Thanks." And then it hit her: he used to scooter home after school with a cigarette hanging out of his mouth. "I'm having a show at a gallery in the city. Maybe, if it's okay, I could drop a few flyers here."

Fred—it said so on the name tag she'd just noticed—brightened. "Sure, yeah, no problem."

Veri felt horrible for thinking he was a creeper, even though he still kind of was.

"And just so you know, all this stuff is final sale."

"Really?" She'd spent hundreds of dollars on supplies already, and even though Charles Winthrop kept promising he'd take care of everything she needed, he still hadn't.

"We're closing."

"Aw. Really?"

"Sucks, but yeah." He was back to staring at her boobs, and she wondered if maybe this was just where his eyes naturally rested, like his eyelids could only go so high. Or then again, maybe he was just high.

At least Veri could hand over her card with confidence. The money that Charles Winthrop had sent her for the cat painting was, in fact, a lifesaver. She'd paid her mother back the $5,000 too. It was a mistake, she'd explained. She'd meant to take the money out of her own account but got the bank cards mixed up.

"Okay, well, have a good one!" Veri waved halfway out the door.

The air smelled like the promise of rain when she walked toward the brownstone. Veri knew that her time living there was limited. Charles hadn't mentioned anything about buying it again, and she'd been telling the truth when she told Allison that Carol Pellowith had promised it would be off the market soon. Painting the Le Brun was going to take at least a few more weeks, though.

A lockbox was hanging off the front doorknob today. It was the kind Realtors used to hide the key for other Realtors to get inside for showings. *Great,* she groaned. This meant she'd have to worry about someone walking into her studio now.

In the kitchen, a bag was on the table that definitely hadn't been there this morning. It was from the Artist's Hive, an overpriced art supply store in the city, and filled with oil paints, turpentine, brushes— pretty much the same final sale items that she couldn't return.

Her studio was stuffed with more art supplies. Dozens of oversize canvases were piled up next to three new easels with stools. Plus there were sketchbooks, erasers, chalk pencils, and rulers. It had to be thousands of dollars' worth of supplies.

Her phone pinged.

Hello Veri. Some new supplies for you. Major Cohen is expecting you at his Park Avenue address tomorrow at 10am. I'll have Tate pick you up. Fondly, Charles

Her stomach flipped. Tate. The Liar. The Faker. Walking around out there in the world like he hadn't made her believe he actually liked her. Kissing her like that. Every time she saw a black town car in the city, which was pretty much always, she felt sick. And sad.

Veri: Sorry can't make it. Have things to do.

CW: I'm afraid I insist.

Veri: I said No!

She deleted the last text before sending it and stepped back into the kitchen. Fine. She'd go. Because actually, Tate had a few things he needed to explain.

THIRTY FIVE

At nine thirty the next morning, Veri sat at the bottom of the stairs and stared at the front door. Any minute, Tate would knock on it. Her stomach felt like she'd eaten spicy mustard for breakfast. The most she'd managed to consume was coffee. All night she'd kept imagining what he was going to say. *She* planned on saying nothing. *She* wasn't the one who had lied.

The doorbell startled her. She stood and threw back the lock.

"Hey, Veri."

"Hi." Damn, he looked good. Of course he did. His perfect face. His perfect broad shoulders. His perfect cute accent. She rushed past him. "Let's go."

He beat her to the car and opened the passenger door for her.

"I think I'll sit in the back, if that's okay," she said.

"Not at all." *Not at all.* She slid into the back seat, trying not to remember in detail the two times he'd kissed her.

"All set, then?" he asked after he'd started the car.

"Yup," she answered, very aware of the American trash she'd just spoken.

"Shall I turn on some music?"

"Whatever." She scrolled through her phone.

After a pause, he said, "Look, Veri, I know there's nothing I can say except that I apologize for misleading you. I don't expect you to believe me."

"Are you even in business school?"

"Yes. It's a requirement for special agents in the intelligence field." He caught her eye in the rearview mirror. "And I am very sorry, Veri." He smiled at the double *very*, which only made her burn hotter. Did he really think he was the first to say this?

"Why would I take your apology seriously when you only pretended to like me so you could frame me? No pun intended." That *was* kind of funny, but she crossed her arms and legs and stared straight ahead.

"I get it. I shouldn't have spent so much time with you. I shouldn't have—"

Kissed her. Yeah, *you got that right*, she said with her eyes when he caught them again in the mirror. "But you did, Tate."

"I know. But I couldn't help it. I've never met a girl like you, Veri. I kept wishing it was under different circumstances the whole time."

"Yeah, well, I thought it was *real*, the whole time."

She watched the back of his head nod. His gorgeous stupid head. "Would you ever consider letting me take you to dinner sometime? Even if it's just so you can tell me how horrible I am?"

"Were you in the brownstone?" She couldn't answer his question. She couldn't even think about accepting his offer. Yet. Maybe never.

He nodded again. "Your sketches are incredible. Your painting is going to be brilliant."

She hid her grin by looking out her window. "I mean, thanks, I guess." She paused. "So, how's um, school?"

"Top notch." His kid-like grin was at odds with everything else about him—a sexiness that made people walk into walls. "I love it, actually. Maybe I won't even stay an agent. There's a lot more money in finance."

She nodded absently, but there went that ping in her belly button again—the thought of him being in a normal career like finance. Would it make her trust him again?

"Why am I going to see Major Cohen, anyway? I assume you know."

"I think he has something to give you. But that's all I was told." He maintained eye contact with her in the mirror. "Honestly, that's all I was told."

They drove on in silence until Tate seemed to understand there was nothing left for them to talk about and turned on some music: Drake.

"It's really nice to see you, Veri," he said as they pulled up to Major Cohen's address.

"Yeah, you too. Kind of," she said, opening her door before he could get out of the car.

He shifted his body around to face her. "Would it be okay if I texted you about that dinner?"

"Probably not."

She didn't dare look back to see his expression when she stepped out.

Veri knocked on Major Cohen's front door for two minutes. Why would Charles Winthrop insist she go see him if he wouldn't even answer? Just when she was turning to leave, the door cracked open.

"Major Cohen. It's Veri Sterling?"

"Christ. Just a minute." Major Cohen shut the door on her.

Veri looked up at the blue sky framed by the perfectly aligned Upper East Side apartment buildings, once again amazed that an art forger could make enough money to live here.

The door opened a second time, revealing Major Cohen in a gray terry cloth bathrobe and worn-out slippers. His drooping eyes considered her for a moment before he grunted, "Come in."

"Thank you."

The studio looked to be in the same chaotic state. Canvases and paint cans were strewn across the floor. He shut the door and went back to doing what he most likely had been doing before: sipping from a homemade-looking ceramic mug with *Grandpa* on it and staring at an empty canvas on an easel. "You here for some tips, art grad?"

"No?"

"Code for yes. Listen, art grad, I only do twentieth century, and Le Brun is a giant. A master of masters. You probably can't get her right. That's my tip."

Veri's heart sank. Major Cohen was gruff and rude, but he was also potentially correct.

He turned his canvas sideways on the easel and continued staring at it. "I assume Winthrop's got you the right supplies. The frames were all screwy in 1783."

The canvases. That was why they didn't look right in her studio. They were authentic European canvases. American canvases were 24 by 30, or any even-numbered sizes. European canvases from the last two centuries were uneven numbers: 17 by 32 and so on. "How did he find authentic ones?"

Major Cohen slurped his coffee. "Simple. Buy any old painting from the eighteenth century done by some poor sucker that never made it, strip the paint, cover the canvas with gesso made from boiled rabbit skin, then sand it down, apply white paint, leaded but still available in Europe, and you got yourself an authentic canvas."

"Oh."

"Ah, I remember why he sent you." He shuffled over to the other side of his studio and sifted through some boxes, while Veri walked closer to a new David Hockney he was working on. *Portrait of an Artist.* "Masking tape. He used tape to make those perfect pool lines."

"Isn't that kind of cheating?"

"Why?"

"I guess it's kind of *aided*?"

"Show me an artist who cheats in the interest of beauty, and I'll show you a great artist. Here." He shuffled back over and handed her a tightly sealed plastic bag. "There's a shirt in there, more like a tunic. Put it on when you're painting the portrait."

"Why?"

"So microscopic pieces of fiber will get onto the canvas as you work."

"Jeez." She frowned. "It's all so scientific and forensic-y."

He glared at her, and it felt like someone had poured ice water down her back. "Do you think this is a game?" He didn't wait for an answer. He turned away instead. "They'll be looking to see that everything's authentic, and that tunic's from the eighteen hundreds, so be careful with it."

"Do . . . do you know who 'they' are?" she asked carefully. Did *he* know who Charles was trying to trick into getting the Rembrandt back?

Major Cohen sat on his stool and coughed. "Hell do I know, art grad. I would have told you to part ways with Winthrop by now, because if you keep working for him . . . well." He motioned around his studio and then studied her for an uncomfortable moment. "It's too late, though, isn't it?"

Veri looked down. She wasn't exactly sure of what he was implying, but she also didn't want to know. She just needed to get the portrait done, and then she could put this all behind her, forever. "Thanks, Mr. Major Cohen."

He groaned something, and Veri let herself out.

THIRTY SIX

The Blue Unicorn was livelier than usual today. Even the people standing in line in front of Veri seemed more upbeat than normal. It must have been the weather, Veri guessed. It was still February, but the snow was melting outside, and the sun was blaring. It wouldn't last long—all New Yorkers knew it—but they would definitely appreciate it today. On the way to the PATH this morning, Veri had even passed a few runners wearing shorts.

"Hey, love," the barista said. "Myra's order's all ready. I saw you when you walked in."

"Thanks, Connor. Have a good day." She scanned her phone and moved down to the other end of the counter to wait for the order.

There was a TV screen in the corner of the coffee shop, usually showing TikToks, but today it was on *Good Morning New York*. The sound was off, but something on the screen caught her eye. A close-up of a Marie Antoinette portrait filled the screen.

She walked across the room to get a closer look. Closed-captioning ran along the bottom of the frame: . . . *stolen last night while on loan to the National Gallery. The portrait was painted by Élisabeth Vigée Le Brun, also known as Madame Le Brun, Marie Antoinette's portrait artist. Marie Antoinette in a Chemise Dress was painted in 1783. Authorities suspect an inside job but as of yet have no leads.*

Veri grabbed Myra's coffee, walked outside, and clicked on her phone. "So that's it, then. It's over."

"Hello, Veri," Charles said. "I'm around the corner. We'll drive you back to the gallery."

Veri transferred Myra's searing-hot coffee into her other hand—she'd forgotten to bring gloves to work today—and the town car pulled up. Tate jumped out in his usual driving clothes and opened the door for her. "Hello."

"Hey," she greeted him. After driving her to Major Cohen's apartment all those weeks ago, he'd texted her a few times asking about dinner. She didn't respond for days, but every time, when she finally did, she told him she wasn't ready. He might have only been doing his job, but leading her on like that was cruel. So now they weren't friends, and they weren't going to be friends, and he should stop contacting her. She'd seen him a few more times since then as well, but always with Charles, and always in the town car, where she forced herself to remember that behind all that hotness was a liar.

"You can put the coffee there." Charles pointed to a cupholder.

"I can't let it get too cold."

He nodded. Tate started driving.

"So everything went as planned?" Veri asked.

Charles looked relieved. "It did. The painting, *your* painting, was stolen last night, just as we expected it would be. The real one is in a safe location offshore."

Veri nodded. She was relieved too. "Do you know when they'll make the trade for the Rembrandt?"

"I'm afraid I can't say anything about that, Veri. You understand." She hadn't been told the specifics of the setup for her own sake. In fact, Charles and Tate were the only two people who knew that Veri was the artist behind the copy. If anyone else, even anyone in the FBI, found out about Veri, she would need a security detail. "But trust me: the whole world will know if the Rembrandt gets returned to the Gardner Museum." That was all she was going to get. Painting a fake Marie Antoinette by Vigée Le Brun only got you so much undercover information.

Veri cleared her throat. "Cool. So now you'll let me get on with my life." She said it loud enough for Tate to hear.

"Yes," Charles said. "You've kept your side of the bargain. Your obligation to me, and to us"—he nodded up to Tate—"is complete." These were the words Veri had been waiting to hear for so many nights while she painted the portrait, and so many days while she worked for Myra and lied to her mother about all of it.

Tate slammed the brakes at a red light. "Sorry," he apologized.

Charles seemed a little annoyed but brushed it off when he looked back at Veri. "I'm looking forward to your show," he said in a bright new tone.

Her *Walk Out* series was opening tomorrow night at the Hattfield Gallery. Her mother was coming up from Cape May and spending the weekend with her. Every time Veri saw her now, she was more surprised. Belinda Sterling looked like a brand-new woman. The dim haze of sadness that had surrounded her since forever was gone. Owning Divine Homes with her partners had changed her life completely.

Just after Christmas, Charles had bought the brownstone under an LLC, which meant that no one, not even Carol Pellowith, knew who the actual buyer was. Veri could only imagine Carol peeing in her pantsuit the day the buyer offered $650,000 over the asking price. Carol told them it was because of their ceiling; the buyer absolutely had to have it. At first, her mother refused to consider using the extra money to buy into the store. That money could be saved for emergencies, for both of them. But Veri FaceTimed her that night, and after three failed attempts on her mother's end to answer it, Veri made her sit down and listen. "Here's the deal, Mom," Veri said to her mother's ear. When she'd finally framed her face in the camera, Veri continued: "Everything that you've done for me—working all those jobs for the mean Janets, being a single mom, taking out the school loans for me, all those things that you did—I never believed it when you told me that you were happy to do them. It was all worth it. I couldn't understand how you didn't secretly resent me for killing your dreams. You're an amazing artist, Mom—"

"Oh, I don't know about that, honey—"

"But now I do. Now I totally believe you. Because you taking the money to buy into Divine Homes makes me happier than I've ever been in my whole life. And if you've felt even a speck of that for me—"

"Of course I have."

"Then please, I'm begging you, let me keep this happiness like you kept yours. Use the money to buy into the store. Otherwise, I'll live my whole life knowing that I missed out on what true happiness really feels like."

Her mother's face fizzled into tears. "Really, honey? Are you sure?"

"I've literally never been more sure of anything in my life," Veri answered through a few tears of her own.

The LLC behind the buyer would be happy to rent the brownstone out for a while, too, Carol Pellowith had told them. Her mother didn't like the idea of letting Veri rent it back from the mysterious new owner, but she'd been warming to the idea of late. Veri made it mission number one to sound happy every time she talked to her mother, and so far, it was working. Divine Homes was doing better than she, or her partners, could have expected. They'd hired a manager named Jane. Her mother still did the window designs for the store, and her beach-themed Christmas scene had been written up in the *Cape May News*. She'd returned to the brownstone only twice since November: a weekend visit, plus Christmas. Veri had had to stop working on the Marie Antoinette portrait in the garage, but they'd had a great time. Allison stayed at the brownstone whenever she and Saggy Dick were fighting, which was often, so Veri had yet to feel lonely. They'd even started going to trivia nights together at the Hoboken Sip. Allison was terrible at it, with the exception of one topic: history. She'd meant it when she said she needed to brush up on it. Veri would usually go all in on the art history questions, until one of the questions was about Marie Antoinette and who painted her famous portraits. After that, she kept quiet and watched Allison have the time of her life.

"I'm excited," she told Charles now. "We're hanging the series up this afternoon." She caught eyes with Tate when he looked back for a lane change. The truth was that lately, whenever Charles took her to another "private auction" or to see an "up-and-coming artist," she'd started softening toward Tate. She was still furious at him for all his lying, but she was no longer feeling as humiliated. Charles had not-so-subtly mentioned all these things to her whenever Tate was not with them. "He's a genuinely great guy," Charles had told her more than once over the last few months. "And he's wrecked that he had to lie to you for so long." Veri responded that she couldn't even begin to forgive him. Or either of them, for that matter.

"Veri," Charles said now. "There's another situation we're watching."

It took her a few seconds, but she'd seen that look on Charles's face before—or maybe she'd already recognized it as her own. It was a question, framed as a statement. "No way." Veri held up her palm. "One painting. I agreed to *one*."

"I know." Charles frowned deeply. "And I will keep my promise. The Dufy in the Guggenheim was painted by Dufy. But would you at least let me tell you what we need?"

"Fine. What is it?" Veri asked, crossing her arms and legs at the same time. Tate caught her eye in the rearview mirror.

"A Cézanne."

Veri's heart raced. Paul Cézanne. One of her favorite painters. Charles must have spotted the spark of interest in her eye.

"*The Bathers*. 1906."

"*The Bathers*?" she repeated. How could they have known how much she loved that painting?

Charles nodded. "Shall we discuss tomorrow?"

Veri shook her head but didn't say no, and Charles grinned. Tate caught another glimpse of Veri in the rearview mirror. This time, she felt one of the icicles around her heart break off, and she smiled at him.

Charles fiddled with his leather gloves. "All right, then. I'll mention to Myra that I'd like your opinion at a private sale uptown tomorrow so we can discuss the details."

Veri groaned. "You're going to get me fired, again, you know." She never knew what Charles had said to Myra to get her rehired, but whatever it was, it had worked. Myra resented Veri even more afterward, though. A few weeks ago, she'd finally said, "Charles Winthrop is too old for you, you know." Veri assured her that she was not into older men, but Myra rolled her eyes and slammed her office door on her. Myra's new face made her look like she was constantly surprised.

"Don't worry about Myra," Charles said, pulling a tissue out of his coat pocket. "I'll just have to . . . promise her . . . something—"

He sneezed three times. "Excuse me," he said at the same time Tate said, "God bless you."

Veri stared at Charles, speechless for a moment. "Does . . . that always happen?" she asked.

He looked at her, confused.

"That—" *you sneeze three times in a row?* "That, um, that you have to bribe her with something?"

"Oh," he said, blowing his nose. "She can be a child like that."

Charles tucked the tissue into the small compartment in front of him and looked out his window, while Veri's eyes burned. If the three sneezes were an inherited trait from him, then she could only imagine how many others there might be. The way he sat with both his arms and legs crossed, the way he nodded along to the person on the other end of his cell phone, the way he cleared his throat when he got ready to ask a question—did she do those things too? And then there was the simple DNA of it all. The deep lines in between his eyes—should she prepare for those when she reached his age? Her tonsils that had to be removed when she was in middle school had to be part of his genetic makeup because her mother still had hers. If his parents were still alive, would she ever get to meet her grandparents?

She felt a lump in her throat. It was all so overwhelming. She'd learned early on to compartmentalize her worries—Was *this* an inherited trait from him too? Her mother usually wore her worries on her sleeve—but this time it was going to be tough. Every little habit and idiosyncrasy that Charles had, his disposition and temperament, all the things that made him *him* would make her question whether it made her *her* too. There was something he'd said that haunted her now as well. *"You have quite the criminal mind, Veridian Sterling."*

And there was one more thing she needed to know. "I've been meaning to ask you, Mr. Winthrop—do you have any children?"

"I don't, no," he said. "It wasn't in the cards for me, I guess."

She nodded and looked down at her phone.

The day would come when she'd tell him the truth, but that day was not today. She scrolled through her phone and stopped at her voice recorder. After Allison had texted her that terrible day in the Guggenheim, she'd secretly kept her phone on and recorded the rest of what Charles was telling her—especially the part about keeping her mother's painting a secret. If the day ever came when Charles threatened her again, she'd have his words on record.

They pulled up to the Hattfield Gallery, and out her window, Veri could see the post office worker leaning up against his building on yet another one of his forever smoke breaks.

Tate opened the door for her and then shut it as soon as she'd slid out.

"Do you mind if I come to your opening night too?" he asked. "I'd really like to."

New Show Coming Soon was in the front window of the gallery. Below it read, *Walk Out Series by Veridian Sterling.* Her stomach flipped every time she saw it. There was already buzz about her in *Artforum.* She'd done two interviews and a podcast for *ARTnews New York.*

Veri looked up at Tate. She'd waited so long for this moment. She slipped her hand into her pocket and handed him a penny. The Penny. "We share a penny, Tate. Of course you can come."

He flashed that perfect smile again, and Veri headed into the gallery, where Beck Becker was waiting to help her hang her paintings.

Acknowledgments

My palette is full of colorful characters who brought this book to life. My mentor, Caroline Leavitt, is always the first set of eyes on my work, and I owe her endless thanks for her generosity and time. My agent, Jennifer Unter, has been in my corner from the beginning, and I am so thankful that she took a chance on me. Alicia Clancy, the editor whom I've dreamed of working with since I was seven years old, is even better in real life, and my gratitude for her is immeasurable. So many thanks to Jeniffer Thompson, my website designer, who has the eye of a master artist herself, and to Tanya Farrell at Wunderkind PR, who spins magic for me. My mom, Jinxie, was the *least* fake person I've ever known, and my dad, John, is perhaps the most sanguine. I am lucky to have them as parents. Writers live with one foot in a made-up world and the other in the real one, and as such, it must be frustrating to live with us at times. My everlasting thanks go to my daughters, Madison, Daisy, and Tatum, who are my greatest works of art, and to my husband, Craig, my never-wavering champion and greatest love.

About the Author

Photo © 2023 Anne Rose

Jennifer Gooch Hummer received her BA in English from Kenyon College before moving to Los Angeles to work as a script reader for a variety of production companies. She is the award-winning author of *Girl Unmoored* and *Operation Tenley*.

When she's not writing, Hummer spends time with her husband and three daughters and tries not to trip over their two little dogs, who are the same color as their floors. She lives in Los Angeles.

ABOUT THE AUTHOR

Author photograph © Bob McDevitt 2022

Lisa Gray is an Amazon #1, *Washington Post*, and *Wall Street Journal* bestselling author and has sold over one million books. In 2020, she was longlisted for the McIlvanney Prize. Lisa previously worked as the chief Scottish soccer writer at the Press Association and the books columnist at the *Daily Record* Saturday Magazine. She is also the author of *Thin Air*, *Bad Memory*, *Dark Highway*, *Lonely Hearts*, *The Dark Room*, and *To Die For*. Lisa now writes full-time. Learn more at www.lisagraywriter.com and connect with Lisa on social media @lisagraywriter.

Follow the Author on Amazon

If you enjoyed this book, follow Lisa Gray on Amazon to be notified when the author releases a new book!

To do this, please follow these instructions:

Desktop:

1) Search for the author's name on Amazon or in the Amazon App.

2) Click on the author's name to arrive on their Amazon page.

3) Click the 'Follow' button.

Mobile and Tablet:

1) Search for the author's name on Amazon or in the Amazon App.

2) Click on one of the author's books.

3) Click on the author's name to arrive on their Amazon page.

4) Click the 'Follow' button.

Kindle eReader and Kindle App:

If you enjoyed this book on a Kindle eReader or in the Kindle App, you will find the author 'Follow' button after the last page.